SICK TO DEATH

ANDY HAYES MYSTERIES

by Andrew Welsh-Huggins

Fourth Down and Out

Slow Burn

Capitol Punishment

The Hunt

The Third Brother

Fatal Judgment

An Empty Grave

Sick to Death

SICK TO DEATH

AN ANDY HAYES MYSTERY

ANDREW WELSH-HUGGINS

SWALLOW PRESS
OHIO UNIVERSITY PRESS
ATHENS

Swallow Press
An imprint of Ohio University Press, Athens, Ohio 45701
ohioswallow.com

To obtain permission to quote, reprint, or otherwise reproduce or dis-
tribute material from Swallow Press / Ohio University Press publications,
please contact our rights and permissions department at
(740) 593-1154 or (740) 593-4536 (fax).

This is a work of fiction. The resemblance of any characters
to real persons, living or dead, is purely coincidental.

Printed in the United States of America

Swallow Press / Ohio University Press books are
printed on acid-free paper ∞ ™

Library of Congress Cataloging-in-Publication Data available upon request.
Names: Welsh-Huggins, Andrew, author.
Title: Sick to death / Andrew Welsh-Huggins.
Description: Athens : Swallow Press, Ohio University Press, 2024. | Series:
    Andy Hayes mysteries ; 8
Identifiers: LCCN 2024022830 (print) | LCCN 2024022831 (ebook) | ISBN
    9780804012539 (paperback ; acid-free paper) | ISBN 9780804012546
    (pdf)
Subjects: LCGFT: Detective and mystery fiction. | Novels.
Classification: LCC PS3623.E4824 S53 2024 (print) | LCC PS3623.E4824
    (ebook) | DDC 813/.6—dc23/eng/20240517
LC record available at https://lccn.loc.gov/2024022830
LC ebook record available at https://lccn.loc.gov/2024022831

In memory of Mark Gillispie:

colleague, curmudgeon, friend.

How I miss our talks about life,

literature, and everything in between.

And when they had assembled, and the gathering was complete, swift-footed Achilles rose and spoke: "Son of Atreus, if war and plague alike are fated to defeat us Greeks, I think we shall be driven to head for home: if, that is, we can indeed escape death."

—Homer's *Iliad*, A. S. Kline translation

1

SEEING WHAT'S right in front of you can sometimes save your life.

It can also get you killed.

This was the third time in as many days that I'd spied the woman at the museum. Today she was staring at me across the Modern wing, just to the left of a bickering couple on the cusp of being too loud. Curiosity piqued, I met her gaze and she immediately dropped it, adjusted her face mask, and turned toward the Bellows on the wall beside her. My security antennae went up, but only a little. The last serious virus surge was in the rearview mirror by several months. Though mask wearing in the museum had become hit or miss, it wasn't unusual by any stretch. It was a perfectly natural thing to do. I still kept my eye on her.

She was young, early twenties or so, athletic looking with the frame of a runner. Short black hair with a hint of curl. Possibly a Columbus College of Art and Design student, though they usually came armed with sketch pads and pencils and ran in pairs or trios or more recently small packs following the Bellows acquisition. The problem was there was also something familiar about her that I couldn't quite place, even though I was positive we'd never met.

I examined her discreetly as she studied the Bellows with her back to me. Maybe I had it wrong. Was it possible I did know her? Perhaps someone I met on a case? That list was long and prone to gaps. A friend of a friend? That list was short and easy to recite. An ex-girlfriend? At least I could cross off that possibility. My love life makes the *Titanic* crossing look like a pleasure cruise up the Danube. But I gave up dating women that young when I was, well, that young. I had just decided to satisfy myself and put it to her directly when Patience approached.

"What's up?"

"Nothing. Just trying to figure out if I know that person."

"Who?"

I nodded across the room at the young woman.

"Who is she?"

"No idea. But she keeps looking at me."

"It's that animal magnetism, Andy. You need to rein it in."

"Sorry, but I think my poles are reversed."

"I'll be the judge of that," she said with a smile. "Actually, I'm making sure everything's okay with . . ." She glanced at the bickering couple.

"So far, so good, but thanks."

"Great. In that case, give me your phone."

"Not again."

"It's worth it, I promise."

Patience—Patience Hampton—was, like me, a Columbus Museum of Art security guard. Or "gallery associate," as the museum prefers. It was one of the odder jobs I'd ever held. I supposedly protected millions of dollars' worth of art, yet the most common question I fielded was "Which way to the restroom?" A knowledge of art wasn't a prerequisite, which was a good thing in my case. But whereas I was a private eye pondering a career change while clueless about the difference between Monet and Manet, Patience was an actual artist. She'd shown me some of her watercolors. Even with my limited knowledge I could tell they were good.

Of course, given her Botticellian curves and glow—see, I did know something—I wasn't looking to upset the apple cart by offering ill-informed criticism. The idea of elevating our relationship to the life-drawing phase was never far from my mind—or hers as well, as far as I could tell from her recent advances.

"Here," Patience said, handing my phone back after a minute and sidling close enough for me to detect a hint of lavender perfume. "This is that Henri painting I was telling you about. See how similar it is to *The Boulevard?*" She pointed at the George Bellows painting across the room, the one we were meant to pay extra attention to given how much the museum paid for it. "You can see how Bellows incorporated some of his technique."

I didn't see, really, but decided to take her word for it and made a mental note to research Robert Henri, who, according to the link she pulled up, was a founder of the Ashcan school movement. At least I'd heard of that. If he were important to Patience, I reasoned, it wouldn't hurt to know more about him.

"You'll make an art historian out of me yet."

"Or something like that," she said, giving my arm a squeeze. "Good luck with the mystery woman."

"Thanks." I studied Patience with artistic appreciation as she moved out of the gallery and disappeared into the hallway.

After she departed, I beelined for the young woman. It was a kill-two-birds move anyway. We were supposed to give *The Boulevard* extra TLC given its price tag. Patience liked to point out that most of what I knew about art could be written on a brewpub napkin. That's why, according to her, she was always seizing my phone with gusto—she was on a self-imposed social media diet and so kept hers in her locker—to look up names and artistic movements and thrust the results in my face. But even I understood Bellows's significance and his reputation in the art world.

The painting in question was a recently acquired 1920 treatment of a crowded New York City boulevard. Its purchase was considered a coup for the museum and its collection, especially given Bellows's roots in Columbus. Most of that credit went to board chairwoman Eleanor Seward, who championed its acquisition, in part in homage to her grandfather, a minor Ashcan school painter who'd known Bellows briefly in New York. It hadn't come cheap—estimates whispered by my fellow gallery associates pegged the cost in the healthy seven-figure range.

"Excuse me?"

Hearing my voice, the young woman turned, eyes widening in surprise. I saw her shift her body to leave the gallery. She needn't have worried. Before I could approach any closer, my attention was distracted by the bickering couple, whose harsh whispers had morphed into a loud argument. I turned and glared at them. Glaring back, the woman stalked from the gallery. Her male companion checked his watch impatiently and followed in close pursuit, practically shouting.

I glanced back and saw that the young woman, like everyone else, was staring at the spectacle. Reluctantly, I turned and followed the couple, figuring that duty called.

"Dammit, just listen," the man was saying in the next room, the walls lined with Impressionists with a couple random Realists thrown in for good measure. His volume would have turned heads at a Clippers game, let alone the art museum. Already most visitors had interrupted their contemplation of artistic meaning to stare like kids rubbernecking at a schoolyard brawl.

Neither the man nor woman seemed likely candidates for a public shouting match. He was trim with dark hair and beard, wearing tan chinos, a French blue button-down shirt, and a tailored navy jacket. She was part of a matched set with thick honey-blond hair pulled back from her face, wearing designer jeans, a gold blouse, and over it a beige wrap. Both mask wearers. The perfect picture of hip, COVID-respecting thirtysomethings taking in an afternoon at the gallery. Except for the fact they appeared to be losing their shit, they blended right in.

"No, you listen," the woman said, facing him as they stood in the middle of the gallery. "I'm tired of your nonsense."

"My nonsense?" he said, checking his watch again. "My nonsense?"

"You heard me—"

"Okay, folks," I said, pulling up next to them. "Let's take this outside, shall we?"

"Mind your own business," the man said.

"Happy to once you're minding yours. This is an art museum, not divorce court."

"Screw you."

"Sorry, but you're not my type," I said, gesturing at the gallery exit.

"The hell with this," the woman shouted. "The hell with all of you. And especially you." The comment was directed at her companion, who out of the blue grabbed her arm. She screamed, pulled free, and started to run. He went after her with a final glance at his watch, swearing loudly. Maybe being late for something would take them off my hands faster.

I expected them to bolt for the stairs and the exit. Instead they moved on to the next gallery, which brought us up to the latter half of the twentieth century. As I followed them inside, two things happened almost simultaneously.

First, upon approaching them, I saw the pair exchange a glance before resuming their fight. An exchange like a couple onstage breaking character for an instant. I was just processing this observation—was this a put-on?—when I heard someone shouting behind me.

"Hey! Help!"

I pivoted and ran back in the direction I'd come, nearly knocking Patience over in the process.

"Andy, what are you—"

I loped through the Impressionists and arrived back in the original gallery in time to see a man sprinting from the room, something tucked against his chest.

"The painting—he took it."

The young woman I'd caught watching me. She pointed at the fleeing man. I glanced at the wall. I stared in disbelief. The Bellows was gone. Less than a month after its much-heralded acquisition. Snatched—on my watch. I ran.

"Andy, no." Patience, behind me. "You know the rules. No pursuits."

"He's got *The Boulevard!*" I shouted.

"It doesn't matter."

"Yes, it does."

"Rules, Andy."

"Fuck that shit," I said, arriving at the top of the stairs and bounding down two at a time, the thief already through the museum's glass doors and running up the walkway toward Gay Street.

"Andy—"

Now I was outside too, ignoring the startled looks of arriving patrons as I bolted up the walk as best I could. My knees weren't what they'd once been: back in the day, I and my No. 9 jersey had gone down on too many gridirons too many times. I struggled to match the speed of the man ahead of me. But I knew I had to try.

Reaching Gay Street, he angled right and headed east. White, young looking, thin face hidden by a mask and sunglasses, wearing black jeans and a black T-shirt. On-point disguise for an art museum snatch-and-grab. Out of the corner of my eye I saw a dark van rolling toward him up Washington. I picked up what little speed I had and closed the distance. This was more like it. I yelled at him to stop. But it was too little too late. There was no way I could catch him. Instead, I pulled up and dug out my phone, hoping to at least grab a picture of the license plate.

"Stop!"

I looked to my left. To my astonishment, the young woman from the gallery dashed past me. She was moving fast, knees high and arms pumping. A moment later she reached her quarry, grabbed his waist, and spun him around. As the van rolled to a stop behind them, the man raised the painting over his head as he struggled to free himself.

"The hell, bitch. I didn't sign up for this shit."

"Then give me the painting."

"What shit is that?" I said, rushing to join the fray. Before the man could respond, I heard my name called—by the young woman.

"Andy—the picture."

She had managed to wrest the Bellows from the thief and was now struggling to get loose herself.

"Here," I said, holding out my arms.

To her credit, she hesitated only a second before tossing the painting into the air. I leaned for it, stumbled, righted myself, and caught it just before it hit the pavement.

"Oof!"

The thief backed up, hunched over, hands between his knees where the woman had connected with a well-aimed kick.

"Come on, dammit." The driver of the van, shouting through the rolled-down passenger window. The thief paused, unsteady on his feet, then recovered, dead-eyed the woman, and jumped into the already rolling van. The door slammed shut and the van roared away toward Broad Street. I watched it disappear to the left with a screech of tires before turning to the young woman.

"Jesus. Are you all right?"

"I'm fine. Just winded."

"I bet. You were flying. I never would have caught the guy. You saved the day."

"Thanks, I guess."

"It's the truth." I examined the painting. Not a blemish on it, as far as I could tell. In the distance, I heard sirens.

Suddenly, something dawned on me. "Wait a second. You shouted my name."

Panic flitted in and out of her eyes. "Um, maybe."

"Not maybe. You definitely said Andy. Do I know you?"

"Sort of?"

"What's that supposed to mean?"

"Nothing." Panic replaced by a hard-edged resolve. "You've been in the museum the past few days."

She acknowledged it reluctantly. I peered at her more closely, studying her now mask-less face.

"Why?"

Behind us, the sound of a crowd approaching. I turned and saw Patience trailed by a crowd of visitors. A moment later a Columbus police cruiser tore up Gay from Ninth.

"I need your help with something."

"My help?"

"Andy, are you okay?" Patience, arriving at my side.

"I'm fine." To the woman, I said, "What kind of help?"

"I want to hire you."

I stared at her. "Hire me? For what?"

She hesitated, eyeing the crowd closing in around us.

"I want you to find the person who killed my mother."

Another police cruiser, this one rolling down Washington. More footsteps as the throng continued to grow.

"Someone killed your mother?"

"Hayes. What the hell is going on?"

I turned and found myself face-to-face with Lillian Melnick. The director of security and visitor engagement. Also, my boss. Not a fan of mine on the best of days. Most days, the feeling was mutual.

"What about the police?" I said, turning back to the young woman.

"They're doing what they can. But it's been almost five months with no answers. That's why I need you."

"Me?"

"Yeah, you."

"I'm not really taking cases right now—"

"That doesn't matter. You owe me."

"Hayes." Melnick again.

"Hang on," I snapped. To the young woman, I said, "I owe you?"

"That's right."

"Owe you why?"

Her eyes brightened, and the resolve melted away momentarily, replaced by an expression halfway between sorrow and rage.

"I'm waiting," I said.

She shook her head, wiping away a tear.

"You owe me, because you're my father."

2

I BLINKED, stunned.

"What did you say?"

Before she could respond I heard Lillian Melnick again, this time up close and personal.

"Hayes. Let's go."

"Go where?"

"To my office. You're suspended."

"Suspended?"

"You heard me. Effective immediately."

"Suspended?" This from Patience, standing beside me.

"You stay out of this," Melnick said.

"I just saved the Bellows. *We* saved the Bellows," I said, gesturing at the young woman whose name I still didn't know. Who had just told me I was her father.

"*No pursuits. No apprehensions.* First rule in the handbook. Who knows what could have happened? You jeopardized an extremely valuable piece of art."

Outrage flared in Melnick's eyes. Sorry—Dr. Melnick's eyes. A tall, thin, always fashionably dressed woman someplace in her late forties whose aloofness was matched only by her superiority complex. Today, neatly tailored slacks were met by a fussy high-collared top. Did I mention there was no love lost between us?

"Jeopardized it? What about the clown who tore it off the wall?"

"For your information, thieves aren't in the business of harming the art they steal."

"Give me a break."

"Andy," Patience said, touching my arm. "Relax."

"Relax after being suspended for doing my job? I don't think so."

"Okay. Just hang on."

The comment from a cop, approaching from one of the newly arrived cruisers.

"Nobody's going anywhere until we figure out what happened and take some statements."

"I beg your pardon?" the museum head of security and visitor engagement said. "Do you know who—"

"Let's go," the uniformed woman said, ignoring Melnick as she steered me toward the museum.

THEY STAGED the inquisition in the museum's now-closed café. The questions from the on-call detective, a harried-looking guy named Denny Tipton, got a little harder once he figured out who I was. But my story—and the young woman's—held up after they looked at the gallery security cameras, which captured nearly everything. I'd been right: the robbery was a setup. The arguing couple—faces concealed under their COVID masks—positioned themselves as a distraction while the smash-and-grab guy swooped in for the Bellows and hightailed it. If not for the young woman, the plan would have succeeded perfectly and the museum would have been out a chunk of change, not to mention huge amounts of bragging rights.

"'I didn't sign up for this crap?'" Tipton asked me. "You sure that's what he said?"

"'Shit,' not 'crap.' But yes, I'm sure."

"Any idea what he meant by that?" He was tall with a slight stoop, dark hair frosting his sideburns, dressed in khakis and a yellow oxford shirt with a dark tie a centimeter or two from fully knotted. I tried not to let it bother me.

"The obvious, I'm guessing. Someone hired him to pull a painting off a wall and deposit it in a getaway van, not be chased down and apprehended. As much as I hate to admit it, Lillian Melnick was right. There is a no-pursuit rule. If I knew it, the thieves knew it."

"So why'd you go after him?"

"I've got a thing about bad guys getting away."

"Even if it costs you your job?"

"I hope not. But, if I'm being honest about it, yes."

He left after making sure he had my contact details and informing me I might also be hearing from the FBI since they often handled art theft when they weren't chasing bank robbers and domestic terrorists. Oh joy. I was on my way to my locker to retrieve a couple of belongings when I heard my name called. I turned and found myself face-to-face with Lillian Melnick once more.

"Yes?"

"Where are you going?"

"The break room."

"I'm afraid not."

"I'm sorry?"

She handed me a single sheet of paper. "I'm here to inform you that your status has evolved from suspended to terminated. Effective immediately."

I opened the paper and stared at the one-line dismissal.

"You have got to be kidding."

"I assure you I'm not."

"I saved a valuable painting. *Really* valuable, from what I hear."

"No pursuits. No apprehensions."

"You don't sound so sure." And in fact, she didn't. Despite the tension that defined our brief relationship, there was a hesitation in her eyes. A moment later, though, it was gone, like a drawn window shade abruptly shutting out daylight.

"I'm sure, Hayes. The door is that way."

"This isn't right."

"That's your opinion."

"At least let me get my stuff."

"The museum is closed, Hayes."

And that was that. I stared at her until she dropped her gaze, and then walked out of the building, doing my best not to skulk.

I was headed to the parking lot and my Honda Odyssey when I looked up and saw the young woman standing by her car. Apparently, she'd been cleared for takeoff by the police as well, minus the whole firing thing. We stared awkwardly at each other for a few seconds.

"Listen, I—"

I raised a hand to interrupt. "Beer?"

"God, yes."

MATT AND Tony's was a quick walk away. We settled at a corner of the bar and ordered. A Heineken for each.

"I thought you were the craft beer generation."

"Sometimes you just need a cold one, you know?"

"Indeed." We clinked glass and each pulled our bottles below the shoulders.

"So."

"I'm sorry, Andy. I didn't mean for it to come out like that. I had a plan, but it all went to hell when that guy grabbed the picture."

"Didn't mean for what to come out?"

"Like I said—"

"That I'm your father?"

"That's right." The resolve crept back onto her face. "It wasn't how I planned to tell you."

"You're serious. This isn't a joke?"

"Yeah, like this is something I'd joke about. Yes, I'm serious. You're my father. I'm your daughter."

"How?"

"You had sex with my mother, that's how. Do I have to spell it out for you?"

"As a matter of fact, you do. Because I have no idea what you're talking about. Or who." I paused. "I don't even know your name."

She hesitated for just a moment. "It's Alex."

"Alex what?"

"Alex Rutledge."

"Who was your mom?"

"Kate Rutledge."

"And you're saying—"

She reached into her back pocket and handed me two pieces of paper stapled together.

"What's this?"

"It's the DNA test results."

"The what?"

"I know this is coming out of left field. I didn't believe it either, at first. So I had the test done."

"You tested my DNA?"

"Yup."

"How?"

"A month back—you were eating breakfast at Stauf's. You had a cold."

"I remember. So what?"

"So you blew your nose and threw the napkin away. I fished it out of the trash when you weren't looking."

"You stalked me at my neighborhood coffee shop?"

"What do you call the on-the-job surveillance you do?"

"Professional tracking."

"Whatever. I sent in the samples and it came back 99.99 percent. That's good for any court in the world. But I understand if you're skeptical. Like I said, I didn't mean for it to come out this way. If you want to do another test, no problem. I'll pay for it," she added. "I'm not trying to create any problems here."

She took a long pull on her beer, bringing it to low tide. I followed suit.

"It won't be necessary," I said, examining her face for a second before returning to the results.

"You believe it?"

"Yes."

What I didn't say: DNA results or not, there was no question. The reason she looked familiar was because I stared at a similar face every morning in the bathroom mirror. And if my face and hers didn't convince me, those of my mom and my sister and at least one aunt would. The family resemblance was overwhelming. I sat quietly for a moment, mind reeling.

"Your mom—Kate?"

"What about her?"

"When . . ."

"When did you have sex with her?"

"That part, yes."

"You don't remember?"

"I'm sorry."

She shook her head, pulled out her phone, swiped here and there, and handed it to me. A dark-haired, dark-eyed woman stared back at me from the screen. Practically Alex's much older sister. Attractive, but with a stern expression that hinted at deep waters it would take a lifetime to plumb. I didn't recognize her, although there was also something familiar about her face, just as there had been about her daughter's when I first saw it.

My daughter's face.

"You really don't remember?"

I shook my head.

"Well, that's just great."

"I'm sorry, Alex. I wish I did."

"It's not that."

"What then?"

She looked over my left shoulder. "She would never tell me the details. All I know is you met somewhere in Columbus, probably someplace she was waitressing."

"You don't know where?"

She shook her head. "She wouldn't tell me, and if her parents, my grandparents know, they're not saying either. I guess that part doesn't matter." She paused, seeming almost on the verge of a grin. "Other than being crucial to my origin story. Which I was hoping you might know."

"When was this?"

"How's twenty-five years and eleven months ago sound?"

I sighed. "About right, unfortunately."

Even though I couldn't remember Kate Rutledge, I recalled the era. Boy, did I ever. The mess that was my life during my short-lived career with the Cleveland Browns. The disaster of my flameout at Ohio State during my senior year barely behind me. A summer bender back in Columbus before the Browns' training camp started up again. There had been a lot of bars and a lot of women.

"I'm sorry, Alex." The name awkward on my tongue, like a word I was afraid to mispronounce. "I don't remember. I wasn't in a great space back then, for what it's worth. Did she try to contact me? I don't remember that either, but I promise you that if she had, I would have—"

"She didn't. At least that's what she told me."

"Why not?"

"I don't know. She wasn't in a great space back then either. No surprise, if she was getting off on one-night stands with guys like you."

I played with my Heineken bottle, slowly twirling it on the bar top.

"She left town right after. She had a girlfriend who'd moved to Indianapolis. She followed her and stayed. She found out she was pregnant over there. Her parents wanted her to come home, to come back here, but she refused."

"Did she ever say why?"

"Not in so many words. I pieced some of it together over the years, talking to my grandparents and connecting the dots. Half of it was how headstrong she was, always saying she didn't need any help. She was also embarrassed, and I don't think she wanted to be around people who knew her. Getting knocked up at nineteen had definitely not been part of the plan."

I nodded, looking at the photo of Kate Rutledge again, trying as hard as I could to recall the woman and our meeting and what happened afterward. There was nothing there, the memory lost in a haze of alcohol and late nights and more mindless rutting in strange bedrooms than I cared to remember—or possibly could.

"Andy?"

"Sorry," I said, handing her phone back. "Go on."

"When I was a few months old, she enrolled in nursing school and ended up getting a job in Indianapolis."

"Where?"

"Methodist Hospital. She was an emergency room nurse."

"You were born there? In Indy?"

"That's right. Her parents pleaded with her, told her to get an abortion, that they'd help, but she got into this mindset that she had to own what happened. They reconciled, but she refused to ever tell them about you. They still don't know."

I sighed, unable to help myself. I thought briefly of my boys, Mike and Joe, and how I was going to explain this latest development in my rollercoaster life.

"Your grandparents—they're around?"

She explained they were in a retirement home in Westerville, ailing but hanging in there.

"How did you end up here?" The bartender circled and I nodded, pointing at both our beers.

"My grandma wasn't doing so well for a while and needed help. My uncle lives in Texas and my aunt in California, and they weren't around much. My mom was over here so much she decided to just move back."

"She never married?"

"Once. I've got a half brother, Steve. He's a couple years younger. But she and Steve's dad divorced pretty quickly."

"And you?"

"What about me?"

"What do you do?"

She hesitated. "I'm a security guard."

"Where?"

"Securitas. I've got an overnight warehouse gig right now. But it's only temporary, until January."

"What happens in January?"

"I start at the police academy."

"Columbus?"

"That's right."

I raised my eyebrows. "I hear that's hard to get into. Congratulations."

"Thanks." She looked away, but I caught a glimpse of a smile nonetheless.

The second round of beers arrived. We each took another long pull. I thought about my day so far. A slow walk down the street and back with Hopalong first thing, followed by a jog around Schiller Park. Post-run pushups and sit-ups in the living room, then shower, breakfast, and the headlines. Reading a couple chapters of Good Kids, Bad City, then a bike ride up to my shift at the art museum. A slow day at work, all things considered. Light crowd for a Saturday. A chat with Patience on our break while she furthered my art history education, dialing up Cubism on my phone. Two PB&Js gulped down at lunch, followed by the rescue of a million-dollar-plus painting from an art theft ring with help from my long-lost daughter.

"You okay?" Alex said.

"I'm fine." Not fine. "The academy thing. That's great. Have you—did you always want to be a cop?" Even as I asked the question, I felt the stirrings of parental concern. The normal reaction to your child announcing they want to be a police officer, combined with the current law enforcement climate. A series of police shootings of Black men and kids in recent years had the department and the community on edge.

"Yes and no."

"Meaning?"

"I kind of floated around in college. English, psychology, thought about nursing, like my mom. Then I took a criminal justice class and that was it. It just clicked."

"Where?"

"IU Bloomington."

"Good school." Also where my ex-girlfriend, Anne Cooper, got her English PhD. Yet another relationship I'd let slip away. No need to dwell on her now. Nothing to see here, folks. Just move along.

Alex acknowledged the compliment. "I was looking for work in Indy, but I was here visiting my mom and went to a job fair and talked to somebody with the Columbus police and decided to apply. Seemed like a pretty good deal."

Silence settled over us. On the TV in the corner, the Guardians were down 4–2 in the second game of a Yankees series. In Columbus, I was unemployed and dumbfounded. I twirled my beer bottle some more.

"Alex. Short for Alexandra?"

"Yes."

"Anybody ever call you that?"

"And live to talk about it? Not a chance. Anybody ever call you Andrew?"

"Touché." I let another few seconds pass, and said, "Your mother. You said she was—"

"She's dead. Hit-skip car accident."

"When?"

"Last May. She ran most mornings after work. After her night shift. She was maybe a mile from home when it happened."

Of course. That's why Kate Rutledge's face looked familiar. I'd seen it on multiple TV broadcasts and in the paper.

"I'm so sorry."

Alex bit her lip and waved away the sentiment.

"Where did she work?"

"St. Clare–North. The intensive care unit."

"And where did she live—if I may ask?"

"She rented in Westerville. The two of us. It's close to the hospital and my grandparents. I'm not really a suburbs person but it worked for her. The plan was I'd get my own place once I started at the academy."

More silence while the implication of that plan's disintegration settled over our corner of the bar.

"How did you find out about me? I take it she never said anything?"

She shook her head. "When I was younger, she told me you were a jerk she didn't want around. That I was the only good thing he—you—accomplished in life. Later on, she said she might tell me someday, depending on the circumstances. Honestly, though, I didn't want to know. I had you painted in my mind as this bogeyman for so long that I stopped caring."

"Not that I'm not a bogeyman, but what changed?"

"After she died—after she was killed—I came across a file. It was filled with clippings of you. Some old ones, back when you played for the Browns. But more recent ones too. Some of the cases you worked on. I knew immediately. The file gave it away because it was the only thing like it in her possessions. She wasn't a sports person. But I mean, come on. Look at us. You'd have to be an idiot not to see the resemblance." She laughed dismissively.

"What?"

"I was really proud of my career decision. Getting into the academy. Becoming a cop. Then I found that file and realized I was doing the most unoriginal thing in the world. Like daddy, like daughter."

"Don't kid yourself, Alex."

"What's that supposed to mean?"

"First off, I'm a private investigator, not a cop. Secondly, it was literally the only thing left for me before skid row or the cash register at Speedway. The last job I had before getting my license was shoveling pig shit on my uncle's farm for twelve hours a day. There's a lot of people in town who think that overqualified me for my present career."

"Don't be absurd. The things you've done."

My turn to wave away a sentiment. "This isn't false modesty and it's not humble bragging and it's not an attempt to bullshit you. It's reality. I've done okay. But I fell into this job by accident. That's a far cry from getting accepted into the Columbus Police Academy. I've worked a lot of security jobs in this town. I know plenty of people who tried for years to get in. Who *never* got in. Don't downplay your success just because life's slot machine came up with my face on it. You have a lot to be proud of."

"Thanks, Andy," she said after a moment.

"So. Back to your mom."

"What about her?"

"You said before you wanted to hire me. To find her killer."

"Yes. And I still want to."

"What can I do that the police can't?"

"Did you mean what you said, before?"

"About what?"

"False modesty and all that."

"Sure."

"In that case, you could do what you always do. At least according to what I read in my mom's file."

"Which is?"

"Make a big fucking mess of everything. And then save the day."

3

I PULLED into a McDonald's parking lot in Westerville shortly after ten the next morning. I'd offered to pick up Alex—to pick up my daughter—on the way but she declined, saying she'd meet me there. As I parked, I spied her studying her phone inside her car, a red two-door Chevy Cruze that looked shiny from a recent car wash. The air was cool, in keeping with the early October Sunday morning. On any other day, I might have admired the foliage on my drive up the highway, the rich reds and yellows of the color-shifting leaves. But everything had gone to hell for me, again.

I should have been sitting at home, getting ready to bike up to the museum for my Sunday shift. Thanks to the good doctor—Dr. Lillian Melnick—not today. And not ever again, apparently.

The job hadn't been the most exciting, yesterday notwithstanding. But I'd welcomed the regular hours and steady paycheck—and the chance to get to know Patience Hampton—now that Joe was living with me more or less full-time and I needed a more stable existence. One that didn't come with late hours, broken appointments, and occasional gunplay. The Wednesday–Sunday schedule was unorthodox, but Joe was at his mom and stepdad's most weekends anyway, and increasingly self-sufficient no matter what. Over the past few weeks, I'd even managed to save a little for the first time in my adult life.

Good thing, since that was going to have to float me for a while as I looked around for new investigations to pay the bills.

I was pulled back to the present by the sound of Alex's car door opening. She walked over and stared at my Odyssey.

"Really?"

"Hey, it fits my lifestyle."

"Which is what, soccer mom?"

"Soccer moms are people too."

"If you say so."

"How was your evening, now that we've got that out of the way?"

"Fine. Thanks for meeting me. It's just over there."

All business. Okay. I could roll with that. Would have to, I supposed.

AFTER PARTING ways with Alex the day before, I'd gone home, cracked open a Black Label, went online, and read and watched everything I could about the death of Kate Rutledge. There'd been a lot of coverage initially, which was understandable since her death checked off so many boxes. Westerville was a popular place to live. A lot of people in town jogged. A lot of people worked in health care. Nobody liked the idea of someone leaving the scene of an accident like that. *The Dispatch* ran a long story, including the usual mix of terse police comment and effusive and emotional tributes from friends and co-workers.

"We join the entire community in mourning this terrible loss," said Dr. Christine Coyle, the St. Clare–North administrator. "An absolute tragedy," said Dr. Ryan Ives, a night ICU doctor who had worked with Kate. "Almost like a sister to me," said Natalie Mettler, described as a former

St. Clare colleague. Channel 7 even managed to find someone who'd called 911 from the drive-through of this very McDonald's, but he hadn't seen much.

After the initial flurry of stories, interest predictably dropped off with no arrest in the offing. The paper ran a short story a few weeks later after Crime Stoppers offered a $5,000 reward for information leading to the arrest of the driver. After that—nothing.

"THERE," ALEX said.

We watched traffic move up and down State Route 3, a main thoroughfare running through Westerville, a village-turned-suburb with a cute downtown surrounded by the usual retail and subdivision sprawl. I stared at some of that sprawl now, a jumble of strip malls, fast-food joints, and gas stations, as we stood at the corner where Kate Rutledge died.

According to the bare-bones police account, a dark SUV, possibly black, possibly blue, ran a red light coming south just as Kate jogged across the street at quarter after six in the morning. The vehicle braked before impact, meaning the driver saw her and at least tried to stop, but it was too late and he—or she—struck Kate going forty miles an hour, crumpling her body like tissue beneath the wheels. She was dead on impact. The car raced away, barely slowing its speed, and disappeared down the road. The working theory was the driver headed onto the nearby 270 Outerbelt to merge into the beginnings of rush hour traffic. No suspects and no leads.

The only video was footage captured from a BP gas station on the far corner. I watched the clip several times the night before, my stomach clenching each time. Despite the video's poor quality—grainy and fuzzy—it was still a graphic film of a woman dying. The mother of my daughter being killed.

"Just the one video?" I said to Alex.

"That's it. And it didn't capture the plate, as I'm sure you saw."

"Unfortunate," I said, stating the obvious.

"It was too far away. The camera's meant to check activity at the pumps. We were lucky it captured anything at all."

"She'd just gotten off work?"

"That's right."

"And she usually ran then?"

"Yup. She had her routine down pat. On the nights she worked, she wore her running stuff under her scrubs. She'd come home, drop her things on the counter, and head out for thirty minutes. She liked to get it done then, so it was out of the way. Plus it was a chance to clear her head. She'd shower, eat something, and sleep for five or six hours."

"Always the same route?"

She confirmed it. "She said she needed to be on auto-pilot by that point. She'd loop around that subdivision a couple of times"—Alex pointed across the thoroughfare—"and come back. It's safe and well lit."

"That morning. How did you find out? About the accident, I mean."

"She had one of those ID bracelets. Cops came to the door, woke me up."

"And they haven't found anything?"

"Squat, basically." She looked to her right as she spoke, watching the traffic move up and down the five-lane road. "People called in a bunch of leads initially. Neighbor's car had a funny dent, that kind of thing. They're pretty sure it's a Chevy Blazer, but older model. Turns out that's a needle-in-a-haystack kind of thing, especially without the plate."

"Who's the lead?"

"Doug Shortland. He's Westerville's traffic investigations guy."

"Are you satisfied with him? Or is that why . . ."

"Why I want to hire you?"

"I guess."

"He's done his best, I think. There wasn't a lot to work with, and they got bad breaks because of the video thing. I don't know how much more they could have done, really."

"You're sure about that?"

"As sure as I can be. Billy complained a couple times about the lack of progress, but in the end, even he saw how little there was to go on."

"Billy?"

"Sorry. Billy Chowdhury. Well, Iqbal, but everyone calls him Billy. This guy she was dating. He's a night pharmacist at St. Clare."

"They were dating when she died?"

"It was over by then. Mom broke it off."

"Any idea why?"

She shook her head. "She didn't talk much about stuff like that to me."

"Was he a suspect?"

"Billy? You'd have to ask Shortland. I know they talked to him because he didn't work the overnight before she died."

"Why not?"

"He called in sick, which didn't look great. But it checked out as far as I know. Plus, it doesn't seem likely. He's a sweet guy, from what I could tell the few times I was around him."

"Got it." I made a mental note to double-check that with the Westerville detective. In my experience, sweet guys usually rose to the top of the suspect list. "Anybody else?"

She hesitated. "No."

"You sure?"

"I'm sure."

"Okay." It felt like she was holding something back but I didn't push it. "Was everything all right at work? With your mom, I mean?"

"Yes and no. No feuds with co-workers, if that's what you're implying."

"But?"

"But nothing, except it was super stressful. That's why she ran after work."

"ICU. That must have been hard."

"It was, but normally she thrived on that stuff. Then COVID changed everything. It was like nothing she'd experienced."

"How so?"

She gave me a pitying look. "It was bad from the start, beds filling up like crazy. Things tapered off a little once the vaccines came along. When the variants hit, it started right up again. Only this time, everybody who was sick was unvaccinated, and they could be a handful. St. Clare had to hire all these outside nurses to help with the crush. That's the only time I ever heard her talk about doing something else."

"Like what?"

"Anything, as long as it didn't involve COVID. I mean, community health care was her first love. She felt like she made a difference in people's lives. But once the lines were drawn over vaccines? The abuse she took was unbelievable. She and others. The anti-vaxxer crowd." Alex made a face. "She tried to understand where they were coming from, but some days it was almost too much. A good friend of hers decided to bail. Said fuck it and started applying for jobs in home health care. Was going to take a pretty big pay cut, according to Mom, but she said it'd be worth it."

"Do you remember who that was?"

"Natalie. Natalie Mettler. I think she finally left a few weeks after Mom died."

I remembered after a moment her quote in the *Dispatch* story. *Almost like a sister to me.*

Alex said, "Mom thought briefly about leaving when Dr. Coyle did. Some people told her she was crazy not to—this was when it was really bad. Shouting matches on the ward and all that."

"Coyle—the hospital administrator?"

"Used to be. She just opened a clinic in New Albany."

"What kind of clinic?"

"I'm not sure. I know it pays a lot more and patients don't scream at you if you suggest their dying mom might have the coronavirus."

"Obviously Kate decided not to go that route, though."

Before Alex could reply my phone buzzed. Joe was calling. "Hang on," I said, and answered.

"Everything okay?"

"Any chance you could come get me a little early?"

I glanced at Alex. "Probably. What's going on?"

"It's really bad here. I don't even want to leave my room. And I'm worried about Lyndsey. She's been crying all morning."

"I'm wrapping something up, and then I'll be right there." I paused. "Lyndsey could come with if she wants. At least for the day?"

"I'll ask her."

"Everything all right?" Alex said when I disconnected.

"Yes and no. That was Joe—he's your half brother. One of them, anyway. Things aren't great at home right now." Understatement of the year. His mom, my ex, Crystal— one of my two exes—was struggling to save her marriage to her plastic surgeon husband, Bob, who was only half-heartedly dealing with his recently acknowledged porn addiction. The situation was hard enough on Joe, who spent weekends there, living with me the rest of the time. But it was hell on Lyndsey, Crystal and Bob's daughter.

"Joe—I know."

"You do?"

"Yeah. And Mike too."

"How?"

"Google—how else? Mike especially. All the football stuff."

Of course. Mike was now the starting quarterback at Thomas Worthington. The press couldn't get enough of the idea of my son following in my footsteps, especially considering how badly I'd screwed up my once-promising career. Mike was a far different person than me, with much better prospects in life, if not on the field, but that was a distinction lost in many of the reports.

"Have you told them about me?"

"Not yet. I was thinking maybe we could all grab dinner."

"That'd be cool. Together at last, your three kids. That you know of."

"I'm pretty sure this is it."

"But can you be certain? What if someone else is keeping secrets? Or is worried you might deny it?"

I stared at Alex, not sure I'd heard correctly. "Listen— you said your mom didn't want to contact me."

"That's what she told me. Maybe there's another side to the story I never heard. If she wouldn't even tell me where you two met, what else was she hiding?"

"Meaning?"

"Maybe she thought you'd fight her. Famous football player and all that. On your guard for those kinds of claims."

"That's not true. And it's not on me that your mom never reached out. I would have helped—I promise."

"Don't talk about my mom like that. What do you know?"

I kept still, feeling the anger practically spill out of her. The sudden misery in Alex's eyes in contrast to the beauty of the autumn morning. I realized how hard this must be for her—all of it. I'd gained a daughter, but she'd lost her mom, and the consolation prize—me—wasn't what she was hoping for.

"I didn't mean—"

"Maybe this was a mistake. Maybe I shouldn't have bothered."

"It's not a mistake."

She bit her lower lip, studying the traffic rushing past us.

"I'm not sure anymore. It's a lot, all of a sudden."

"I get that. It's a lot for me too." I could tell it was the wrong thing to say as soon as the words left my mouth. The look of disdain on her face confirmed it.

"I've got to go." She walked toward her car.

"Alex?"

"Don't," she said, cutting me off with a flick of her hand.

"Wait. What just happened here? I thought we were working on this. On your mom's case."

"Like I said, I'm not sure anymore."

"Why not?"

"Because I said so, that's why."

"Please. I want to help."

She stopped, car door open, and looked at me, eyes bright. But with tears or anger or something else, I couldn't tell.

"I'm not sure I want it now."

A moment later she was in her car and pulling away.

4

I BARELY had time to ponder this turn of events when my phone buzzed again. Caller ID blocked. I answered anyway.

"It's Cindy Morris. Do you have a second?"

"Do I have a choice?"

"Of course you do."

"Good one. Anyway, I was expecting your call. What do you need from me?"

"What do you mean you were expecting my call?"

I explained to FBI special agent Cindy Morris what Columbus detective Denny Tipton told me yesterday at the museum, about the agency's interest in art theft.

"In fact, that's why I was calling," Morris said, sounding a little deflated. "Was hoping we could ask you a few questions."

"We?"

"A colleague of mine. Works on art theft."

"Attempted theft, you mean."

"Thanks to you, apparently."

"And a little help from my friends. When did you have in mind?"

"No time like the present. Those guys are still out there, whoever they are. Be good to get a jump on them."

"On a Sunday?"

"It's a priority case."

"I assume you know I was fired?" I pictured Lillian Melnick, the tall, elegant security director, and how white her face was as she told me I'd been terminated.

"I heard that rumor. Sorry."

"Me too. This morning's not good. I have a family matter to attend to."

"This afternoon?"

"To repeat, you do know it's Sunday?"

"I'm aware of that fact, Andy. You'd be doing us a favor."

"How?"

"You might have some insights into what happened. Because of your background."

I sighed. Where Morris was concerned, the line between doing her a favor and being served with a subpoena was thin. "I can give you an hour around one. Would that suffice?"

"I guess it'll have to. We'll see you then. You know the address?"

"Yes. It's 837 Mohawk. My place—I'll have kids with me by then, and I can't leave them alone."

To my surprise, rather than fighting me on it, Morris agreed and said they'd stop by my house at one o'clock. I disconnected and rose to return to my van, then thought better of it. I scrolled through my contacts until I found the number for Patience Hampton. She answered on the second ring. I apologized for interrupting her Sunday morning and told her why I was calling.

"Home visit, huh? Lucky you. I'm supposed to give them a statement next week at their offices. Not the personal touch you're getting. Course I wasn't in the thick of it, either."

"I should have taken your advice and let the guy go."

"I'm sorry about that, Andy. Melnick, I mean. She didn't need to do that—fire you and everything. But kind of typical. Stuck-up bitch, pardon my French."

"H_2O under the bridge. Plus, technically, she was right. 'No pursuits.' Just because she's a stuck-up bitch doesn't mean she doesn't have a job to do. I'm not happy about it, but I'd be lying if I said I hadn't read that in the handbook on day one."

"That's generous."

"Pragmatic, more like it. So, small favor?"

"Anything for you, my friend."

"Any chance you could grab my stuff? I left a bag and a book and a coffee mug there. I can meet you someplace."

"No problem. I'm back this afternoon."

"Thanks, Patience. Really appreciate it."

"Like I said, no problem. And I am sorry, Andy. I'm gonna miss you, be honest about it. Hanging with you was half the fun of coming to work."

Me too, I thought, wondering if we had a post-work future together. But what I said was, "And schooling me in art history?"

"That too. Which reminds me, you're still coming to my opening?"

"Wouldn't miss it."

Patience had secured an exhibit at Nature Morte, one of the oldest and most prestigious galleries in the Short North Arts District. It wasn't New York, but the owner also had galleries in Manhattan and Los Angeles. From what Patience had told me and I'd learned online, a pipeline east and west existed for a fortunate few if their Nature Morte exhibit went well. Shuffling from painting to painting with a plastic cup of white wine in one hand and a plate of dry cheese in the other wasn't exactly my thing, but if it kept me in Patience's good graces, count me in.

We said goodbye and a few minutes later I was on my way north to Crystal and Bob's, wondering what kind of mess awaited me. Traffic was light on 315 and soon I was parking outside their house, an oversized pile that always made me think of what might be produced if a Mediterranean villa and a Georgian mansion hooked up and had a kid. I glanced at my phone before walking to the door and saw I had a text from Alex. The message was short and to the point:

> This was a mistake. Please don't contact me again

CINDY MORRIS made good on her word and arrived promptly at one. She was accompanied by a male agent she introduced as Adam Fawcett, a tall, hale-looking fellow with a G-man central casting face that looked like it had been sculpted into symmetrical planes by a trowel.

I let them in and introduced them to Joe and Lyndsey, who I'd settled in the living room in front of *Frozen* along with a takeout pizza from Plank's. The movie was Lyndsey's favorite. A good egg, Joe hadn't blinked when she requested it. Crystal hadn't blinked either when I suggested Lyndsey spend the afternoon with me, which told me all I needed to know about the state of affairs at home. I hadn't even seen Bob.

Morris, Fawcett, and I moved into the kitchen and sat around my small table. Hopalong joined us a minute later, settling himself at my feet with a sigh.

"So," Fawcett said, opening a notebook and clicking a pen. "You'd never seen these guys in the museum before?" Like Alex this morning, straight to business.

"Not during my shifts."

"You're sure?"

"Positive. That doesn't mean they weren't there. I just never saw them."

"Go over what happened again."

I repeated the spiel I'd given the day before to Denny Tipton, the Columbus detective who caught the case. The squabbling couple, their argument growing louder and louder. The man's repetitive checking of his watch, which made more sense now. Following them into the

Impressionism room to quiet them down. The shared glance that suggested a put-on. Their departure into another gallery, followed a few seconds later by the cry for help from Alex back in the original gallery. My ill-advised pursuit. The tussle on the street, ending with the successful return of the unscathed Bellows.

"This girl." Fawcett checked his notes. "Alex Rutledge. Did you know her?"

"Not at the time."

"Had you seen her there before?"

I hesitated. "A couple times, yes."

This piqued his interest. He asked me the particulars and I told him my experience of seeing her in the gallery previously.

"Any idea why she did what she did? Got involved like that?"

"Possibly."

"What's that supposed to mean?"

I leaned back in my chair and peered into the living room. Joe and Lyndsey were absorbed in the film, though I had to figure they'd each seen it half a dozen times minimum, likely more for Lyndsey. Nevertheless, maybe it hadn't been such a great idea to invite the FBI to my house under these circumstances.

I lowered my voice and said, "Alex Rutledge is my daughter."

Surprise on her face, Morris said, "I thought you just had the two boys."

"Until yesterday, I thought so too. And I'd appreciate you keeping your voice down." I nodded toward the living room. "I haven't told them yet. It was a bit of a surprise." A notch or two above a whisper, I explained about yesterday's revelation. Morris seemed genuinely taken aback by the story. If Fawcett felt similarly, he didn't show it.

"You think she took those actions because she wanted to help you?" he said.

"Or because she's planning to become a cop and it came naturally." I told them about Alex's acceptance into the Columbus Police Academy.

"Seems like a strange coincidence," Fawcett said. "A daughter you've never met assists you in stopping an art thief like that. Is that the only reason she was there? To meet you?"

I conjured an image of the photo of Kate Rutledge. Recalled the pain in Alex's eyes as she recounted her mother's death. Considered the text she sent me a couple hours earlier. *This was a mistake. Please don't contact me again.*

"I guess she wanted to scope me out. Get the lay of the land before the approach. Police Legwork 101."

Fawcett and Morris exchanged glances. I didn't blame them for the implied skepticism. Even leaving out the primary reason for Alex's outreach—to enlist my help in finding her mother's killer—the episode with the painting did seem like a strange—a very strange—coincidence.

Fawcett said, "When did you start at the museum?"

"Mid-August. The sixteenth, I think."

"Why? Aren't you a private investigator?"

"Still am. Licensed and everything."

"So why this gig?"

"Personal reasons. I needed a more reliable schedule."

"Why?" Fawcett was staring at me closely, blue eyes cold and fixed.

I returned the stare. "My son's living with me more or less full-time now. It's called parenting. Any kids, Agent Fawcett?"

"August 16," he said, ignoring the question. "A month before the museum put the Bellows on display. *The Boulevard.*"

"If you say so."

"Seems like another coincidence. You undertake a major career change just as the museum acquires one of its most expensive art pieces ever."

"First off, I've worked plenty of security jobs, so I wouldn't call this a major change. More of a temporary shift in priorities. Secondly, as my mother used to say, I don't like your tone. What's your point?"

"My point is, it seems questionable that you in particular changed jobs at this juncture, and then were present the day of an attempted robbery of said painting."

"Me in particular. What's that supposed to mean?"

"Someone with your reputation."

"A reputation for saving the day, you mean?" I turned to Morris. "This is your idea of me doing you a favor? Fun and games with George of the Jungle? You can take a ticket next time."

"Andy—"

"Skip it." To Fawcett, I said, "A robbery I thwarted, in case you'd forgotten."

"Helped thwart, right? With your daughter?"

"With a woman I didn't know from Mata Hari at the time. Are you implying I had something to do with this?"

"Did you?"

Fawcett looked at me patiently, the cold blue of his eyes belying his relaxed expression, as though he were quizzing me on my pizza toppings preference.

"Yes. I planned it top to bottom. Starting with arranging to have a daughter who I had no idea existed be standing in the gallery at that very moment, and ending with nearly blowing out my knees trying to do the right thing."

To his credit, he kept his composure. "I'll take that as a no."

"You can tell that Quantico training every time. Of course it's a no. Why in the hell would you think differently?"

"Due diligence. Statistically, more than half of art thefts are inside jobs."

"Which means less than half aren't. That said, I assume you're questioning others?" Besides Patience and me, at least four other gallery associates were on duty yesterday.

"It's a wide-ranging investigation."

37

"So was the Kennedy assassination. And some people still think they got the wrong guy. What about the security cameras? They back up what I'm telling you."

"They confirm your story, from what I've seen," Fawcett admitted.

"That's not good enough?"

"We need to explore all the angles. Art theft's a serious business."

"And also a victimless crime."

"Victimless?" Fawcett leaned forward in his chair and scratched Hopalong between the ears. Always a lousy judge of character, Hopalong leaned his head into the gesture. "Try telling that to the museum's board of trustees, who authorized the purchase. To Eleanor Seward. She's livid. The money to buy it didn't come out of thin air. Plus, it's an affront to the community—the loss of a shared inheritance."

"Foiled loss."

"You know what I mean."

"Do I?"

I knew Seward, the board chairwoman, by reputation only. But it was a big reputation. There were few piles of old family money in town bigger than the one she sat on. She had the ears of congresspeople and U.S. senators, which I'm guessing explained this emergency Sunday meeting and which probably screwed up Fawcett's day as much as mine. If he hadn't more or less accused me of being in on the heist, I would have felt the teensiest bit sorry for him.

Fawcett scribbled something in his notebook and said, "Writing this off as a victimless crime sounds funny coming from a guy who broke all the rules to retrieve it."

"I don't take kindly to people encroaching on my territory, especially turf I'm being paid to protect."

"Even when the museum's rules of engagement specifically prohibit physical confrontation?" Morris said.

"What can I say? It's the principle of the thing. I couldn't stomach someone stealing a painting like that in broad daylight in full view of everyone. Sue me, I guess."

"There are those who would say the effort you put in could be an attempt to throw off suspicion," Fawcett said.

I met his gaze and didn't drop it. "Those people would be wrong. As in, heads-up-their-asses wrong."

"I hope that's true," Fawcett said, leaning over to scratch Hopalong once more. "I think we're done here for now. We may have more questions for you at some point."

"What a coincidence, since I have one for you."

"Which is?"

"Do I need a lawyer?"

Fawcett and Morris exchanged glances again.

"I'm not sure," Fawcett said. "Do you think you do?"

"I think you need to leave. And while you're at it?"

"Yes?"

"Stop petting my dog. I have no idea where your hands have been."

5

"I'M NOT really into sports."

My eyes opened and I rolled over in bed. I checked my phone—just past 5:30 a.m. Time to get moving. Instead, I lay back for a moment, puzzling over the voice I heard in my dreams just before awakening. The utterance of a single sentence. *I'm not really into sports.* Who wasn't? And why? But it was too late. The dream and the speaker's identity—man or woman—were already fading away. Oh well. I swung my feet to the floor and headed for the bathroom.

On a normal day, I would have been out the door with Joe by 7 to deliver him to school on time. That left a wide margin for traffic, meaning I sometimes deposited him on the curb twenty minutes early and sometimes had us rolling into the high school parking lot in the far northern suburbs with seconds to spare. Not today. Both Joe and Lyndsey spent the night with me, and Lyndsey had forgotten a homework assignment. As a result, I had to build extra time in to swing by Crystal and Bob's.

We hit their McVilla by 7:15. Under different circumstances I would have waited in my Odyssey and listened to the news on WOSU while Lyndsey dashed inside. Today, recalling the look of relief on her face when she climbed into my van the day before, I accompanied her into the house and stood in the darkened foyer downstairs while she retrieved a notebook. I heard running water in an upstairs bathroom but spied neither Crystal nor Bob. Back in the van, watching in the rearview mirror, I took in Lyndsey's braces and her unconscious application of lip gloss and thought about Alex at that age and what it would have been like to be there for her.

This was a mistake. Please don't contact me again.

Joe and Lyndsey safely at school, I pulled into a Tim Horton's drive-through, ordered a small black, and parked in the restaurant lot while I figured out my day. After some deliberation, I decided to call the Westerville Police Department. It was probably inadvisable, given what Alex said yesterday and the fact she ignored two texts and a call later on, but I told myself she hadn't technically pulled me off the case. Purely because of the circumstances, and the guilt I was feeling about the entire situation, starting with Kate Rutledge, I knew I'd have to poke around a little to ease my conscience. It was a family matter now, like it or not.

When the call went through, I asked for Doug Shortland, the traffic investigations guy. The woman answering the phone said he was in but unavailable and did I want to leave a voicemail. I declined the opportunity and headed for the highway. I'd risk showing up in the flesh. Sometimes the personal touch, like hand-delivered flowers or a roundhouse kick to the face, earned better results.

While I waited in the police department lobby, I thought more about the visit from Cindy Morris and Adam Fawcett the day before. In addition to bearing all the hallmarks of a ladder climber, Fawcett also struck me as a grade A asshole. With time to reflect—and cool down—I realized that it didn't necessarily make him a bad agent. He was adept at button pushing and had successfully pressed all mine. But why? He couldn't seriously think I was involved in the attempted theft of the Bellows, even if Seward had rousted him from a day off by pulling a few strings and demanding answers.

So what was he probing for? I'd tried calling Morris afterward for an off-the-record debrief between old frenemies, but it went straight to voicemail. I couldn't blame her for not picking up. Her job wasn't to pat me on the back and make me feel better. I'd have to reckon with whatever Fawcett was up to, but that would go on the back burner for now.

"Mr. Hayes?"

I looked up. A man stood at the door leading into the department's inner recesses.

"Detective Shortland. You had a question?"

I stood. "That's right. About the Kate Rutledge case." I presented my investigator's license and a business card. He took the card, examined it with the enthusiasm of someone pulling a parking ticket out from under a windshield wiper, and pocketed it without further glance. He studied the license a few moments and handed it back.

"What about it?"

"Is there someplace we could talk?"

He frowned. He looked to be in his mid to late forties, handsome in a younger version of *Blue Bloods* Tom Selleck sort of way—minus the 'stache—solid build, dressed in civilian garb of running shoes, dark slacks, a collared button-down shirt, and a blue V-neck sweater. "It's an ongoing investigation. There's not a whole lot I can say."

"I get it. I'm not trying to cause any problems. But I have a personal connection to the case." I decided to show my cards and gave him the abbreviated version of my encounter with Alex and her bombshell revelation.

"Okay, I grant you, that's a little different. Not what I expected to hear. Either way, I'm disappointed she didn't give me a heads-up. If she's dissatisfied with the investigation, it would be nice to know that. I'm as frustrated as she is, believe me. But bringing someone else in isn't going to move things along any faster."

Though Shortland seemed like a stand-up guy, I privately questioned if he was a fraction as frustrated as Alex. Aloud, I said, "If she's dissatisfied, it's because she wants answers, not because she doubts you're doing everything you can. The fact her long-lost dad is a private investigator may have seemed like too big a coincidence to pass up. I mean, nearly five months have gone by, and she didn't hire anybody else, right?"

"Not that I know of. That doesn't mean I resent this intrusion any less. I've got enough to deal with without the chance an outsider might screw up my case."

"I'm not going to screw up your case," I said, wondering if I had the authority to make that claim. As Alex pointed out over beers, screwing up cases—and then trying to make things right—was what I did.

Before Shortland could reply, his phone pinged with a message. He retrieved the phone from his back pocket, examined it, and replaced it without changing his expression. "All right," he said. "I can give you ten minutes. But like I said, it's ongoing. Not much I can say at this point."

"I appreciate it."

He settled us in a small conference room down the hall with a window overlooking a parking lot lined with the department's black SUV cruisers. A blank whiteboard covered most of one wall and a framed picture of the state memorial to fallen officers in London, Ohio, hung on the other. Shortland looked at the room's wall clock.

"Shoot."

I told him what I knew about the case, most of which was in the public domain, including Kate's early-morning jogging routine, the existence of the grainy gas station video, yaw marks indicating the driver's attempt to brake, and finally the fact that Kate had been dating a St.

Clare—North pharmacist named Billy Chowdhury—who'd called off the night before the accident—but that things had ended between them before she died.

"So basically you know what I know."

"I doubt that. Can you say if there's any suspects?"

"No."

"There aren't or you can't say?"

"I'm not telling you anything about suspects, nor am I confirming there are or aren't any."

"Is Chowdhury one of them?"

"I just said I'm not—"

"Have you at least talked to him? About why he called off?"

"I'm not at liberty to discuss an ongoing investigation."

"How about this: Can you say whether you think it was an accident, pure and simple?"

"Same answer."

I tried a different approach. "Have you had any luck tracing the vehicle?" I knew sometimes cases like this got hung up when police found the car but couldn't determine who was driving it at the time. Figuring that out could take days or weeks of additional investigation, which might explain the lack of progress.

"Can't say."

"I'll take that as a no." He frowned at this but didn't respond. I trudged on, aware I was most likely on a fool's errand. "Any witnesses other than the guy at McDonald's?" Alex had shared with me a copy of the initial incident report, which was all that was available under Ohio's open records law when criminal cases were pending. The report made mention of a man who was paying for an orange juice and an Egg McMuffin at the drive-through when he heard the thud of the SUV striking Kate. The same man—Leo Brown—had placed a 911 call that made the news, and he'd given a brief interview to Channel 7 when they showed up at his door that afternoon.

"Once again, I'm not at liberty to say."

"Is it just you on the case at this point? Or do you have help?"

"It's an ongoing priority investigation. And that's about all the time I have, sorry."

"You haven't told me a single thing."

"Did I say I would?"

"You get that we have the same goal, right? Trying to nail the guy who did this?"

"I can't speak to your motives, Mr. Hayes, though as a dad myself I'm glad you connected with Alex. At least she's not an orphan."

"That's harsh."

"Sorry. That came out wrong." His expression softened a little. "My dad was an orphan. I shouldn't have said that."

"It's fine," I said, seeing an opening. "So, you have kids?"

I could tell he wasn't happy about the question. "Six," he said at last. He caught the arch of my eyebrows.

"Four of our own, and we adopted twins."

"Wow. Good for you. Lucky man. What's your wife do, if I may ask?"

His discomfort deepened. "She works in Residence Life at Otterbein. How about you?" he said, staring. "What's your wife do?"

Busted. I explained about my sons and my two exes. He kept a stone face, to his credit.

"Not as lucky in love, I guess," I said, to break the silence.

"Back to Kate Rutledge," Shortland said, as if I hadn't spoken. "I can't tell you that much because there isn't that much. If Alex is in touch with Billy Chowdhury then she probably knows we talked to him. We talked to a lot of people, all right?" He hesitated. "I even checked Jamie Thacker out, as awkward as that was."

"Who?"

He looked at me. "Jamie Thacker. Alex's boyfriend? Ex-boyfriend, I guess."

There's a time for bluffing, but this wasn't it. I knew my face had given away my surprise at this revelation.

"She didn't mention him. He's a suspect?"

Shortland paused before replying. At last he said, "He's not a suspect, no. We talked to him because they had a bad breakup and, by Alex's own admission, he and her mom didn't get along. But his alibi is solid. Unfortunately."

"What's that supposed to mean?"

"I've already said too much. It's Alex's business if she didn't mention it. You'll have to ask her."

"How can you have an unfortunate alibi?"

"That's all I can say."

"It's hardly anything," I said, frustrated. But whether with Shortland or Alex, I wasn't entirely sure.

"One other thing, though," Shortland said.

"Okay."

"I'm not happy about you getting involved, but I guess there's nothing I can do about it. To be fair, I appreciate the heads-up. Some of you guys don't even show that courtesy."

"I'm not those other guys."

Ignoring the comment, he said, "Despite the heads-up, I'm hoping I don't need to remind you that this is a one-way street."

"Meaning?"

"Meaning, although I'm not compelled to share anything with you, you are. If you come across something germane to the investigation, you're obliged to tell me. Otherwise, it's—"

"Obstruction of justice. Thanks. I'm familiar with the Ohio Revised Code."

"Good to know. Second, although I've got too much on my plate to warn anybody about what you're doing, if you contact somebody I've interviewed and they call me, I'll advise them not to speak to you."

"Like Billy Chowdhury?"

"Like anybody."

"Thanks a lot."

"You can lose the attitude. My job is to find out who killed Kate. If you do anything that hinders our investigation, or jeopardizes it in any way, I'll shut you down."

"Even if I make progress where you don't?"

I saw anger bloom in Shortland's eyes for the first time in our brief acquaintanceship. "Listen," I added quickly. "I was hoping for more from you, but I get your point. You do your job, I'll do mine. If there's even a job to do. It sounds like this case is as cold as they come."

"I didn't say that."

"You didn't have to. I know ice when I see it."

6

I WALKED out and went back to my van. It wasn't even 10:30 and already I needed a beer. Shortland's lack of cooperation was aggravating, but not unexpected. What really bugged me was Alex's decision to hide the fact that her ex-boyfriend had been interviewed, "unfortunate" alibi or not. Why keep that kind of information quiet on a case like this? Slowly, though, I calmed down. I'd known Alex exactly twenty-four hours when we talked at the scene of her mother's death the day before. None of this could be easy for her. What business of mine was it that she'd had a bad breakup when I wasn't even in her life, especially since Shortland had cleared the guy of involvement? Come to think of it, embarrassment at the thought of having to tell me might explain her change of heart and the darkening of her mood. I was fooling myself if I thought I empathized with a tenth of what she was going through.

Reluctantly, I put the thought of a beer aside, climbed into my van, and made a short list of people to talk to if I decided to carry on with this case, with or without Alex's permission. To call any of these people suspects seemed a stretch. Billy Chowdhury, Kate's former boyfriend who called in sick the night before, was the only one who could possibly fit the bill, but I knew damn well Shortland would have looked hard at him already. Yaw marks or not, he wouldn't have ruled anyone out.

I considered briefly what Alex told me about the antivaxxers her mom and others on the nighttime ICU had to deal with. Was it far-fetched to believe one of them took their frustrations out on Kate? There'd been news accounts here and elsewhere of deniers physically confronting the caregivers of their dying loved ones. It was hard to believe someone would turn that denial into a motive for murder, but I decided not to dismiss it out of hand altogether.

That left the rest of Kate's work colleagues. Natalie Mettler, Kate's friend who left for the calmer pastures of home health care. Dr. Christine Coyle, the former administrator now running her own drama-free clinic. Dr. Ryan Ives, the attending ICU physician on Kate's ward. With Ives and Chowdhury both working overnight shifts and the others gone from St. Clare, there didn't seem much point in stopping by the hospital this time of day. But in the end, I decided to satisfy my curiosity about the place Kate worked. Might as well start someplace.

On the short drive to St. Clare–North, I reminded myself that I had to figure out a time, and soon, to tell my family about Alex regardless of her dismissive text. The truth was out there, for better or worse, and I couldn't sit on it. I wasn't sure how any of them would take it, especially my parents, although I had a feeling, the boys aside, that nobody would be all that surprised. Someone asked me recently what I'd majored in at Ohio State, and for once I gave an honest answer: "I majored in girls and minored in trouble." Post-graduation—and post–federal point-shaving conviction—I elevated my studies to a career choice.

Deep down, I didn't blame Alex for insinuating she might not be my only long-lost child. There'd been a lot of Kate Rutledges over the years, not to mention two divorces and a broken engagement, before that summer on my uncle's pig farm finally cleared my head. I would always be grateful for those muck-filled months of grace. Although to this day I'm not a huge fan of pork.

I PULLED into the St. Clare's parking lot ten minutes later and assessed my surroundings. The hospital sprawled over a large campus, a conglomeration of older, largely brick buildings—the original central facility—supplemented by more modern-looking structures of glass and steel as the facility grew. Kate's hospital was part of a medium-sized health system with Catholic roots that also included its downtown headquarters, a hospital on the South Side, and a big operation on the eastern side of the city. Up here, services included a traditional emergency room, a cardiac unit, and an ob-gyn center, along with an extension of the downtown nursing college.

I knew that St. Clare–North increasingly catered to a large immigrant population, mainly the growing Somali and Bhutanese-Nepali communities on this side of town, along with aging retirees hanging on in their nearby suburban tract homes, leftover from the city's expansion in the '6os and '7os. Doing my research on Kate, I'd come across news articles suggesting that the area's shifting demographics, which included a heavier reliance on Medicaid and Medicare, were putting a financial strain on the hospital. No wonder its former director had disembarked for greener pastures.

I thought back to my conversation with Doug Shortland and his annoyance at my appearance on the scene. I also remembered his grudging gratitude that I'd at least made contact. On a whim, I masked up, walked inside, and asked the receptionist if the director of hospital security was available. She pointed me toward a bank of elevators and told me to follow the signs.

Brian Riggs turned out to be only slightly less thrilled to meet me than Shortland. He seated me in his office down the hall from a fishbowl room filled with monitors showing security camera views of nearly every angle of the hospital. Two monitors atop Riggs's almost spotless desk broadcast a smaller version of the same views—six screens apiece. I briefly glimpsed my Odyssey when one of the cameras flipped to a parking lot shot.

"I'm fine with ditching these as long as you've had your shots," he said, tapping his mask.

"Works for me," I said, pocketing mine.

"So," Riggs said, rotating my card in his hands like a three of clubs he couldn't decide whether to play. "You're the guy who cracked the Howie Campbell case."

"Guilty as charged. Did you know him?"

"Before my time." He flipped me his own card, which I tucked into my wallet. "I was on the job with guys who did, though. That was good work. A little unconventional. But at least you got to the bottom of it."

I wasn't surprised Riggs knew of the case—the publicity alone had been deafening. Campbell was a Columbus cop who retired on disability after a burglar he caught in the act shot and seriously wounded him in 1979. Then the burglar, instead of being prosecuted, fell through the criminal justice cracks and disappeared. It wasn't until Campbell's son hired me more than forty years later that I managed to find the shooter—and reveal the cover-up that allowed him to escape justice all those years. It was a messy, ugly affair that left three bodies in its wake. Exactly the kind of gonzo detecting that Alex referenced at the bar the day she asked me to find her mother's killer.

I also wasn't surprised that Riggs had been on the job; in my experience, most people in hospital security, at least upper management, had followed a tried-and-true career path from the force to the private sector. The transition seemed to have suited Riggs, a trim white guy who looked less like an ex-cop than an assistant dean, with short, sandy-brown hair—but not as short as a crewcut—a youngish face, hazel eyes, and tortoiseshell eyeglasses. He completed the look with freshly pressed tan slacks, a sky-blue checked shirt, a Celtic cross and diamond-patterned blue tie, and a dark sports coat.

"On the job," I said. "With Columbus?"

"You got it. Beat cop, narcotics, traffic, training bureau, vice. Little bit of everything."

"Why'd you leave?"

"Opportunity knocked. This gig opened up and I liked what I saw, especially after the crap we dealt with in Columbus. Don't get me wrong, we see some serious stuff. But after twenty years of shootings and stabbings, helping a panicked doc find his keys is a nice change of pace."

"A more stable schedule too, I'm guessing."

"Yup. Figured it would be a better way to spend more time with my kid." He paused. "Except now I'm divorced and he's with her."

"Tough luck."

"I suppose. But that's neither here nor there. So you're investigating Kate's death? I thought you were busy protecting pretty paintings."

Talk about deafening publicity. The local media had gone bonkers over the attempted theft of *The Boulevard*, especially given the "oh shit" factor that Eleanor Seward, one of the city's wealthiest and best-known philanthropists, played such a big role in its acquisition. The fact I'd been involved was the icing on the cake. Or blood in the water, depending on how you looked at it. That my connection to Alex hadn't leaked yet was a minor miracle and one more reason I needed to tell my boys, my sister, and my parents about her as soon as possible.

"All the paintings are safe now, thanks. Plus, I'm more into purloined bitcoin these days."

"I heard you were a joker. So what can I do for you, not that it's going to be much."

I explained my mission, concluding with my desire to talk to any remaining St. Clare employees who knew Kate, including Billy Chowdhury and Ryan Ives, the night ICU doctor. I was also forthright about Alex's and my relationship.

"Wow," he said. "You're Alex's father. So you and Kate—"

"Kate and I were never together."

He looked at me skeptically. "Never?"

"Just the once, if you must know. That was it." I wasn't going to mention the embarrassing fact that I had no memory of my daughter's mother.

"You only found out about Alex this week?"

"That's right."

He shook his head. "You don't hear that every day."

"So I'm told."

"I'm glad you connected, I guess. But it doesn't change the facts of the case. Kate's death was an accident. Some coward ran her down and fled. Alex's father or not, why would you need to talk to anyone here? Not that I'd ever grant you permission."

"It's the only place I have to start. I'm not accusing anybody of anything. But talking to friends and colleagues is all I've got right now. Maybe something might shake loose."

"Something like what?"

"A disagreement Kate had with someone. A concern she had about something. A car in the parking lot that seemed out of place. Anything, really. I won't know until I hear it."

"The answer's still no. It feels like you're dishonoring Kate, to be honest about it. Implying this was anything more than a tragic hit-skip. I'm surprised her daughter doesn't see it that way too."

"She just wants resolution. And so we're on the same page, I didn't need to tell you what I was up to, obviously. I'm doing that as a courtesy."

"Gesture noted, not that it will do you any good. I assume you've talked to Doug Shortland?"

I confirmed it.

"And I'm assuming he told you the same thing about talking to any of these people?"

"He did. But would I be wrong in assuming he already talked to the same employees that I want to talk to now?"

Carefully, Riggs said, "In the immediate aftermath of Kate's death, Westerville PD gathered as much information as possible, partly to track her movements while they established a timeline. Exactly how I would have done it. And yes, they did talk to people here. That's about all I can say."

Something occurred to me. "Are you part of the investigation?"

"What do you mean?"

"Well, ex-cop and all that. You've got a lot of experience. Are you assisting Shortland in any way?"

"Other than facilitating interviews and establishing a timeline for Kate that morning, absolutely not. It was pure coincidence I was even here."

"I'm sorry?"

"I had to come in early that day. There was a breached-door alarm on the ER that wouldn't shut off and I had to deal with it."

"What time was that?"

"I was here at six, whereas normally I start at seven. The only reason I'm telling you this is I got a call right away about the accident because Kate had a St. Clare ID in her running pack. I was able to check her shift status and confirm she'd worked and gotten off at the regular time."

"No other involvement with Westerville's investigation?"

"None. It's their ball of wax. I'm available to offer assistance on an as-needed basis. Which I did when it happened."

"Back to the employees they talked to. Did that include Billy Chowdhury?"

"That's not for me to say. Shortland's a good investigator. He did due diligence and more."

"So what's the problem with me doing it again?"

"He talked to those people within hours of Kate's death, and no more than a few days on. You want to bug them out of the blue after several months. Surely, you can see the impact that's going to have. People have only now started to heal. You'd be picking at a painful scab."

I knew Riggs had a point, even if I didn't want to admit it. I didn't always like this part of my job, but ruffling feathers was an occupational hazard of private investigation. We're the criminal justice equivalent of the obnoxious uncle at Thanksgiving: we show up late, often uninvited, ask questions we shouldn't, make unwelcome observations, read all the wrong social cues, and then on our way out the door leave a wake of destruction that only a marauding herd of elephants could appreciate. And after all that, the answers we find are often as popular as that uncle. Or those pachyderms.

I said, "I have to start somewhere. It's a cold case getting colder by the second. I figured I might as well begin here, knowing full well it was the wrong tree to bark up. But right at the moment, I don't have any other trees."

"No offense, because I know who you are and some of the things you've accomplished, starting with Howie Campbell. But that's lame. Ten minutes online could have given you the same information. A lot of folks here talked to the press afterward."

"But like you said, that was when it happened, what, five months ago? Memories change. People remember something."

"Which they'd be required to tell the police. Not you."

"I'm not keeping anything from the police." I reviewed the one-way street warning that Shortland gave me. "I hear something new, my first call is to Westerville PD."

Riggs leaned back in his chair. "Listen, I'm sympathetic. No one wants the bastard who did this caught more than me. Kate was good people. But I have my instructions, and they don't include ex parte interviews with hospital staff, especially if there's an implication you're looking at them as suspects. Plus, to repeat the obvious: we're not the subject of this investigation. Kate just happened to work here."

He glanced at the monitor on the right, watching people walk down a hall. He relaxed a little and said, "I'd help you if I could. Like I said, Kate was popular. Dr. Ives was devastated, as was Christine. But there's nothing I can offer, and I can't let you interview anyone on hospital grounds."

I let slide the obvious retort, that these people had homes I could visit. Like Shortland, he probably guessed I already planned that and was waiting to shut me down just as quickly if he heard from them.

Instead, curious as to his reaction, I brought up the topic of the anti-vaxx anger Kate and her colleagues faced on the overnight shift.

"It's been overblown by the media, you ask my opinion. But I'd be lying if I said some of it wasn't real. Emotions always run high on the ICU, and especially then. What about it?"

"Did Shortland look into that angle?"

He folded his hands and placed them on the desk in front of him. "You'd have to ask him."

"Okay. But in your opinion, is it possible?"

"Is what possible?"

"That some family member, I don't know, was so pissed off that they stalked Kate after hours?"

"You can't be serious."

"It's just a question."

"An inflammatory one. I mean, think about what you're saying."

"I get that. But you just said some of it was real. There've been stories of doctors and nurses confronted in parking lots, that kind of thing."

"Here?"

56

"I'm not saying that. But it's happened other places. I'm only asking because, like I said, I don't have anything else to go on. As far as I know, it was a random hit-and-run and none of this matters."

"If it helps solve Kate's death, it matters," Riggs said. "But you're on your own here. I appreciate the fact you came to me first. I doubt anyone will talk to you anyway, and I'll tell them not to if they reach out to me. That's true for Christine, even though she doesn't work here anymore."

"I appreciate the honesty."

"Really?"

"No," I said, excusing myself and walking out of Riggs's office.

7

ANNOYED AND also hungry, I left the hospital and drove to a Waffle House on Route 3 where I ordered waffles, eggs, and smothered and covered hash browns, then scrolled through my messages while I waited for my food. Still nothing from Alex. It occurred to me I might be sitting only a mile or two from her apartment, the one she'd shared with her mom. I thought about inviting her to join me for lunch and then remembered she worked the overnight shift and was probably still asleep. Plus, the specter of her newly discovered dad tromping around on her turf in defiance of her wishes might not put her in the best of moods.

Instead, I texted Mike, asking if he'd be free the next night for an unscheduled dinner with me and Joe. It was a gamble, since I wasn't sure I could wrangle Alex into attending. But I couldn't sit on our news much longer, regardless of whether she was present for the big reveal. With him in class I didn't expect a response right away. Just to be safe, I followed up with a text to Kym, his mom, letting her know about the request without explanation. She responded almost immediately.

Everything OK?

Over the past few years, our relationship had settled into a détente focused on what was best for Mike. But she never entirely forgave me for the way I betrayed our brief marriage with my affair with Crystal—not that I thought she should—and any change in the routines we'd established with our son tended to raise suspicions. And often for good reason.

> Right as rain

I knew immediately my response was a mistake, since Kym was also no fool.

> Now I'm worried

> No need

My food arrived just then and I set the phone down, thankful for the reprieve. As I ate, I reviewed my conversation with Riggs. On the one hand, he'd been more welcoming than I expected for an ex-cop-turned-hospital-security-director who couldn't be thrilled about a private eye digging up something that might give St. Clare a black eye. In the unlikely event an anti-vaxxer nut job did kill Kate, it wouldn't look good if it turned out their relative had been treated at the hospital. It wasn't fair. But neither was life.

On the other hand, Riggs's obstinacy in denying me official access to people like Billy Chowdhury and Ryan Ives seemed contrary to his desire to find justice for Kate. Almost five months in, with no leads, you'd think any help would be welcome. I supposed the blue code ran strong even if you weren't on the force. He'd rather take his lumps from me than Doug Shortland, honked off that Riggs let a civilian muck up an official police investigation.

No matter what, there was nothing Riggs could do to stop me from contacting people off St. Clare property. The clinic started up by Christine Coyle, the former administrator, was a boutique emergency room in New Albany called 21st Century Care. I called the number and, to my surprise, after a transfer reached Coyle herself. Further to my surprise, she agreed to a meeting first thing the next morning, though not before confirming I was both vaccinated and boosted. Either Riggs hadn't called her yet, or he had and, unlike him, she decided that talking with me had merit of some kind.

I still had a few hours before I needed to pick Joe up from school. It was too early in the day yet to bug Dr. Ives, the ICU doctor, who was likely sleeping after the overnight shift. Ditto with Billy Chowdhury. That left one other person I was hoping to talk to—the one person who had a direct connection, however tenuous, to Kate's death: Leo Brown, the man who'd been sitting in line at the McDonald's drive-through when the accident happened and had then called 911.

The one person other than Kate's killer, of course.

ACCORDING TO the police report, Brown lived in a duplex in Linden off Cleveland Avenue. Not that many miles down the road from where Kate died, though a far cry from comfy Westerville. The only interview I'd seen of him was a short clip on Channel 7 when he said something about being on his way to work at the time. I wasn't surprised when I saw which reporter tracked him down. The shelf full of Emmys at Suzanne Gregory's house wasn't there by accident. Checking with her was an option except for the little matter of her being my ex-fiancée. Which meant that contacting her came with complications that made the Yalta Conference look like a friendly poker game. I decided to leave her out of it for now.

After parking and finding the address, I knocked on the door and then rang the bell a couple of times. I waited a minute and tried again. And figured I was out of luck. Either no one was home or Brown wasn't coming to the door.

On a whim, I tried the opposite door. After a long minute, I found myself looking at a heavy-set young woman with fuchsia-colored hair pulled into a topknot and wearing a set of tight-fitting beige sweatpants and sweatshirt that left almost nothing to the imagination.

"What."

"How's it going?"

"Shitty. If you selling something, I'm not buying." Music played behind her and the smell of fast-food burgers filled the air.

"No worries there. I'm looking for Leo Brown. He's supposed to live here?" I nodded at the opposite apartment.

"Why you looking for him?"

I told her the truth, as far as it went. The fact I was a private investigator didn't seem to impress her, starting with the way she glanced at my business card as if it were a warrant and handed it right back. When I was finished talking, she gave me the exact look you'd expect a strange white man asking questions in a poor, predominately Black neighborhood to receive.

"He ain't around."

"Any idea when he might be back?"

"I mean, he ain't *around* around. I haven't seen him in weeks. I think he moved out."

"Any idea where he went?"

"Nope."

"Know anybody who might know?"

"Nope."

"Any idea when he left? You said weeks ago?"

I braced myself for another monosyllabic response. Instead, she crossed her arms and said, "This is about some lady that got run over?"

"That's right." I repeated my spiel about Kate's death.

"And he witnessed that?"

"Witnessed it, or at least heard the impact, looked over and saw the car leaving the scene."

"He in trouble?"

"Not as far as I know. I'm just trying to re-create what happened that morning. He's the only person who saw anything."

"I don't know nothing about any of that. But it was about then, I guess."

"About when?"

"You listening, mister? When you're talking about. I haven't seen him since. He was here, maybe a year, and then he was gone. Way back in May, at least."

THE FACT that Leo Brown, the one witness to Kate Rutledge's death, left the address he gave police almost immediately after the accident struck me as weird. It could mean nothing, since the textbook definition of what polite society referred to as a "transitional" neighborhood was that people were, well, in transition. But Brown had been living there a while, according to the girl, Ja'Nyah—she wouldn't give me her last name—which didn't jibe with a guy regularly on the move. As a result, the tidbit took on special significance, if only because it was the first fly in the ointment I'd come across. I'd wanted to talk to Leo Brown about what he saw that morning. Now, I needed to ask him that plus why he pulled up stakes right after witnessing a fatal hit-and-run.

The one other item I pried out of Ja'Nyah was that she thought Brown had been working construction someplace on the northeast side of town. The supposition made sense: he could have fallen into a routine of stopping at that McDonald's on his early-morning drive from Linden into the burbs. Canvassing central Ohio construction sites wasn't an option; the region was under assault from front loaders and cranes as developers took advantage of a booming local economy to throw up apartment complexes faster than you can say luxury square footage. It would make finding a needle in a haystack a welcome diversion.

If I located Brown, it would have to be the old-fashioned way: through an internet records search.

AFTER ALL my running around, it was late enough in the day that it wasn't worth going home and then turning around to pick up Joe after cross-country practice. I had no regrets about the decision to change the terms of my custody agreement with Crystal and let Joe live with me during the week. And sometimes weekends too, as had happened the day before thanks to whatever the hell Crystal and Bob were going through. You knew things were bad when a kid was better off with his underemployed private eye dad in his small rental home than with his mom and stepdad in a supersized McMansion in one of the priciest zip codes in town.

Benefits of the switch aside, the rigors of schlepping Joe up and back each day were starting to take a toll. If the arrangement stayed permanent, it might be time to broach the topic of him transferring to a closer school.

A few minutes later, I found a place at the bar at Temperance Row Brewing in the old part of Westerville they call Uptown. It was time for that beer I'd been yearning for since 10:30 that morning. No sooner had I ordered than my phone went off. It was Alex.

"Hey, Andy. I saw you called."

"Hi there." I wondered how long I'd go by my first name with my daughter. Maybe forever, at the rate things were proceeding. Before I could say anything else, she said, "I thought I told you to drop things with my mom."

"What do you mean?"

"You've been talking to people. Doug Shortland texted me. Told me you came by the station. Said he was making sure I was okay with it. Why did you do that after I asked you not to?"

I wasn't sure how to answer. Why had I disobeyed her instruction, if that's what you called a one-off text message

telling me to go away? And why hadn't I figured that somebody would out me to Alex? I surprised myself by what I
said next.

"Guilt, I guess."

"Guilt?"

"About me and your mom. About the fact I had no idea
about you all these years. About her death, as irrational as
that sounds. About a lot of things, honestly, some of which
have nothing to do with you. Because I can't do anything
to rewind the clock, I figured I'd at least try to get some
answers. For you, but also for me."

"You should have told me you were going to go ahead. I
felt blindsided, hearing from Shortland like that."

"You're right. I'm sorry."

I glanced at the TV closest to me. Two sportscasters, a
woman and a man, prime-time sexy and hunky, respec-
tively, were dissecting the Browns' narrow victory over the
Steelers the day before. Both had probably been in elemen-
tary school—at best—when their forebears picked over
my last pro game: the day I set the Cleveland franchise record for throwing the most interceptions in a single game.

"Andy? You there?"

"Sorry. Anyway, like I said, I apologize for not listening
to you. I'll steer clear from this point on."

Her turn not to say anything.

"Alex?"

When she spoke, her voice had gotten smaller. "So, did
you find anything?"

"I'm sorry?"

"I mean, as long as we're talking. Did you learn anything interesting?"

"Well, on the surface, no." Carefully, aware I may have
been granted a reprieve, I went over my conversations
with Doug Shortland at the Westerville Police Department, with Brian Riggs at St. Clare–North, and with my
good friend Ja'Nyah, Leo Brown's neighbor.

"So, nothing," Alex said, discouragement in her voice.

"Not exactly. The thing about Brown is a little odd. It might not mean anything. But I'd still like to talk to him." Even as I spoke, I realized something from my conversation with Riggs was also bothering me, but like a word on the tip of my tongue I couldn't come up with it.

"You don't think he had something to do with it, do you? I never heard that, from anyone."

I told her I didn't. "It wouldn't make sense, anyway. He was interviewed by the cops at the scene, where he was sitting in his own car."

"And Shortland. He confirmed it was an accident, right?" Her voice somewhere between defiant and fearful.

"In so many words."

"Meaning?"

"Meaning he wouldn't tell me anything, and he wouldn't show me squat. But he didn't take issue with anything you told me. The yaw marks kind of make it clear—whoever it was tried to stop but it was too late."

"And as for why they'd keep driving afterward?"

"We didn't talk about that. But as I'm sure you're aware, it happens all the time. People panic. They think they can hide. Or maybe they had a reason not to stop—a warrant or something. None of it's something a rational person would do, or a compassionate person for that matter. But adrenaline can mess with the mind."

"Why not turn themselves in, later?"

"It's a good question. I don't know."

Neither of us spoke for a moment. I drank some beer and glanced at the TV again. Like sleek big cats distracted by new prey, the sportscasters had moved on to the upcoming college football matchups. Perfect smiles disguising razor-sharp fangs, they didn't think much of Purdue's chances against Penn State.

Carefully, I said, "One thing?"

"Okay."

"Shortland mentioned something about an ex-boyfriend of yours. Someone they talked to."

A long silence, so long I thought she might have cut the connection.

"Alex?"

"I'm here. What about him?"

"Shortland made it clear he wasn't a suspect, that he had an alibi. But he called it 'unfortunate.' Do you know what he meant by that?"

Another pause. "It's nothing. The guy was a jerk. But he wasn't involved."

"Shortland said he and your mom didn't get along?"

"Drop it, Andy."

I decided not to press the point, even though I wasn't satisfied with the explanation. I needed to be back on speaking terms with my newfound daughter more than I needed the truth about her ex's alibi. For now.

Then, to my surprise, she said, "I don't know what to do next."

"What do you mean?"

"The thing is, I harbored this fantasy that you could fix things. The fact my dad turned out to be you seemed like this weird gift from Mom—like a beckoning from beyond or something. Sorry. I know that sounds weird. Then, when you said that yesterday, about her not reaching out to you about being pregnant, I lost it."

"I'm sorry about that."

"Don't worry. I see red sometimes. Something I inherited from you?"

"It's possible. People often liken me to a bull in a china shop. Except that's probably being hard on the bull."

That won a small laugh. "My friends say I should see a therapist."

"Not a bad idea."

"Except cops don't do therapy, Andy. You should know that by now."

You're not a cop yet, I thought, catching myself just in time from saying it aloud.

"Suit yourself," I said, not wanting to lose her at this point. "If you have one more second? I was actually calling for a different reason." I explained my hope we could have dinner with Joe and Mike the following night. I also asked her permission—perhaps my only smart move of the day—to tell my parents and my sister, and possibly to set up a meeting with them sometime soon. Somewhat to my surprise, she agreed on both fronts. I told her it would be easier with the boys' schedules to meet on the north side and she agreed.

"What are you going to do now?"

"Finish this beer I'm drinking and go pick up Joe, I guess. Why?"

"I mean about the case. About my mom."

"You're okay with me sticking with it?"

"If you think it's worth it, sure. Though it seems like dead ends at this point."

"To be honest, you may be right. I'm not sure what I can do that Shortland isn't. But I've got other folks to talk to, and then I need to track down Leo Brown." I told her about my meeting the next day with Christine Coyle, the former St. Clare–North director.

"What about Billy?"

"What about him?"

"Are you going to talk to him?"

"I'll try. If it's all right."

"It's all right with me," Alex said. "But so you know, I just got a text from him. I'm guessing the security guy reached out."

"And?"

"And in so many words he said there's no way in hell he'd ever meet with you."

8

AS MUCH as I wanted a second beer, it wouldn't be proper etiquette, not to mention good karma, to show up at Joe's school with two drinks under my belt. Instead, I traded up to a Dr Pepper, placed a to-go order of sandwiches to cover dinner, and reviewed my conversation with Alex. I could hardly fault her for the on-again, off-again confusion about her decision to ask me to look into Kate's death. Twenty-six years old and a successful Columbus police recruit or not, Alex had been through things in the past half year that beggared the imagination, from her mother's death to her discovery that I was the swine who fathered her.

I recalled her dismissive comment—*Cops don't do therapy*—and hoped she'd rethink it. Of course, how much therapy had I done, my backbreaking summer on my uncle's farm notwithstanding? Then there was her reluctance to talk about her ex-boyfriend, though that wasn't all that surprising. I'd played the lout in enough relationships to know how unwelcome my name was in multiple circles. At least she agreed to dinner with Joe and Mike the next night, and to my talking to my parents and sister. In fact, at that moment I was seized by a sudden desire to call Shelley and spill the beans, just to relieve myself of the burden I'd been carrying around for two days.

I never got around to it. As I waited for my sandwiches a text popped up from Patience, wondering if she could bring my stuff over around noon the following day, as she'd be in my neck of the woods. She said she'd bring lunch. I told her that was fine and thought, *At least one bright spot to the week.* Two minutes after that, Mike returned my text from earlier in the day about dinner the next night.

> I was gonna study with Hannah. Another night?

Hannah, his latest girlfriend. Together over two months now, so practically married by Mike's standards. I explained that it had to be tomorrow. He asked if Hannah could come.

> Family only

Boy, was that ever true.

> Please?

I stuck to my guns, with no response. Then, a few seconds later, his answer arrived.

> LMAO

Laughing my ass off. Except that in our exchanges, as both of us knew, it had come to mean the exact opposite: Screw you, Dad.

"I'M NOT *really into sports.*"
"*Is that so?*"
I opened my eyes. I lay still, afraid if I moved I would scare the dream off. It almost worked. For just a moment, shards of images floated before me and . . . there. A woman's face. Someone I recognized. But who? Was I finally recalling Kate? Or no—was that Alex's face? Or—and I found myself oddly disappointed by the thought—was it Patience?

I strained to hold onto the visage, but it vanished as the day started in earnest. Hopalong shifted beside me with a low growl, which meant I had only a minute or two before his aging bladder caused a mess I didn't have time to clean up.

"Thanks a lot," I said, rushing to open the bedroom door.

AT 9:30, the trek to Joe's school behind me, along with another coffee at Tim Horton's, I pulled into the parking lot of 21st Century Care. The contrast with St. Clare–North, showing its age on the distressed north side, couldn't have been more striking. The modern, gleaming two-story building sat on a couple of acres of former green space off Hamilton Road on the outskirts of New Albany, a section of town exploding like yeast proofing in a cup of warm water. Back in the day, the city wasn't much more than a one-stoplight village that I passed through driving from my flyspeck hometown of Homer on the way to Ohio State. Now it boomed like a modern-day Dodge City with tony subdivisions, light manufacturing, retail plazas, and medical facilities like Dr. Coyle's new venture.

It was easy to see the appeal of the clinic. Not only was it visually striking, 21st Century Care was safely removed from the humdrum world of community health. Poking around online, I'd determined that the shorthand for Coyle's facility was a FSED—a freestanding emergency department. More prosaically, it was a specialized operation that catered mainly to people with private health insurance. As a result, her patients were moneymakers loved by investors, which I assumed Coyle had as well. Her clinic even showed up in a *Columbus Dispatch* article weighing the merits of such facilities, which, despite mission statements to provide medical care in underserved areas, often ended up in affluent parts of town.

Dr. Coyle herself was waiting for me in the lobby, which looked like a cross between a Starbucks and an

IKEA showroom if you placed the results in the middle of a plant-filled conservatory room. She stepped forward with a smile and we bumped elbows.

"Dr. Coyle," I said. "Thanks for agreeing to see me."

"It's my pleasure. Glad you've had your shots—my policy is mask-free if that's the case. Let's talk in my office."

Coyle was trim, strawberry blond hair done up in a French braid, wearing a white coat over a beige blouse and dark slacks. Late forties or early fifties, and fit-looking. Very much the confident medical professional on the move. Her office matched her vibe of success: a spacious suite on the second floor with windows that overlooked an artfully landscaped drainage pond and a small stand of maples that escaped the bulldozer. A tray holding a coffee carafe, sugar, cream, and glass mugs sat on her desk. She closed the door behind her.

"Coffee, Mr. Hayes?"

"Black, thank you. And call me Andy."

"So, Andy," Dr. Coyle said, handing me the coffee and pouring herself a cup. Also black. She settled herself on a small couch without, I noticed, offering her own first name in return. "You've got some questions about Kate Rutledge. Such a tragedy."

"That's right." Sitting in a chair beside the couch, I reviewed Alex's request that I look into Kate's death.

"I understand you've talked to Doug Shortland and Brian Riggs," Coyle said when I finished.

So much for flying under the radar. I confirmed it. "I assume one of them called?"

"I spoke with Riggs after you stopped by St. Clare. He wanted to give me a heads-up. Professional courtesy—we worked together for quite some time. He also shared your personal connection to the case. I'm sorry for your loss as well."

"Thanks." I left it at that. Confirming in so many words to Brian Riggs that Alex was the result of a one-night stand was one thing. I couldn't see getting into that kind of detail with Coyle. Instead, I said, as politely as possible, "Brian didn't tell you to decline my invitation?"

"He did, in fact. Who I talk to is my own business."

"I appreciate it. I'm also guessing you know I'm starting from scratch here. And that I wanted to speak to him, and to you, and"—I hesitated a moment—"people like Dr. Ives and Billy Chowdhury, to get a better sense of Kate. Not because I think anyone from St. Clare was involved," I added quickly. "But because I don't have any other place to start."

"You're a private investigator, is that right? How does that work? Do you coordinate with the police?"

"Not exactly. I'm conducting my own independent inquiry. But the goal's the same: to find the driver of that SUV. If I manage it, my first call is to Doug Shortland."

"Even before Alex?"

"Depending on the circumstances, yes." I wondered if that were true and what I would actually do in that moment.

"As long as you're not impeding the police, I'm happy to help. I can't say I knew Kate all that well. But I want justice for her as much as anyone does. She was well liked, good at her job, and a hard worker. In addition to being a tragedy, it's a travesty they haven't caught anyone yet."

"I think they're doing their best."

"You'd hope so," she said, with the tone of someone used to getting her way and offended that not everyone felt similarly.

"I'll start with the obvious, then. Given all that, was there anyone you know of who might have wanted to hurt her?"

She seemed taken aback by the question. "Are you implying Kate's death wasn't an accident?"

"There's no evidence of that. In the absence of anything else to go on, I figured I'd ask."

"To be honest, Doug Shortland asked me the same thing right after it happened. The answer's the same. No one."

I mentioned the stories from Alex about occasional confrontations on the ICU ward with anti-vaxx family members.

"There were a couple unfortunate incidents. But it's a preposterous theory. As I told Brian when he relayed it to me."

"Frankly, I agree. But I think it had to be asked."

"If you say so."

As she spoke Coyle looked at her watch, pulled the screen close, and tapped out a response to some message or other. I was reminded that possibly the only thing Crystal and Kym had in common—other than their brief marriages to me—was that both were fans of their smart-watches. Kym used hers to keep track of exercise via various apps whereas Crystal seemed mainly to check social media, but still.

"More to the point of why I'm here, what can you tell me about Kate?"

"Well, hard worker, like I said. Devoted to her patients but, from what I could gather, also able to leave her work on the ward. Burnout is always an issue in the medical field, but it was especially acute during COVID. Kate seemed like she struck the right balance."

I recalled what Alex said about Kate and the anti-vaxxers. *She tried to understand where they were coming from, but some days it was almost too much.* Not for the first time in the past seventy-two hours, the thought occurred to me that Kate seemed like a special person. Someone I would have liked to get to know beyond the single encounter that brought us together a quarter century earlier.

"Anything else?"

"Well, this is a little morbid, given what happened, but she and I both liked to run. I'm in a running group, and every so often, her schedule permitting, Kate would come along. We meet at Antrim Lake most Saturdays and go north or south on the trail depending on the day. Alex has been there too, a couple times. Though not so much since . . . Anyway, we were friends on Runnrly. Always giving each other a thumbs-up." She laughed. "Kate was faster than me, which was annoying. Of course, she was a little younger too."

"Runnrly?"

"It's an app?" She raised her left arm and gestured at her watch. "Kind of like Facebook for runners. It tracks your workouts, compares your times on different routes. People friend each other and see how they're doing."

I nodded. It sounded like something Kym would use. As for me, I was happy with my ten-year-old Timex. Then something occurred to me.

"It tracks routes?"

"That's right. There's a mapping component, via GPS."

I recalled the circumstances of Kate's accident. Killed just as she crossed the intersection. A freak occurrence— the SUV approaching just as Kate left the curb.

"Are your routes visible to your, whatever you call them, Runnrly friends?"

"They are, depending on your privacy settings."

"I mean, speaking of morbid, could someone have looked at Kate's route and, I don't know, followed her? She ran the same time every day, right?"

"It's not morbid at all. I think about it all the time. I was running myself about the same time that day. You can't help but wonder what if. I know Doug Shortland was aware of Kate's use of Runnrly. I think at some point she turned the mapping function off. A lot of women do, for the exact reason you're thinking of."

"You included?"

"I probably should. But I compromise. You can disguise your start and finish, which I do. Since I don't always run the same route, it makes me feel a little safer. Though I'm sure anyone could still figure out approximately where I go."

"Someone could still see when you started, though, right?"

"Not in real time. It's not like the tracking in road races, where you can actually follow a runner around the course and watch their avatar move. Runnrly doesn't offer that. I suppose you could see afterward when they started their run." She fiddled with her watch. "Yes. This says I was out at 6:15 this morning."

Exactly the same time Kate started her runs. Including the day she died.

"You could detect a pattern, in other words."

"That's true. But like I said, Detective Shortland looked at all that."

I found myself wondering whether Alex used Runnrly and made a note, with my concerned father hat on, to ask about it. I also wondered about Billy Chowdhury. I put the question about both to Dr. Coyle.

"I believe I am friends with Alex." She checked her watch again. "Yes, we are. But we don't interact much. Some people, if I don't get a thumbs-up after a run, I actually worry if they're okay." She laughed again. "That's social media for you. I'll see Alex's runs occasionally, but I don't think she activates it every time."

"And Billy?"

"We're not connected. I didn't know him that well."

"Did you know he and Kate dated? And broke up?"

Her smile turned to a frown. "I was aware of that, yes. And before you ask, yes, I know he called in sick the night before. That's all been looked at."

I realized I'd run out of questions. I found the concept of the Runnrly app and its tracking capability disturbing. But as Coyle said, it wasn't in real time. All it did was show you a route. You could estimate when someone might pass a certain point, but down to the second? Which is what would have been needed for someone to target Kate. And there was no evidence of that kind of stalking.

"Was there anything else?" she said, glancing at her watch.

"How did you find out?"

"I'm sorry?"

"You said you were out running that day. How did you find out? About Kate, I mean. Was it later?"

"Oh. That was such a horrible morning, it all sort of blurs together. But yes, it wasn't for a couple of hours. My phone started blowing up at some point."

"That must have been traumatic. I mean, both of you out running like that."

"Yes. It made a terrible day all the worse."

"Worse for Kate, of course."

Her face fell as she considered her choice of words.

"Of course, of course. I'm sorry I said that. Of course it was worse for Kate."

Indeed, I thought.

9

I LEFT 21st Century Care unsettled by my conversation with Coyle. I didn't begrudge the administrator her move to boutique medicine. We all have our different paths, and it was easy to see the appeal of the upper-class setting without the headaches of a come one, come all facility like St. Clare–North. But thinking about Kate, and the affinity she had for community health care, it was hard not to take the high-horse position and see Coyle as a sellout.

Then there was the issue of Runnrly. I was familiar with the pros and cons of GPS and had used it myself more than once to track spouse cheaters and others. A few years back, smartphone tracking technology also allowed me to save the life of Theresa Sullivan, a prostitute–turned–social worker helping me investigate a serial killer stalking streetwalkers in town. Without the GPS on her phone, I'd never have found her in time after she walked into a trap the killer set.

But the implications of Runnrly for Kate's death were troubling, despite Coyle's assurances that Kate's map settings were turned off. Her Runnrly "friends" could still get a sense of her routine just by the time she left each day. I thought of my anemic Facebook account; even with how little I did with it, I still had dozens of connections. Had Doug Shortland checked out every single person with access to Kate's routines? It seemed a stretch to suggest that someone on Runnrly would have gone to those lengths to track Kate and run her down. But could I completely rule it out? Pondering all this, I headed for my unscheduled next appointment—one I hoped might bear more fruit.

"I WOULD have appreciated it if you called first. You're lucky I was even at home."

"I apologize. Sometimes I get a little ahead of myself."

I was standing on the stoop of a split ranch in a subdivision off Linworth Road. Standing before me was Natalie Mettler, garden trowel in her right hand, dirt muddying the knees of her jeans, a hint of impatience in her eyes. Her face shone with perspiration despite the cool temperature.

"You might as well come around back, as long as you're here. Alex told me you might be contacting me." She brushed a loose strand of straw-colored hair out of her eyes, tucking it under the brim of a canvas gardening hat. "Although I admit, this is a little much for my day off."

"I don't mean to intrude. I know it's a lot, coming out of the blue like this."

"Oh, I think you did, or you wouldn't be here," she said in a light voice. "It's okay," she added, cutting off the apology she saw forming on my lips again. "Alex told me the big news, that you're her long-lost dad. That's enough to cut you some slack. And if it helps with finding Kate's killer, I'm fine with it. Would you like some water? Anyway, I do. I've been out here a while. One sec."

She entered the house without inviting me to follow. She returned in a couple of minutes, handed me a glass, and waved for me to follow her around back. She seated us on folding chairs on an open brick patio beneath a large wooden pergola, a chiminea sitting just outside, surrounded by more chairs. The yard was small but filled with well-groomed flower beds, many of them adorned with late-season mums. She caught me admiring the scene.

"My husband's the handyman. He built all this," she said, gesturing at the pergola. "Our COVID project. I'm the one with the green thumb, I guess."

"I'd say you are. It's beautiful." I thought of my bare, postage stamp–sized yard in German Village and the pots of wilted begonias in the far corner.

"So, you're helping the police find whoever killed Kate?"

I corrected her and re-explained Alex's desire to have a fresh pair of eyes on the investigation. I told her about talking to Shortland, Riggs, and then Christine Coyle earlier this morning.

"And what did the good Dr. Coyle say?"

"That Kate was a hard worker, loyal, well liked. She also said she found it annoying that Kate was a faster runner." I told her about the Runnrly conversation. "Then she made a point of noting that Kate was younger than she is."

"That's Coyle to a T," Natalie said, shaking her head. "Hypercompetitive. What a thing to say."

"Not a fan?"

"I'll plead the Fifth. I didn't know her all that well and our paths rarely crossed. St. Clare's not huge but it's still a busy place, plus I worked nights until I left. I probably saw her husband more than her. But let's just say I'm not surprised she said that."

"Her husband?"

"David Coyle. He's a cardiologist. He's still at St. Clare, at least the last I heard. Which is kind of funny."

"Why?"

"He was an investor in 21st Century Care. Well, one of several. You don't launch something like that on a shoestring. Seemed odd that he stayed in the trenches while his wife moved uptown, so to speak."

At least my assumption about investors had been on point. "Maybe he likes his work?"

"It's possible. Or maybe they decided it was better to stay in their own gardens. Sometimes marriages work better that way."

I tried to decide if it was strange that Coyle hadn't mentioned him during our conversation. Maybe she thought it wasn't relevant and, frankly, it was hard to disagree. But Natalie's remarks had at least triggered one thought.

"Christine Coyle. Was she why you left?"

"Her? Hardly. I left because I couldn't take it anymore."

"What do you mean?"

She took a drink of water. "I'm guessing Alex has already told you this. Everything changed during the pandemic. Well, obviously. But things got turned upside down because of politics. We're used to emotion on the ICU—people are at their most vulnerable, and they're confused and scared. And it can get nuts. One minute you're doing compressions on someone who coded out of the blue, and a minute later a patient's screaming at you because you're late with their apple juice."

"That sounds unpleasant."

"It was. It was also part of the job. Some people, like Kate, handled it better than others. Grace under fire and all that. She was in line to be a preceptor, which made sense."

"A what?"

"Like a supervisor to newer nurses. She would have been great. Anyway, COVID kicked the drama to a whole other level. We were getting crushed by all the people coming through. Record-high numbers of patients on ventilators. We came close to running out a couple of times. The hospital hired tons of travel nurses to keep up, at a hefty price tag, by the way. It still wasn't enough. We thought the vaccine would change all that. It never occurred to me that people would walk away from the one thing that could save them."

I told her how Alex mentioned what a hard time it had been for her mom because of the anti-vaccine crowd.

"It was crazy, to be honest. The patients that came in then, a lot were in complete denial, not to mention their families. I decided to leave after somebody on a ventilator hit me while I adjusted their propofol drip. I mean, enough's enough."

"It's understandable."

"Just for the record, that was the last straw, not the impetus. I was well past burned-out by that time."

"Do you mind if I ask if Kate's death affected your decision?"

She studied a rose trellis for a few moments. "I was going to leave regardless. Kate knew that. But not having her around my last couple of weeks erased any doubts."

"Better situation now?"

"Home health? It's got its challenges, like anything else. But yes, by a mile."

"Back to St. Clare. Did you work with Dr. Ives?"

"Of course. Why?"

"He's still there, right?"

"As far as I know."

"How'd he handle all that? The COVID stuff you're telling me about."

She grew quiet for a moment. "He got frustrated, like everybody else. And he had it worse, in my opinion, because of his personal situation."

"Which was?"

"He lost both his parents in the first wave. And his wife's a coronavirus long-hauler. It left her nearly disabled—couldn't drive anymore, couldn't be in front of a screen. She worked at Nationwide but had to retire. Ives and his daughter care for her at home. His daughter's a nurse, which helps. But still."

"A nurse at St. Clare?"

She nodded. "She only works part-time because of her mom. Anyway, Ives is a saint. He kept plugging away, even in the face of all that crap, and all the hours." She paused. "And all the dying." Her voice dropped. "So many deaths."

"And Kate too," I said carefully. "She seemed like she could handle it?"

Natalie didn't speak for a moment. She took another drink of water. She looked out at her lawn and watched a squirrel do that run-freeze-look thing, like it just spotted a *Tyrannosaurus rex*.

"Kate was remarkable. She thrived on it. I mean, don't get me wrong. It took a toll on her, like everybody else. She got as much crap thrown at her as any of us did. And she took patients' deaths hard. Almost personally. There was this one . . . anyway, she just showed up next time, raring to go. She was also good at the stuff we all hated, like calling docs at 3 a.m. because their patient coded. And she was always on the administration to get things right."

"Like what?"

"Oh, minor technical stuff. Not sure it matters."

"Try me."

"Well, our IV pumps were supposed to communicate with a back-end recording system to track medications, but the two parts weren't always talking. Not a biggie, but it mattered to Kate. That's just the kind of nurse she was. Which reminds me, you know Alex is going to be a cop?"

I told her I did.

"Like mother, like daughter. All the turmoil made Kate work even harder. Perseverance in the face of adversity—it must run in that family."

For better or worse, I thought. I said, "Just now. You said, 'this one.' A patient? Someone who died?"

She hesitated. "Well, yes. Kate took it hard, is all. Like I said before."

"Was there something unusual about the case?"

"Not especially, I guess. I don't remember a lot of the details. I don't think they were vaccinated, but that wasn't unusual. I happened to see Kate as she left that day, and I could tell she was upset."

"Do you remember who it was?"

"Why does it matter?"

"I have no idea. It probably doesn't. I'm just exploring all angles."

"I'm not sure I should tell you. It's not really my place, and there's patient confidentiality . . ."

I looked into the yard at the squirrel, which was back to darting to and fro, and said nothing.

"Shirley Vanhouten," Natalie said after a moment. "I only remember the name because my mother had a cousin with the same surname. But you can't do anything with it—you have to promise."

"Just between us." I added quickly, "You were talking about Kate's perseverance?"

"That's right," she said, relief on her face at the change in subject. "It's like that old saying: 'Adrenaline either makes you sick or it stimulates you.' Definitely the latter for Kate."

Once again, I advanced my theory, which felt lamer each time I spoke it aloud, about an anti-vaxxer stalking Kate. I also mentioned my fears about Runnrly.

"Wow," she said, shaking her head. "I don't know where to start."

"I know. It's just all I've got right now. What you said about Shirley Vanhouten made me think of it."

"I don't know about Runnrly, but maybe my kids do. When I go for walks, the last thing I want is to worry about stuff like that."

"Me too."

She glanced over at the squirrel, which was now eyeing a bird feeder. "I suppose anything's possible, anymore. I did hear that someone followed Dr. Ives to his car once. But from that to murder? I don't know."

"Any idea who that was?"

"Just somebody having a bad day. Security was on him in a flash. Nothing came of it, as I recall. And trust me, we saw plenty of asshole family members before COVID."

"Sure," I said, but made a mental note to ask Brian Riggs, the St. Clare–North security director, about the incident. I wondered why he hadn't mentioned it.

"Did you and Kate talk much about this stuff? Or, did she ever tell you, I don't know, how she dealt with it?"

"Not really. Kate could be circumspect at times. Sort of inscrutable. She was a born nurturer, but she also had an outer layer, a thick skin, that you weren't going to get past. You know what I mean?"

"Like she was hiding something?"

"Nothing like that," Natalie said, adjusting her sun hat. "She was just very private. There were certain places you couldn't go. Like, I'd talk about things with my husband, and she'd talk about . . . well, she'd talk a little too, and listen, but it's like you hit an invisible wall at a certain point. That's what made the thing with Shirley Vanhouten stick out. She was really upset."

I thought about Alex. Her own reticence made a little more sense now.

I said, "Did Kate ever talk about Billy Chowdhury?"

She looked at me. "You should leave Billy out of this."

"Why?"

"He was very upset about what happened. He's still not over it—not that I suppose you ever could be."

"I'd still like to speak with him. I promise to tread lightly."

"That's up to him. But, I have to be honest, I don't think it's a good look."

"What isn't?"

"Implying that someone at the hospital had something to do with this. Patient, family member, or employee. This was a random hit-and-run by some cowardly shithead, right?"

"That's the way it looks," I conceded. "It's just—"

"Just what?"

"It's just that this is the only way I know how to do something. Start at the beginning, even if there's absolutely nothing there."

"Why not let the police do their job? What is any of this accomplishing?"

"I promised Alex. She's frustrated and wants answers faster than she's getting them."

"She's just a kid—she'll get over it," Natalie said, and then from the look on her face immediately regretted it. She reached behind her and fingered the trowel stuck in her rear pocket as if rubbing a talisman for support. "I'm sorry. I didn't mean it like that."

"It's okay. I understand what you meant. I should go—I've kept you long enough." For a moment I considered asking about Alex's boyfriend and his negative relationship with Kate. I thought better of it at the last second, realizing there was no point in aggravating things with Alex should Natalie mention our conversation.

Instead, I pulled a card from my wallet and rested it on top of the glass-topped coffee table sitting between us. "This is how to reach me. Let me know if there's anything I can do to help."

She picked it up without speaking, examined it, and placed it back on the table. "With what?" she said, a quizzical look on her face.

"With figuring out who the cowardly shithead was who killed Kate. It's the least I can do at this point."

10

BACK IN my van, I thought about calling Brian Riggs and asking him about the incident Natalie mentioned, of someone following Dr. Ives into the St. Clare's parking lot after his shift. But I decided it would be better to ask Ives about it first, assuming I ever got the chance to talk to him.

From there I headed home. Patience was due shortly after noon with my stuff from the museum. I was looking forward to seeing her for purely personal reasons. But I was also interested in any gossip she had on the fallout from the attempted theft, especially now that the FBI was taking such an interest in it.

I tried to stay focused on Kate's case as I drove, but distractions got in the way, starting with tonight's dinner with Alex and the boys. It was hard to predict how it would go, though one thing in my favor was that my career choice already trended toward surprises and unexpected outcomes. As a result, this news, if not prosaic, might not be the most outlandish piece of information I'd burdened my sons with. Maybe if I—

A horn behind me interrupted my reverie. I glanced in my rearview mirror and saw a car that had stopped just before crossing the intersection I'd driven through. The subject of the driver's ire was a car coming up behind me that must have run the light as it turned red. I did the math and figured both cars were at fault: the guy behind me for pushing it through a freshly turned red light, and the guy entering the intersection the instant the light turned green.

I shook my head, thinking both of traffic idiots in general and, naturally, Kate's death more specifically, when I noticed the car behind me had slowed. Odd, I thought. Not the move you'd expect from someone so in a rush they risked running a red. As a result, I kept an eye on the car—a small light-colored SUV—as I drove down the street to 315. Within a couple of minutes on the expressway, I decided I'd picked up a tail.

This is not a hard science. Interpret traffic patterns long enough and soon you're imagining yourself on your favorite cop show trying to outrun whoever's after you. Except nobody is. But there was something about this car that checked some boxes. The way it clung to me, two, three, even five cars back sometimes, all the way past the exits for Ohio State and then closer and closer to downtown. A couple of times I lost track of the car altogether, only to see it reemerge as the accordion of midday traffic elongated to the point that making up lost ground was possible again. I could have been overthinking things. But I didn't think so. The fact the driver wore sunglasses and a COVID mask disguising his features only strengthened my suspicions.

As we neared downtown I decided on a little test. A redesign of the road in recent years allowed people who had merged onto 315 from 670 the opportunity to exit onto Broad Street about a mile west of downtown. The same exit was prohibited if you were coming straight down the expressway, as it entailed moving too quickly over too many lanes of traffic to the right. The restraint was probably a good thing since the cut-over was a recipe for an accident under the right conditions. But I was hardly the first person to violate the rule.

I waited until the last second possible, assisted by clear lanes to my right, then swerved my van hard across the double line meant to dissuade the move. I tapped my brakes as I approached the light at Broad going far too fast. But the move was worth it. Just as I hit the ramp, I looked in my rearview mirror and saw the SUV react, attempting to follow but just as quickly shifting back into the regular flow of traffic moments before what would have been a nasty encounter with a bridge abutment.

So, someone had followed me from Natalie Mettler's house. But who? And why?

PATIENCE'S EYES widened as I related the story thirty minutes later as we sat at my small dining room table. She'd brought two Styrofoam boxes of Hot Chicken Takeover with sides and two sweet teas along with the string bag of my things from my museum locker.

"Wonder what kind of car Dr. Melnick drives?" Patience said.

"You're not serious."

"Why not? She's still up in arms. There's no telling the lengths she might go to punish you."

"I don't think her dislike of me goes that far."

"Please, Andy. It's the good doctor we're talking about here. Has PhD, will retaliate."

"Now you're just picking on her. Not that I mind." But Patience also had me wondering if the tail could in fact be linked not to my investigation into Kate Rutledge's killing, but to my role helping thwart a major art theft. Joking about Lillian Melnick aside, it was conceivable the FBI might put me under surveillance if Agent Adam Fawcett considered me a suspect. I told Patience what I was thinking.

"If that's true, another brilliant use of our tax dollars, my friend. On the other hand, that sounds less scary than if whoever was following you is connected to this other thing you're working on."

"It's also possible I'm imagining things."

"Really?" She reminded me of the detail I'd provided of losing them at the last second at the illegal Broad Street exit.

"I like to play devil's advocate with myself. Sometimes it's the only conversation I have all day."

"Good one, Andy. Thanks for reminding me why I miss having you around."

The feeling's mutual, I thought. I realized I'd never seen her in civilian clothes before—a pair of nicely fitting jeans, an embroidered peach blouse, and a flowing multicolored wrap suited her fine, as did her earrings and a necklace of silver sand dollar–shaped disks. Her brown hair, normally bound tightly at work, hung full and relaxed around her shoulders.

"So, back to me," I said. "What's the temperature like at the museum after Saturday? And did you give the feds your statement yet?"

"This afternoon. As far as the temperature goes, I think boiling hot just about covers it."

"That bad?"

"For starters, chasing you across town or not, the good doctor's in a bad way."

"I'm not surprised. It is a pricey painting, and it's her job to protect it."

"True. But things aren't going down exactly the way you might think. The problem is, Melnick's taking a lot of crap for letting you go."

"Really? She had me dead to rights, not that I'm happy about it. Maybe she was just looking for an excuse, the way she felt about me."

"Well, it's not like she got along with the rest of the staff any better, including me. I told you about the diet thing." I nodded, recalling the story Patience once related about Melnick, who was tall and thin, casually asking Patience if she'd ever tried any of those weight-loss apps. A classic Melnick cheap shot. While Patience could fairly be called a hippy person, she was hardly obese.

"A class act, as always."

"Spoken like a gentleman," she said with a wink. "But in this case, she underestimated you."

"What are you talking about?"

"Turns out a couple of the museum trustees had kids or grandkids at Red, White & BOOM! a few years back. They're pissed they weren't consulted about you being let go."

"The gift that keeps on giving." Though my tactics had been questioned, the fact that I'd thwarted a white supremacist from detonating a van-sized bomb in a crowd numbering in the tens of thousands at the city's annual fireworks bash had won me a few goodwill points over the years.

I said, "Do those trustees include Eleanor Seward?"

"The dowager countess?" Patience said dismissively of the board chairwoman. "Fortunately, I'm not sure she cares about peons like us. No, she's focusing all her anger on the good doctor herself. Lots of questions about how this could have happened. And that takes me back to the mission Melnick's on."

"Mission?"

"You heard me. Melnick's response has been a whisper campaign, supposedly."

"About what?"

"About you maybe being involved in the heist."

I put down the chicken leg I'd been about to bite into. If that was true, it might explain the grilling I'd undergone with Special Agent Adam Fawcett at this very table two days earlier. Dr. Lillian Melnick, up to her usual tricks.

"We all know it's bullshit," Patience said. "But Melnick's still got enough juice that the police supposedly heard her out and took it seriously. Either way, work's not a pleasant place to be right now."

"All the more reason I appreciate you getting my stuff."

"Anything for you, my friend," she said, eyeing me for a moment before scooping a spoonful of mac and cheese.

"Those are nice," I said, changing the subject, if only slightly. "Your earrings, I mean."

"Thanks. Made them myself. Test driving them before the opening." Her jewelry was a conglomeration of jade, silver, and what appeared to be teakwood. Just for a moment I imagined her wearing them and nothing else. The picture was not displeasing.

"How's that going? The show, I mean."

"A little stressful, to be honest. I could use another week, easily. You're coming, right? I want at least one other person there besides me."

"Don't be absurd. It'll be a hit."

"You never know, my friend. Art appreciation is a fickle business."

I had my doubts, but decided not to dispute what I didn't really know anything about.

"Back to Melnick for a second?"

"If you insist."

"Whether that was her behind the wheel or not, she could land me in some serious shit if she keeps it up—maligning me, I mean."

"Look at you and your detective skills. I think that's the goal, obviously. Anything to distract from the fact they nearly lost the Bellows on her watch. She knows damn well she's out on the street if the dowager countess decides it's time for a personnel change."

"Tough crowd," I said.

"Meh. That's the art world. Beware the pat on the back since it may come with a knife thrust. Honestly? My guess is it'll just fade away after a couple of weeks. Some bruised egos and, well, your job, but that'll be about it as far as collateral damage. I mean, they didn't lose the painting, right? And bonus, attendance is way up. Everybody wants to see the one that almost got away."

"You'll be sure the FBI gets that memo?"

"Not sure how much sway I have in that direction. And what exactly did they tell you, when they were here? I mean, do they have squat?"

"They didn't tell me anything. Fawcett made it clear he didn't like the fact I'd traded my private eye gig for a security job around the same time the museum put *The Boulevard* on display."

"He can't possibly believe you'd be involved. For one thing, you don't know anything about art."

"I know that beauty is in the eye of the beholder," I said, catching her blue eyes for a moment.

"They say that's half the struggle. I was teasing, by the way."

"Don't worry about it. I know I don't know anything about art. Or didn't, before I met you. But the thing is, with Seward on her own mission, there's extra pressure to figure this one out. From what I've heard, she gets calls to the Oval Office returned by someone within twenty-four hours. That's enough juice to get some trees shaken." I recalled the momentary pity I felt for Adam Fawcett, figuring he somehow owed Seward's influence for being rousted on his day off to roust me in turn.

"I don't envy you. Fighting off the good doctor on one side and the dowager countess on the other."

Patience stayed a few minutes longer, chatting about the museum and her gallery opening as we ate our chicken. I tried to imagine the two of us together as more than ex–museum guard pals. I didn't find the thought too taxing. She had an artist's earnestness about her that I thought might get old at some point, but the fact she was passionate about her craft was something to admire.

"I should go," she said at last. "I've got an appointment with the feds I probably shouldn't miss."

"Good luck with that."

"Appreciate it. See you at the opening?"

"It's a date."

"Promise?"

"Promise," I said, walking her to the door.

"I'm glad," she said, and then to my surprise leaned in and kissed me on the cheek. She lingered just for a second, long enough for me to smell her perfume and feel wisps of her hair fall against my face.

"See you round, my friend."

11

I WAS still thinking about Patience's kiss twenty minutes later, straightening up after lunch and strategizing next steps. I wondered what would have happened if I'd returned the gesture. The fact was, I was between girlfriends and trying to decide how I felt about it. My most recent ex, Anne Cooper, was a distant memory best not dwelled on, though we still ran into each other from time to time, for better or worse. My unorthodox friends-with-Sunday-morning-benefits relationship with Judge Laura Porter was on hold, thanks both to my museum job, which often found me working all weekend, and to her recently announced run for the Ohio Supreme Court.

Staying single was probably just as well. I had Joe and Mike to think about, both of whose schedules were increasingly taking up a lot of my free time. Mike was looking at colleges and Joe wouldn't be far behind. And of course, now there was Alex. So yeah, single. For sure.

I filed the thoughts into my "what if" folder for now, sat down at my laptop, and, slightly against my better judgment, ran a quick search of Alex's ex-boyfriend, Jamie Thacker. His social media presence was sparse—his Facebook page zipped up tight, though I knew that generation wasn't much for the site anyway. A search of muni court records was more fruitful, showing a speeding ticket, a DUI, and a drunk and disorderly citation. It was hard not to look at that record and wonder about Kate. Asshole ex-boyfriend with a drinking problem takes his anger over a breakup out on his girlfriend's mother? But angry drunk or not, he had the "unfortunate" alibi, according to Short-land, who struck me as a thorough if not forthcoming investigator, at least with me—our uncomfortable chat about our vastly different family situations notwithstanding. Plus, Thacker was just eighteen when he earned the drunk and disorderly charge, putting him in the same category as jillions of other heavy-footed young men showing bad judgment. But for some lucky breaks, including several football-loving cops, I would have been in jail five times over at the same age.

I dropped that inquiry and returned to the hunt for Leo Brown. It was a long shot. But short of a random mention of someone who followed Dr. Ryan Ives into the parking lot during a high-stress period of COVID care, it was the only lead I had.

Except Brown didn't want to be found. After pulling up a composite history on him via a records database I subscribed to, I tried several people associated with him—mom, dad, siblings, roommates, and so on. I soon learned there were a lot of disconnected numbers out there. I was ready to call it a day when my phone went off.

"What's going on? I leave you alone for five minutes and you're back in the news."

"Sue me—I get bored easily. Everything okay?"

"Highly copacetic. Wondering if you're free this afternoon. I could use a little help."

"With what?"

"It ain't protecting art, Woody, I'll tell you that much."

Otto Mulligan was on a list shorter than surviving astronauts who walked on the moon who I permitted to call me by my long-ago nickname. With a last name like

Hayes and the ability to throw an inflated pigskin accurately enough that people considered me the best thing since sliced pumpernickel, it was natural that from high school on I was known as Woody in commemoration of legendary Ohio State coach Woody Hayes. The glow of that origin story dimmed after my point-shaving conviction my senior year and my Hindenburg-like stint with the Cleveland Browns. As a result, I tended to discourage the nickname's use. Most people could take a hint. But most people weren't Otto, a bail bondsman not used to letting things go.

"All right. Give me the details."

When he was finished I disconnected and went back to work. I had ninety minutes before I had to meet up with Otto. I spent the remaining time back on the internet, searching for details about Shirley Vanhouten, the patient whose death Natalie Mettler said hit Kate especially hard. It wasn't hard to find the online obituary, which listed her age as seventy-eight and described her as a beloved mother and grandmother. No cause of death. As I read the notice, I realized she died just three days before Kate was killed. A coincidence?

Vanhouten's first survivor listed was a son, Jeff Heaton. I called the number I found for him but had to leave a message. Just as well. It felt like the wildest of wild goose chases.

A little later on, my afternoon schedule turned inside out, I walked into a laundromat in a low-rent shopping plaza off James Road carrying a basket of thrift-store clothes that Otto handed me a minute earlier as we slid out of his Tahoe. Otto followed close behind with his own basket.

"Play it cool now, Woody," Otto whispered.

"Always, boss."

I stationed myself between our mark, who was standing by the counter scrolling through his phone, and a young woman next to him folding what looked like both their sets of laundry. As I watched, Otto nonchalantly dumped his clothes into a washer, added some detergent, and then made a show of patting his pockets.

"Aw shit," he said.

I kept my eyes on the mark, who looked up at Otto's comment but didn't say anything. He was thin, with a scraggly beard and equally scraggly brown hair the color of a lawn after grubs have taken over. I noticed a tremor in his hands that could have been drink or drugs or almost anything in between. He didn't look mean so much as unsteady, but both qualities could lead to unfortunate outcomes, in my experience.

"Hey man," Otto said to him.

"Yeah?" His face twitched as he spoke.

"Got any quarters? Forgot I played pinball last night—used them all up. You can have this for anything you got," Otto said, reaching a twenty toward him.

The mark, who was white, looked nervously at the brown-skinned Otto for a moment. The trembling in his hands worsened and I worried he might be on the verge of a breakdown, or some kind of ill-judged racial comment. But in the end, the color of green was all that mattered to him.

"Lemme see," the guy said, reaching for the bill, which was all Otto needed to lickety-split slap a cuff around his wrist, jerk him around, bend him over the counter, and apply the second cuff. That's where I came in, holding the line by taking up a stance between him and his girlfriend in case she objected to his apprehension. For the moment, she just stared, open-mouthed.

"The fuck?" the twitchy guy whined, squirming unsuccessfully beneath Otto's iron grip.

"You forget about last month's appointment with Judge Armstrong?" Otto said. "Two counts of receiving stolen property?"

"That's all bogus. My lawyer told me—"

"He told you squat, because I've already talked to him," Otto said, marching the man toward the door. I was following close behind when a voice caught me up.

"Hey." The girlfriend.

"What?"

"Where you taking him?"

"Jail," I said, keeping my eyes on her hands. "He jumped bond."

She stared at Twitchy's back as Otto shoved him through the door, planted him against the Tahoe, and waited for me to help insert him inside.

"Good." She turned back to her laundry. "Keep him there for a change, why don't you. I'm fucking sick of his shit."

"YOU DON'T have to do this," I told Otto forty-five minutes later as he stood me a beer at Thunderwing Brewing around the corner from the new county jail. We'd deposited Twitchy there after a twenty-minute drive across town listening to him whine and moan the whole time. I gestured at the four bills Otto slid across the table after we sat down.

"Do what?"

"C'mon. You could have done that job with one hand tied behind your back."

"I've actually done that and it ain't that easy. As far as who I hire, that's my prerogative."

"I feel like a charity case."

"Oh, you are, Woody. Make no mistake about that. But you're my charity case, which is all that matters."

"I appreciate it. I'll make it up to you."

"Do that and I might sock you. We're all good, Woody. This is just until you get back on your feet. Plus, I appreciate the backup. This time the girlfriend was happy to sit back and watch me take out the trash. But it doesn't always work out that way. The angry fiancées are the worst, trust me."

We toasted pissed-off lovers and dropped our beers a fathom or two.

"My charitable foundation aside, you working on anything else, Woody? I mean, besides stolen art? I might have a couple more things coming my way if you're interested."

Without giving it much thought, I came to a sudden decision. "As a matter of fact, I am," I said, and proceeded to tell him about Alex.

"Holy shit," he said when I finished. "That's a legitimate mindblower."

"And one I need you to keep quiet about for"—I checked my watch—"three more hours." I told him about the family dinner I'd arranged.

"I'll keep it off Twitter until then."

I laughed, but knew I didn't have anything to worry about. If anyone knew about keeping family secrets, it was Otto. His own kids were grown and out of the house when he finally learned the identity of his father—a white Franklin County judge who'd fallen for Otto's Black jazz songstress mother decades earlier at the downtown steak joint where bigwigs went after work. Otto's mother told him the truth as Judge Patrick Mulligan lay on his death bed with cancer, giving father and son exactly one week of together time. Rather than be bitter, Otto, one of the more forgiving guys I'd ever met, expressed only gratitude for the last-minute gift.

"So," he said, as if reading my mind. "You've got a daughter you never knew about, which is enough to handle for a whole year in my book, except she comes with a murder case not going anywhere fast. You always were an overachiever."

"It's a hit-and-run, not murder. A jerk who left the scene. Vehicular manslaughter at best."

"Yeah, I read about it. It was bad, whatever it was. And you don't remember her at all? Kate Rutledge, I mean?"

I explained that to my everlasting shame, I didn't. I didn't mention the strange voice in my dreams the past couple of days.

I'm not really into sports.

"That's a tough one, Woody. At least try to remember you're not the guy you were back then."

"It's a losing battle some days. This pretty much makes me want to throw in the towel."

"Don't. I may need you for some more charity work. In the meantime, you got anything on this driver?"

"Nothing, basically." I explained my theory about a riled-up anti-vaxxer, mentioning the incident Natalie Mettler related to me. I also told him about Leo Brown and concluded with the incident of the person who tailed me from Natalie Mettler's house.

"A tail, huh? Don't like the sound of that. Me, I'd put my money on the feebees. They want to see who you're meeting up with, that kind of shit."

"Not a bad theory."

"Course it ain't. Let's see. Leo Brown." He pulled out his phone and tapped at the screen for a minute. "Nope, nothing right away. That doesn't mean much. I can run his name through a few places if you want."

"More charity?"

"If that's what you want to call it, sure."

"What do you call it?"

"What do I call my old pal Woody Hayes waking up to a new kid who's going to be a Columbus police officer? Who once she's in uniform may have some tips she can throw Uncle Otto's way now and then? I call that a vested interest."

12

AFTER ARRIVING home, I had just enough time to push Hopalong out the door and make it halfway to Schiller Park, which was all the distance he needed anymore for his afternoon dump. It was one of the advantages, if you could call it that, of having a twelve-year-old Labrador whose best days of squirrel chasing were years behind him. Five minutes after that I was on my way to collect Joe and Mike. Ninety minutes later, we were seated at a Donatos in Powell as I tried to keep my cool while looking up at the entrance every fifteen seconds.

"What's the deal?" Mike said. "Are they coming or not?" He'd nearly drained his Coke already.

"They'll be here."

"Who's they?" Joe said. "Is that their pronoun?"

"Just someone I need you to meet."

"I still don't see why I couldn't bring Hannah," Mike said. "I thought you liked her."

"I do like her. She's way smarter than me, which is a plus in my book. But this has to be just family."

"I'm hungry," Joe said. "Can we order?"

Ten minutes passed. I had almost given up hope when the door opened and Alex walked in. I waved her over to the booth, feeling both relief and trepidation.

"That's who we're waiting for?" Mike said. "Wait, is she a new girlfriend? How come you can—"

"She's not a new girlfriend."

"Then who—"

"Sorry I'm late," Alex said, sliding in next to me.

I took a deep breath. Over the years, I'd faced down my share of stone-cold killers and stared into one too many gun barrels for my tastes. But somehow, right at the moment, those incidents felt like welcome diversions to the task ahead of me.

"Joe, Mike . . ."

"Hi guys," Alex said, interrupting. "I'm Alex Rutledge. I'm your half sister—Andy's daughter." She reached out a hand and shook both of theirs in quick succession. "He just found out, so don't blame him for not knowing about me. Well, don't blame him too much. It's really nice to meet you. You okay with sausage and onions?"

No one said anything for a moment. As our personal world stopped, the world around us continued with a steady buzz of conversation, refills, and clinking utensils. It was like that moment of disassociation that happens as a car spins out of control, except with fun family dynamics.

"Holy shit," Joe said at last. The reaction was so uncharacteristic of my younger son that I laughed in spite of myself.

"You're our sister?" Mike said, looking from Alex to me and back again.

"That's right."

"Who's your mom?"

This was the moment I'd feared the most. Neither of my boys was stupid. They were well aware of my track record with women, in generalities if not the gritty details. Each lived with one of my ex-wives, after all, and each had been introduced to more than one of Dad's "friends" over the years. Once again, I needn't have worried.

"Her name was Kate Rutledge. She and Andy weren't together very long. She's dead now—someone ran her over when she was jogging and then drove away. Andy's helping me find the person who did it."

More silence. Two tables away, a pair of tween girls dissolved into giggles at something a grinning boy across from them said. After another long moment, it was Mike who broke the tension.

"Okay, then. Nice to meet you too. I'm okay with sausage and onions. But what about mushrooms?"

From there, the evening went better than expected. After a few minutes of awkward conversation, the boys warmed up to the incredible development in their lives and peppered Alex—and to a lesser degree me—with questions. I kept my mouth shut for the most part, mainly because I was learning a lot myself. Alex told them she'd played basketball in high school and also run track, which impressed both Mike, the sports-crazy football player, but also Joe, a cross-country runner. She was into video games, especially *The Walking Dead* and *World War Z*, which was a big hit. She'd read all the Harry Potter books and seen all the movies, but preferred the *His Dark Materials* worlds created by Philip Pullman. I could tell that Joe and Mike were secretly pleased when they found out that neither my sister nor my parents knew about Alex yet.

Dinner over, I walked Alex to her car while the boys situated themselves in my van after exchanging semi-clumsy hugs with their new sister and pledging to get together soon.

"I thought that went well."

"Yeah. I like them. It's cool to have new brothers."

"And a sister for them. I'm glad this worked out. Listen, while I've got you." I gave her a quick rundown of the interviews I'd done in the past two days.

"That incident with Dr. Ives? Where he was threatened in the parking lot? Do you remember your mom talking about that?"

She didn't say anything right away and I could tell something was on her mind.

"Everything okay?"

"I guess," she said, not convincingly. "Did you talk to Ives?"

"Not yet. I'd like to at some point, if I keep going with this. Why?"

She folded her arms across her chest. "Nothing. It's stupid."

"What's stupid?"

"I guess I should have told you before."

"Told me what?"

She looked past me. "Do you remember the thing about my boyfriend? And his alibi?"

"Sure. What about it?"

"The thing is, Dr. Ives has a daughter. Taylor."

"I know. Natalie Mettler mentioned her. She helps her dad take care of her mom. The poor lady can't even drive anymore because of COVID."

"Here's the thing." An expression someplace between resignation and embarrassment crossed her face. I waited, sensing her discomfort.

"She's the alibi. She was with Jamie the morning my mom died. They'd been sneaking around behind my back."

13

AFTER LEAVING the restaurant parking lot, Joe and I dropped Mike off in Worthington. I walked him to the door and lingered for a few minutes inside while I told Kym about Alex, leaving out the bombshell she'd dropped in the parking lot about her ex and Taylor Ives. Kym responded about how I figured she would, with curiosity tinged with compassion. After everything I put her through, Kym still managed to show me grace in our relationship that I didn't deserve. I knew I couldn't expect the same from Crystal, but I'd deal with that when the time came.

An unfortunate alibi. Talk about an understatement. It turned out Kate's instincts were on the mark when it came to Jamie Thacker. Alex wasn't sure how long the affair had been going on, and I didn't press the point. Alex had gotten to know Taylor casually through Dr. Coyle and her Saturday morning running group. At some point, Taylor had met Jamie. Things happened, as they sometimes do. I could tell it was agony for Alex to explain this to the father she'd known all of four days.

"I don't have to talk to Dr. Ives," I told her. "Not if it's going to make things worse."

"Things can't get any worse, Andy. Not after Mom. And I really don't care one way or the other. If we're going to do this, we need to follow all the trails, no matter where they lead. Don't worry about me."

"You're sure?"

"Stop asking. Just do what you have to do."

Back home, Joe settled on the couch with his tablet and finished some homework. I thought about calling it a night. I was tired after a long day and the conversation with Alex about her ex hadn't helped matters. I felt horrible for her even as I suppressed a desire to find Jamie Thacker and push him up against a wall. But for better or worse, now Dr. Ives was on my mind. As irrational as it sounded, Alex's revelation almost felt like a sign that I needed to speak to him sooner rather than later. I checked the time. Not quite ten. Late by normal standards, but in Ives's case I figured the window might be open for me to catch him before he left for the night shift at St. Clare.

From what I could tell he still had a landline in addition to a cell phone. You don't see a lot of those anymore—my parents and my uncle and aunt were the only ones I knew who still had them—but I figured it might make sense for a doctor as a backup.

"Hello?" A young woman's voice. Had I reached Taylor Ives first? How perfect.

"It's Andy Hayes. I'm trying to reach Dr. Ryan Ives."

Nine times out of ten, introducing myself up front got the desired effect. The worst thing you could do, I'd learned over the years, was simply ask for someone. That was the verbal equivalent of pasting the word "telemarketer" on your forehead. But I was out of luck this time.

"What's this in regards to?"

I hesitated, wondering the best way to approach this.

"I'm a private detective," I said at last. "I'm looking into the death of Kate Rutledge. I'm introducing myself to as many of her friends and colleagues as possible to let them know what I'm doing and to see if there's any help they think they could offer. I've already spoken to Brian Riggs at St. Clare, just so you know. I'm sorry to call so late, but I was hoping to set up a time to speak to Dr. Ives." I left out any mention of Alex.

"You talked to Brian Riggs? He said it was okay to call?"

Carefully, I said, "He knows what I'm up to."

Silence ensued, so long I thought she might have hung up after realizing I hadn't really answered her question. "One sec," she said at last. Another minute passed.

"This is Dr. Ives."

I repeated the spiel I'd given to the woman I presumed was Taylor.

"It's a little late to be calling, don't you think?"

"I apologize. I was hoping to catch you before your shift."

"Well, you managed it, not that I'm happy about it."

"I'm sorry. With your schedule, I wasn't sure the best time to reach you."

"It's all right. Taylor said you've already spoken with St. Clare security?"

"That's correct."

"So, what is it you want to know about Kate? She was a wonderful person and a devoted nurse. Beyond that, I don't know how much help I can be. I've told the police everything I know, which wasn't much."

"Is it possible to meet? It might be easier to go over everything in person."

"I'm afraid not. My wife is ill, and it's difficult for me to get away. It's just my daughter and me taking care of her."

"I completely understand. In that case, if you have a quick second, is there anything else you can tell me about Kate that I should know? If you don't mind?"

"Related to what? To her work, you mean? I only know what I read about the accident."

"To her work, sure."

"But why? You're not suggesting someone at St. Clare—"

"Not at all. To be honest, there's so little to go on I'm starting from scratch. Anything could help at this point."

"You're a private investigator, you said?"

I confirmed it.

"Are you working with the police? Or who hired you?"

I hesitated, but only for a moment. Unburdening myself to my boys tonight had eased some of the pressure I felt to keep quiet. "I'm not working for the police, although they're aware of my involvement, and anything I learn goes straight to them. I'm actually working for Kate's daughter, Alex."

"I see. And she thinks you can find something the police can't?"

"That's the hope. There's one other thing I might as well mention."

"Which is?"

"I'm also Alex's father."

I gave him the quick rundown of how we'd found each other, emphasizing that Alex hadn't known of my existence until Kate's death. I was honest and said it was hard to say I'd really known Kate.

"That's quite a story. I can see now why you're involved." Some of the suspicion had left his voice, which I realized with a twinge of guilt had been part of my motivation for spilling my secret. I hated to trade on Alex's and my relationship, even though using it to my advantage was probably inevitable on this case. I also wondered if it were possible that Ives didn't know about his daughter's betrayal of Alex.

When he didn't say more, I figured he was in the dark. What twentysomething woman would spill those kinds of embarrassing details to her father, especially since they overlapped in a cruel coincidence with a tragedy like Kate's death? Beyond that, I was guessing father and daughter had plenty to do just taking care of Taylor's long-haul-COVID mother.

"I'm still not sure how this doctor can help," Ives said after a moment.

I paused, not sure I'd understood him correctly, before realizing he was referring to himself. "Well, let me ask you this. I know from talking to Alex, and some others, that things were particularly rough because of COVID—"

"Others who?"

"Other people who worked with Kate. Christine Coyle, for example. And Natalie Mettler."

"You talked to Coyle?" he said, the disdain obvious even over the phone.

"That's right."

"And she mentioned the burden we were under? That's rich."

He had my interest now. "Why do you say that?"

"It's not important. Things were difficult, yes, I acknowledge that. But again, what's that to do with Kate?"

"I heard that some patients, and some family members of patients, could be"—I searched for the right word, recalling what Natalie Mettler said about Ives losing his parents to the virus in pre-vaccine days, and the ongoing health problems of his wife—"difficult at times."

"Difficult how?"

"Over the issue of vaccines."

A long silence. "We had our challenges, yes. What about it?"

"It was mentioned to me that at least one person, a family member, was so angry they followed you into the parking lot after work?"

"Who told you that?"

"It doesn't matter. But I'm wondering, if it's true, whether in the absence of any other leads . . ."

"Wondering what?"

"If someone like that could have been so angry at staff members, that they . . ."

I realized I didn't want to spell the suspicion out, especially to the attending physician on an ICU ward, especially to someone like Ives, who'd suffered so much himself, and especially at this time of night. Unfortunately or not, I didn't have to worry.

"You're suggesting someone took their anger over vaccines out on Kate? Is that it?"

"It's just a question."

"An offensive one, to say the least. These were extremely ill patients, many of them dying. Their family members were distraught. The losses they suffered were unimaginable."

"Losses that were preventable," I said, unable to help myself.

"Maybe so." He paused for several moments as if composing himself. "It's hard to fault someone for lashing out under those circumstances," Ives said, so clearly angry that his voice had changed pitch.

"That's a generous perspective. I respect that."

As if he hadn't heard me, he continued: "No one should judge someone for reacting to what he perceived as an affront to his own morality."

He, I thought, the word registering. Had Ives just given me a clue as to the identity of the person who confronted him?

"I'm not judging anyone."

"It's obvious you are. I think we're finished here. I hope for Kate's sake, and for Alex's, that you find out what happened. Just don't drag blameless people down with you."

And before I could say another word, Dr. Ives hung up on me.

14

DR. IVES'S words were the last thing I thought of as I drifted off to sleep an hour later. *It's hard to fault someone for lashing out under those circumstances.* Talk about grace under fire. Ives had lost both parents to COVID, had a wife disabled perhaps forever by the same virus, undoubtedly took plenty of shit from anti-vaxxers as he tried to save their lives or those of their relatives, and still wouldn't pass judgment. A better man than me, I thought.

Considering all that, I wouldn't have been surprised if his comments followed me into my dreams. Maybe they did. But instead of his voice, what I heard echoing in my foggy brain as the alarm went off the next morning was something a little more familiar.

I'm not really into sports.

I sat up.

Shit.

I finally remembered.

DAMON'S, THE ribs restaurant, up at the Continent. The faux-European entertainment district was a ghost town now, but still a semibusy concern in those days. I'd been hunched in a booth with a couple of buddies, one a former third-string defensive back at Ohio State already going to seed as a car salesman, the other a high school pal working construction. After my senior season blowout that cost Ohio State the Michigan game and a shot at the national championship, they were some of the only guys willing to be seen with me in public. I'm sure the fact I always bought the drinks had nothing to do with it. And arriving at our table to take our order as the Macarena blasted over the restaurant speakers, a stern-faced, raven-haired, dark-eyed beauty whose name badge said "Kate."

"You know who this is, right?" Tony, the ex–defensive back, elbowing me.

"*The* Andy Hayes." Tim, my high school buddy. "He plays for the Browns. The *Cleveland* Browns."

Kate looked at each one in turn and gave me the eye.

"I'm not really into sports."

That caught my interest. Call it sexist, but up until that night it had been my experience that many women, even or especially the ones who knew of my past, were willing to overlook my college-era sins and indulge a desire to take care of me, figuring—wrongly—they could change my errant ways. Recently, my pro football player status was the catnip that sealed the deal. And yet, sitting in a back booth in a Damon's at the Continent, I appeared to have found the exception to the rule. Even more intriguingly, in the form of a waitress not inclined to suck up in hopes of a big tip.

"Is that so?" I said.

"That's so."

I smiled at her. "So what are you into?"

"I like to read."

"Like what?"

"Like books."

That won guffaws from Tony and Tim, whose reading preferences, to my knowledge, started and ended with *Playboy* and *TV Guide*.

"What kind of books?" I said, even more curious now.

"Thick ones. With lots of words."

"Can you be more specific?"

"Ones you haven't heard of."

"Try me."

"Okay." She put a hand on her hip. "How about *Dinosaur in a Haystack?* It's about science." She looked at me with a challenging gleam in her eye. "It's really good."

Without looking away, I reached down, found my backpack, unzipped it, and pulled out said volume, which I'd specifically asked for the previous Christmas.

"Yes," I said. "I've heard that."

The table went quiet. She stared at me. She took her hand off her hip. I stared right back.

Uncharacteristically—for me, anyway—we talked for two hours back at my apartment that night after her shift ended—talked and argued and cajoled and sparred over everything from books to politics—emptying half a bottle of Dewar's in the process before we eventually tumbled into my bedroom.

I awoke to sunlight streaming into the room and the bed empty beside me. Later that day, I found a number for her and tried calling, but she didn't call me back. Two nights later I went to Damon's but the manager said she was off. Two nights after that, the manager said she'd quit. I tried half-heartedly for another couple of days to find her, but to no avail. The day after that, pissed off and feeling sorry for myself, I bellied up to the bar at Hooters on Route 161, where a bartender with the requisite grapefruits-sized bosom, long lashes, and a pair of big, blue eyes flashed me a smile as she struck up a conversation.

"Football player, huh?" she said. "That's cool."

We didn't talk for two hours beforehand that night.

Or the night after.

Or two nights after that, though by then I was already on to a different girl.

SHIT.

How could I have forgotten Kate like that? Forgotten the electricity between us, the sparks that flew in my apartment as I connected with the first woman in a long time who seemed more interested in what was between my ears than in my shorts. And vice versa. Yet the memory had slipped through the sieve of time and disappeared, buried under too many benders that summer as I tried to put my botched senior year in college behind me—not to mention the eleven months in a federal lockup that followed—and ignore my anemic pro career. Too many benders, too many hangovers, too many hookups with only one goal in mind. So many hookups. What had I been thinking?

How could I have been so stupid?

Reluctantly, I pulled myself together. I had Joe and school to think about. I also had Alex to think about; Alex, and justice for her mom.

I sleepwalked through the usual routine of making coffee, letting the dog out and back in, and shaving. I forced myself to review my conversation with Dr. Ives and how I might have approached things differently. Like everyone else, Ives reacted strongly to my suggestion that an unhinged family member took matters into their own hands, affronted by the care provided by Kate as they rode the high of some internet-fueled vaccine conspiracy theory.

Or was it into his own hands, as Ives obliquely suggested?

Despite Ives's anger, what struck me most was the forgiveness at the heart of his comments. His reaction was like the empathetic cousin to the Hippocratic oath: first, do no harm, then, forgive any harm done to you. Could I be so magnanimous in the face of the abuse that I inferred that Kate and others suffered as they did their best to minister to the sick and dying? Doubtful.

Kate. Shit.

As I dressed I made a point to ask both Doug Shortland at Westerville PD and Brian Riggs at St. Clare–North whether any report was filed on an individual—on a man—confronting Ives in the parking lot. It was hard to imagine that, if there was, it had missed the attention of investigators looking for clues to Kate's death. But weirder things had happened.

That was the last thought I had about my investigation for several hours as someone knocked on the door just then. Hard.

I WASN'T sure who to expect this early, though I half suspected I'd find myself staring at Alex for some reason or another. Instead, Adam Fawcett, the FBI agent looking into the attempted theft of the Bellows painting, stood before me. Next to him was Cindy Morris and, behind her, another woman I didn't recognize.

"Good morning, Mr. Hayes," Fawcett said.

"Speak for yourself. What can I do for you?"

"We have a warrant to search your house." Fawcett handed me two pieces of paper stapled together and folded in thirds. I examined the documents, barely able to decipher the chicken scratch of the judge who'd signed it.

"Warrant related to what?"

"Part of our investigation into what happened at the art museum. Are there young children or pets at home we should be aware of?"

"Yes. I run both a daycare and a kennel. What the hell do you think? You saw both the other day."

As if on cue, Hopalong materialized beside me, looking hopefully at our visitors in case they worked for a dog treat company.

"I'll need you to restrain your dog, and to surrender your laptop and your phone. Do you have any firearms inside?"

I had to believe Fawcett knew that my federal point-shaving plea deal precluded me from owning guns, and he was just messing with me now.

"This is a joke, right? You can't be serious."

"It's all in the warrant. We won't be long. If you could just retrieve those items and wait outside."

I hesitated a moment, processing what was happening. For better or worse it wasn't my first rodeo. I experienced a similar early-morning knock on my door my senior year at Ohio State when agents appeared at my off-campus condo searching for evidence of the point-shaving I'd been reduced to carrying out that fall. But that was a long time ago and the difference was I was guilty of the charges back then—they had me dead to rights. Whereas now, this seemed like part of the vendetta that Dr. Lillian Melnick was waging against me for the sole reason that my presence in her miserable, rule-stickling, covering-her-ass life rubbed her the wrong way.

"Do I at least get one phone call?"

"I'm afraid not. If you would?" Fawcett gestured inside my house.

Ignoring him, I slammed the door in his face, turned the lock, walked through the house, found Joe in his bedroom, and explained what was happening. Although his eyes widened a bit, he took the news in stride, part of the unspoken compact he committed to when moving in with me. *Sometimes things get a little weird at Dad's. It's not like he's an accountant or something normal.* While Joe dressed and gathered his school stuff, I refilled my coffee cup, grabbed a water bowl for the dog, and poured two cups of kibble into a takeout container I found on top of the refrigerator. As I worked, I ignored the pounding on the door.

This was one way to stop thinking about the night I met Kate.

Next, I stuffed a couple of plastic bags in my pants pocket and clipped on Hopalong's leash, feeling guilty at the excitement lighting in his soft, brown eyes. I found my phone and set it beside my laptop on the kitchen table. Then, and only then, did I return to the front door and let Joe precede me out as I pulled Hopalong past the agents.

"We almost broke the door down," Fawcett said.

"With your head or your ass?"

"Andy," Morris cautioned.

"Enjoy my underwear drawer." I brushed past them with a stone face.

"I need to borrow your phone," I said to Joe as we stepped to the curb and got into my van. He nodded without comment and handed it to me while he started the ignition, happy for the learner's permit driving time.

Over the years I'd prided myself on memorizing the important cell phone numbers in my life, guarding against just such an occasion as this. My boys, my mom, and my sister. Kym and Crystal. Otto Mulligan. A couple other friends and a basketball team's worth of ex-girlfriends, not that those did me much good at this point or, frankly, ever. But of course, the one number I needed right now was not among my collection.

Tamping down irritation at myself, at the FBI, at Lillian Melnick—especially Melnick—I used the browser on Joe's phone to look up the office number for Burke Cunningham, the lawyer who got me into this mess by hiring me as an investigator years earlier.

Naturally, no one answered at 6:45 in the morning. I left an urgent message with Joe's number. I felt defenseless, exiting my house as agents pawed through my belongings, but there wasn't much to do about it. Joe needed to get to school.

CUNNINGHAM STILL hadn't called by the time I dropped Joe off. He offered to let me keep his phone but I decided against it. I had enough to worry about without obsessing over my son not having a telephonic lifeline. Instead, I asked him to look up directions to the nearest Walmart. Twenty minutes later I sat in my van in the store's parking lot charging a new burner phone. At 8:15 I called the lawyer's office again. This time LaTasha Harris picked up after one ring.

"I just got your message. Are you okay?"

"Not exactly. I really need to talk to Burke. I know it's early."

"Hang on, champ."

Over the years I'd enjoyed a rapport with Cunningham's longtime secretary that sometimes bordered on flirting. I guess you could say she was my Moneypenny except with a flair for kente blazers. But at times like this, she had a way of snapping into a formal efficiency that I found comforting.

"Andy," Cunningham said a few seconds later. "What's the deal?"

He spoke slowly and his basso profundo voice sounded even more gravelly than normal. I had a sneaking suspicion that LaTasha either awakened him or caught him barely into a first cup of coffee. The defense attorney was one of the hardest-working people I knew, but also a night owl from way back. If Cunningham had his kryptonite, it was any time the clock's hands read pre–9 a.m.

I apologized for the early-morning interruption and filled him in, starting with the attempted theft of the Bellows and moving on to the search warrant underway at my house.

"Are you there now?"

I explained that I'd had to take Joe to school. I could tell he wasn't happy with my response but also that he knew there was nothing he could do about it.

"All right. I'll make some calls. I'd advise you to go home and see what the situation is. It sounds like a fishing expedition. If they were serious they'd have arrested you. Oh, by the way."

"Yes?"

"I take it you're not part of an art theft ring that targeted The Boulevard by George Bellows?"

"Only in my dreams."

"I was hoping you'd say that, since the painting is one of Dorothy's favorites. Call me when you get there."

To my relief, the block was clear of black SUVs by the time I pulled up to my curb. I lifted Hopalong out of the van, set him on the brick-lined street, and approached the empty-looking house. I heard my name called and saw Cindy Morris emerge from a small beige sedan; her personal vehicle, I realized.

"If you're here to arrest me, my lawyer's advised me not to say anything. If you're here to walk my dog, he's already been out today."

"You shouldn't have left like that."

"I had to get Joe to school."

"Adam had some questions for you."

"Boy is the same ever true for me. He can go through Cunningham."

"You're not under arrest."

"For now. The fact that this is utter bullshit notwithstanding. What evidence could you possibly have that I had anything to do with this? Other than whatever crap Lillian Melnick's been feeding you."

Morris's poker face had always been good and she didn't disappoint now. "I stayed as a courtesy. We didn't have a key to lock your door."

"Good for you. If I had a gold star I'd paste it on your forehead."

Morris blinked, and for just a moment something like anger flitted across the stony expression I'd come to know so well over the years. The snow in the short-cropped hair she refused to dye spoke of how long we'd been butting heads. Despite our run-ins, I'd always respected her, though I doubt the same was true for her and me. Hunter and prey. I knew she was just doing her job, but I wasn't ready to throw her that rope quite yet.

"It's routine, Andy, as you well know."

"Routine is interrupting my Sunday afternoon to ask about what happened at the museum. This is harassment. Try looking for the real thieves, why don't you?"

Morris looked as if she wanted to say something, then thought better of it. Instead, she returned to her car without a word and drove off.

FIFTEEN MINUTES later I was sitting in Cunningham's office in his law building on Front Street while LaTasha handed me a cup of coffee. She left and returned a minute later with a slip of paper.

"What's this?"

"It's the details of the appointment LaTasha made for you at the Apple Store," Cunningham said. "You're going to need a new smartphone and a computer. A burner's not going to cut it. It's on me."

"You don't have to do this."

"An accurate statement, but in this case expediency trumps good intentions. I need you to have a smartphone and a computer. So, tell me what you know."

I explained what happened Saturday in further detail, including the revelation about Alex. Then I went over the bare-bones inquiries I'd made into Kate's death, including my curiosity at the disappearance of Leo Brown, the sole witness, and my certainty that I'd been tailed leaving Natalie Mettler's.

"Where to start," Cunningham said when I finished. "First off, congratulations are in order, I believe, even under these circumstances. Discovering a daughter like that—it's remarkable."

"Yes," said LaTasha—a single mother of four—chiming in. "That's so amazing."

"It feels that way."

"It should," Cunningham said. "We'll have to meet her when all this is over. Until then, you're sure she hasn't been contacted by the FBI?"

"She was interviewed by Columbus police that day. Beyond that, not as far as I know. I didn't have a chance to check with her this morning."

"Find out, would you? As soon as possible?"

"For sure." Then I remembered something else. I told Cunningham how Patience dropped my things off the day before and stayed for lunch, ahead of her visit to the FBI office.

"You trust her?"

"Yes," I said, thinking about the kiss on my cheek as she left my house—though I didn't mention that detail to Cunningham.

"It's possible they're keeping an eye on her too. If they saw she visited you, I can see how it might have raised red flags. Maybe she's been followed too. Can you find out if she got a similar visit this morning?"

I told him I would.

"So how bad was the search?"

I recalled the general untidiness of my house when I reentered after my chat with Morris. "It was okay. They took the phone and computer and my files, most of which are old vet bills. But some client stuff too."

"I'll see what I can do about getting them back. Are you working on anything else other than this thing with your daughter's mom?"

"Otto Mulligan's throwing some odd jobs my way. Other than that, no."

"Okay. Try to keep your nose clean until we get this sorted out."

"There's nothing I'd rather do."

"You always say that," Cunningham said. "Let's hope it's true this time."

15

CUNNINGHAM TOLD me to keep a low profile when it came to anything regarding the museum and to call him immediately if I caught wind of the FBI wanting more, including an interview. I assured him I would. I bid LaTasha goodbye, returning to form just enough to compliment her on her colorful blouse, before heading to the Apple Store at Easton. There, I learned I was out of luck; whatever the FBI was doing with my phone meant my contacts weren't going to sync.

Discouraged, I headed home, set up my laptop, and started making calls. I had to leave a message with Patience—one number I'd made sure to memorize, given what I hoped was in our future. It made sense she didn't pick up, given how many times she borrowed my phone as we worked, because she never had hers handy. Then I texted Alex, explained what happened, and asked her to call as soon as she was awake.

Next, I texted Otto to see if he'd run anything down on Leo Brown, the lone witness to Kate Rutledge's death. And then, after setting up my new laptop, I broke my promise to Cunningham and headed to the art museum.

Despite the disdain I held Dr. Lillian Melnick in when I was an employee—and especially now—there had also been times I felt a twinge of sympathy for her. That normally happened around noon, when, on the days I was working, I would spy her eating alone in the museum café, parked by a window as she nibbled on a salad and looked at her phone. It wasn't that she preferred a solitary meal. It's that no one wanted to eat with her. Today, I was grateful for that fact, however painful it might have been for her.

"Mind if I join you?" I said, slipping into the chair opposite her.

She looked up. "My God. What are you doing here? You're not—"

"Not what? Allowed here? You fired me, you didn't excommunicate me. Plus, I've got a thing for the Pre-Raphaelites."

"I'm calling the police."

"Go ahead. Since you called the FBI already."

That caught her attention. I'd interrupted her with a forkful of salad suspended between her plate and mouth, and she set that down now, staring at me through a pair of gray-patterned glasses that set off her wide, perpetually worried green eyes.

"Of course I called the FBI. It's called art theft."

"Called them on me. Which I don't appreciate. I had nothing to do with what happened that day. I tried to save the painting, as you recall." I shook my head. "Wish it had been divorce court—at least I'd still have a job."

"What are you talking about?"

I mentioned my flippant comment to the bickering couple right before the shit went down.

"First time I've heard of that."

"Maybe you'd be in the loop if you'd heard me out instead of firing me."

"I didn't—"

"Didn't what?"

She looked away a moment, refusing to meet my eyes. "Nothing. You need to leave."

I sat back and looked into the sculpture garden outside the café. "I acknowledge you were within your rights letting me go, because we're not supposed to chase people stealing millions of dollars of art."

"You make it sound like I had a choice."

"Didn't you?"

She reddened but didn't answer. I studied her for a moment, enjoying her discomfort.

"I wish you hadn't fired me, because I liked this job, and frankly I needed it." I said. "But you were in the right. I admit that." Just for a moment, her face relaxed, even as I watched her eyes dance to the entrance of the café and back. "Though I hear some people weren't too happy about the decision," I added, recalling Patience's gossip about board trustees angry at the lack of a heads-up. Melnick's left eye twitched at the reminder.

"Rules are rules."

"I also hear Eleanor Seward was especially honked."

Something like alarm crossed Melnick's face.

"Mrs. Seward was understandably upset at what transpired, given her involvement in the painting's acquisition," she said, enunciating each word. "That has nothing to do with you."

"It'd better not. But c'mon, siccing the feds on me? What's that supposed to accomplish?" I told her about the search warrant executed at my house that morning. To my surprise, she looked stricken at the news for just a second before regaining her composure.

"I had nothing to do with that. It sounds as if they're just carrying on with their investigation."

"Nothing to do with it? Really? Feels like you decided to throw me all the way under the bus. Anything to draw attention away from you, maybe? The fact this happened on your watch?"

Her face drained of color. "How dare you."

"Half our job was telling people where the bathrooms are. But wasn't the other half supposed to be loss *prevention?* Half your job, I should say."

"You need to leave, Mr. Hayes. Or I really will call the police."

"I have a membership, you know. I have a right to be here."

"Not for long you don't."

Even though her phone lay beside her plate, she made no move to pick it up. I glanced at it and watched her gaze follow mine.

"Go ahead. Call."

She raised her eyes and held mine for a moment before dropping them again. It was then that I noticed how white her knuckles were as she gripped her fork, as though she were afraid I might grab it from her. Or as if she might need it to defend herself.

"Please, Andy," she said in a voice barely above a whisper.

"Please what," I said, taken aback by her use of my first name.

"Please just leave."

ON THE drive to Joe's school that morning I had fumed at the FBI's intrusion and especially what it exposed Joe to, as unperturbed as he seemed to be about my chaotic life. As I left the art museum and headed to my van, I wanted to fume at Melnick and her interfering ways. Instead, I felt oddly deflated. Despite her anger at my ambush, she hadn't come across as a vengeful art museum security director intent on destroying any and all people responsible for the attempted Bellows theft.

Rather, she struck me as the proverbial deer in the headlights, frozen as larger forces swirled around her. Forces she seemed helpless to control. And nothing affected Melnick more, I knew from experience, than an inability to direct her surroundings. My insinuation that full responsibility for *The Boulevard* fell on her, along with the dig about Eleanor Seward, apparently hit home. It was possible, I realized, that the emotion I detected in Melnick as she pleaded with me to leave reflected the fact she might be on the way out as well. Maybe she needed her job as much as I needed mine.

Both Patience and Otto returned my calls while I was inside the museum. Patience left me a voicemail in her warm voice assuring me she hadn't undergone a similar search and expressing concern at what I'd gone through. She told me to call her as soon as I could. Otto's message was simple: he thought he had a lead on Brown but needed to confirm a couple of things first.

Otto's voicemail provided the first note of optimism of the day, but the feeling was fleeting. As I turned down Mohawk, I saw that the usual parking places on the brick-lined street had been supplanted by TV news vans. As I slowly drove past my house, a reporter walked to the door and knocked while two others stood on the sidewalk doing live shots. Fantastic. News of the search warrant was officially public. Just what I needed. Did I have Adam Fawcett to thank for that too? Or had Melnick dropped a dime on me?

I continued south to Schiller Park, drove around the corner to the recreation center, and found a parking spot. I sat for a moment and admired the colors of the park's towering maples and elms, a swirl of reds and yellows, as the first phase of autumn eased to a close. An idea was forming in the back of my mind, inspired by one of the reporters I'd seen with a microphone in her hand, addressing a camera opposite her. Not a good idea probably. But it might be worth the risk.

Putting my mind to it, I summoned up one of those memorized ex-girlfriend numbers that I saved for special occasions like late-night reminiscences or salvaging my investigative career. She picked up after two rings.

"Gregory."

"Direct and to the point as always."

A pause. "Andy?"

"You got him."

"What number is this? I've been trying to call you." Before I could respond, she continued, "What the hell is going on? I'm at your house right now. The FBI was here, right? Are you okay? And, you know, is there anything you can say?"

Under different circumstances, I might have smiled at the double-barreled question—concern followed immediately by the real reason she was happy to hear from me. But not now.

"I'm fine," I lied. "I might have some information for you. But first, I need a favor. Any chance you could meet me someplace?"

"Now? That's a big N-O. I've got another live shot coming up in twenty minutes and my hair looks like shit. And if I leave, three other stations are going to smell blood and follow. I assume you're not interested in a press conference?"

"Indeed not."

"Good to hear," she said, the competitive edge clear in her voice.

I figured the stuff about her rivals that Suzanne Gregory, Channel 7's lead investigative reporter, had just told me was true. But the thing about her hair was pure malarky. Suzanne was the most put-together woman I knew, not to mention the most beautiful, and her stomach-flipping blue eyes and lustrous blond do were only the beginning. And the thing was, she knew it.

I did too. Her looks ensnared me years ago and led to me planting a rock on her ring finger four times bigger than I could afford. I could handle her beauty; what my Mount Everest–sized ego couldn't handle at the time was her prowess as a journalist, a woman whose voice on the other line led individuals, from Columbus city councilmen all the way up to the governor, to regret ever getting out of bed that morning.

One night we attended a gala where the attention showered on Suzanne was more than I could handle. I retaliated by sneaking into a cloakroom for a make-out session with a curvy Columbus Crew cheerleader who had tagged along that evening with her date, a photogenic midfielder, only to find herself—right or wrong—also feeling left out. Needless to say, Suzanne's discovery of the transgression ended our engagement on the spot, to my everlasting shame. Over the years as she moved on and I grew up, we reached an accord of sorts. Suzanne never granted me the grace I received from Kym. But she didn't hang up on me anymore either.

Mainly because I was a decent source of news tips. Either way, I'd take it.

"Here's the deal," I said. "I'm going to tell you some things, off the record for the moment. Then I'm going to ask you some questions. Then I'm going to ask that favor, but I promise there's something in it for you."

"And we all know about Andy Hayes and his promises."

"At least hear me out."

"This better be good."

I started from the beginning, at the art museum the previous Saturday, and filled her in on most of what had happened since. I told her about Alex, about my investigation into Kate's death, about my 100 percent unproven theory that the family member of a patient might have had something to do with the accident, and about my desire to find Leo Brown. On and on I talked: about the tail I picked up after leaving Natalie Mettler's house, about the search warrant and the seizure of my phone and computer, and about my suspicion that Lillian Melnick, trying to save her ass, was attempting to feed me to the FBI. I left out a few things, such as Patience's kiss and Alex's ex-boyfriend. A guy's gotta have a few secrets.

"Jesus Christ, Andy," Suzanne said when I was finished. "You always have to go big, don't you?"

"That's why I was on the Heisman shortlist. And then in a federal penitentiary. But you knew that already."

"This thing about your daughter. I mean, that's amazing. But, no offense, it also has to be the greatest comeuppance I've ever heard of."

"I was afraid you might say something like that."

"I'm going to have to meet her, and soon. We have so much to talk about."

"I also thought you might say that. The only thing I ask is that you keep it PG-13."

"In your dreams. Okay, it was shitty making all that off the record. But I get it. Meanwhile, clock's ticking. You said you have questions?"

I watched as a pair of retirement-age ladies in workout clothes walked out of the rec center and strolled toward their car. "And the favor. But first the questions. Which boil down to: What can you tell me about the tip that brought everybody to my house?"

"I can't reveal sources. You know that."

"I'm not asking you to. Just the basics. Do they have shit, from what you were told?"

She was quiet for a moment. The workout ladies shared a laugh as they opened the car doors and climbed in.

"It's not much, all right? But word is they're examining your internet search history. That you were looking up stuff about art theft, famous art heists, the price of The Boulevard, stuff like that."

"The fuck?"

"Don't kill the messenger, Andy. You're the one who asked. I take it you're denying it?"

"Off the record, I'm sure as shit denying it." My mind went back to Melnick, munching on her salad in the museum café. Would she go that far to save herself—deliberately lie?

"Can you at least deny it off the record on camera?"

"When pigs fly, et cetera. For now. Okay, I appreciate you telling me that. Now for the favor."

"Like that wasn't a big one right there."

"I'm aware of the imbalance here, Suzanne. I'm going to make it up to you, I promise. But I need to know anything you can tell me about that guy, Leo Brown."

"What about him?"

"Is there anything from that interview you remember? Anything that didn't make it on air?"

"There's always things that don't make it on air. In his case, give me a second." A few moments passed. While I waited I flashed to happier times with Suzanne, which mostly involved her downtown condo and very few clothes. Just as quickly, I shut it down. Talk about a pointless trip down memory lane.

"So, thinking back," she said, resuming the conversation, "all I remember is that he seemed reluctant to talk. Well, that's not unusual. But there was something about that day, being on deadline with a story that big, that made me tell Cap he should be up and running before I knocked on the door. Trusting my gut, you know?"

I knew. There was a reason why Suzanne had to have a new shelf installed at home to hold all her Emmys. A shelf that in an alternative universe I should have installed instead of her husband, Glenn.

"Cap starts shooting, this guy comes to the door, I introduce myself and start asking about the accident." Conrad "Cap" Roller was a longtime Channel 7 videographer, predating Suzanne at the station by a couple of decades and more than a few technological upgrades.

"It's clear Brown was surprised to see me," Suzanne continued. "I think he asked how we'd found him, and I explained about the incident report. We didn't use that part, of course, even though we had it on tape. After that, everything we got you saw, if you've watched that clip.

You could tell he wasn't happy about us being in his face, but . . ."

But what choice did he have. I knew how Suzanne worked. Short of a subject curling into a ball and begging to be left alone, she didn't bother with niceties like asking permission to pose questions. She just did it.

"That's it?"

"Pretty much. He described being at the McDonald's, hearing the impact, looking over, and then telling the kid inside to call 911."

"Hang on. Say that again, about 911?"

She repeated the comment.

"He didn't use his own phone?"

"Apparently not."

"Strike you as odd?"

"I suppose so, now that you mention it. But what does it matter? The point was to get help, and they did." She paused. "Wait a second. Are you thinking he's connected somehow?" You could almost literally hear her reporter's instincts clicking into place like rotating cogs on a machine stirring to life.

"I'm not thinking anything, although that seems a little far-fetched. It does leave the impression of someone who didn't want to get involved."

"That's not unusual, trust me."

"Okay," I said, tucking the thought away. "Anything else?"

"I remember he wouldn't let us get B-roll. It was clear by the end he really wanted us out of there."

"But is that all that unusual either?"

"I guess not. It just jumped out in his case. So, back to moi. What exactly is in this for me, other than the chance to dish about you with your long-lost adult daughter? Which I admit is a reward in and of itself."

"I'll have to take your word for that. All right—I've got two things for you, in fact."

"I'm listening."

"If I figure out who killed Kate Rutledge—and it's a big if—my first call after the ones I make to Alex and to Doug Shortland is to you. Promise."

"Okay. And?"

"Once I'm clear of this art theft bullshit, you can ask me all the questions you want, on camera."

"Not quite as good, but I'll take it. But listen, are you sure you couldn't make a comment on camera today about the search warrant? It seems only fair, after everything I told you."

"Sorry. Turns out my hair also looks like shit."

"Asshole," she said and disconnected.

16

GOING HOME wasn't an option given the activity on Mohawk. I felt bad for my neighbors, but with any luck a bigger story, like a cow on the highway or the announcement of the Michigan game time, would distract the camera crews sooner rather than later and the coast would be clear again. I'd need to walk Hopalong eventually, hopefully before I retrieved Joe from school, but I still had a little time. I was deciding whether to steal the rec center wi-fi long enough to do some work or find another hiding spot when an answer came in a call from Alex.

"That's crappy," she said after I filled her in. "Sounds like that Melnick lady has it in for you."

"Probably because Eleanor Seward has it in for her." I explained about the board chairwoman nicknamed the dowager countess by Patience. "Shit runs downhill, as they say. I take it the FBI didn't knock on your door today?"

"If they did I didn't hear them because I was asleep. They left a message, though. That Fawcett guy. He wants to talk. I was going to ask you about it."

"That's it? Just talk?"

"Had a few questions, that sort of thing." She paused. "What do you think I should do?"

It didn't go unnoticed that Alex was asking my advice for the first time. Thinking about it, I said, "Let me talk to Burke." I explained about the lawyer and the work I did for him. "If it's just questions, it's probably necessary. If they're operating on a theory we were in it together or something, you should get a lawyer."

"Jesus, that's the last thing I need right now."

"What do you mean?"

"I already got a call from the training sergeant at the academy, after Saturday. She said she was just checking in. But it felt like there was something else to it."

"Like what?"

"Like don't screw anything up that would jeopardize me being in the class."

"That's not going to happen. You're the hero here, remember?"

"Not if I've turned into a suspect. I thought I was doing the right thing, but now . . . I'm not so sure."

"You did the right thing, trust me. Nobody's going to take the academy away from you."

"So what am I supposed to do?"

"Sit tight. And listen, any chance I could stop by? I was going to brief you on some of the conversations I've had." I paused. "Like with Dr. Ives."

What I didn't say: and tell you that I finally remembered the night I met your mom.

"Like now? I was about to go running. I'm training for this thing . . . Anyway, sure, I guess."

"Take your time. Don't cut anything short because of me. I'll sit outside and wait if you're not back."

Just under thirty minutes later I was parked outside Alex's apartment—formerly Alex and Kate's. It was a brick townhouse in the middle of a row of similar units, fronted by neatly landscaped beds of mums and trimmed yew bushes. Locust trees shedding the last of their bright yellow leaves ran up and down the sidewalk. Behind me stretched a row of dedicated parking spots shaded beneath a carport. The place looked quiet, well kept, and secure. I could see why Kate would have been comfortable living here. I could also see why it wasn't Alex's vibe.

As I waited, I returned Patience's call. Once again I had to leave a message. I was scrolling through my email when she called me back a minute later.

"Didn't recognize the caller ID, my friend. How's it going? Sounds like a rough morning."

"Shitty, but I've had worse. You didn't get the same treatment, I take it?"

"Fortunately not. My studio's in my apartment—I would have freaked out to have anybody in there. Listen, I can't talk long. I'm on break."

"You're at the museum?"

"My midweek shift, yeah." She lowered her voice. "I heard you came by today. Talked to the good doctor? Speaking of freaking out. Everybody's saying she looked like she saw a ghost. What the heck did you say to her?"

"Nothing much, other than thanking her for calling the FBI on me. How'd your interview go, by the way?"

"Fine. I just went over what happened. Easy peasy. But—you actually said that to Melnick? What'd she say?"

"She denied it adamantly—calling the FBI on me, I mean," I said, multitasking by deleting three Amazon emails in a row. "Like I believe that."

"Yeah, I'd say that's a stretch. Anything else?"

"Not really. She seemed nervous, though, like she might be in the crosshairs as well. Especially when I brought up Eleanor Seward. I could tell that hit home."

"Shit. You don't think—"

"That Melnick was in on it? Seems unlikely, don't you think? She strikes me as a woman who turned in every homework assignment in her life and stops for red lights at country roads in the dead of night. There's Girl Scouts with more larcenous tendencies than Dr. Melnick." That won a laugh from Patience. "I do think she's worried her job might be on the line because of what happened."

"As it should be, my friend, if you think about it."

"Is that fair, though?"

"Facts are facts. It happened on her watch and security's part of her portfolio. Did she say anything else?"

"That's about it."

"You sure? She seemed really shaken."

"Nothing else to report."

"Well, if you think of something, let me know."

"Will do." I found myself wishing there was more I could say about Melnick to sate Patience's desire for gossip about her hated boss. To keep her on the line, I said, "This is probably my new number going forward, so you can reach me here."

"Got it. Still on for my opening?"

Warming at the thought of seeing her again, I told her I was.

"Maybe we can grab a drink afterward, if it doesn't go too late."

"Ten-four," I said, a little too eagerly.

I disconnected, looked up, and saw Alex sprinting into view. For just a second I panicked, thinking she was in trouble, that someone was chasing her. Then I realized she was concluding her run the way I did once upon a time: at top speed. Because why would you do it any other way?

17

INSIDE HER apartment, Alex rolled a yoga mat onto the living room floor and commenced a series of stretches. I sat on a stool at the island in the adjoining kitchen and took in my surroundings. The kitchen wasn't messy, exactly, but some unwashed dishes in the sink and a pile of mail atop the island spoke to a young person's clutter that I was guessing crept in after Kate's passing. I examined some of the photos affixed to the refrigerator door. A few people I didn't know, families posed atop mountains and on beaches, a couple new baby announcements, and then a pair of Kate and Alex, one in the woods somewhere, another at the end of a race. Looking at them, I fought off a bout of wistfulness, thinking about what could have been.

If I was being honest about it, in spite of the spark that Kate and I shared on our one and only night together, with my track record it was unlikely she and I would have connected long-term. But the thought of missing out on getting to know the mother of my daughter saddened me deeply.

"What's this thing you're training for?" I said, returning my attention to Alex, who was currently on her back with her legs extended over her head and toes touching the floor. "By the way, I'm impressed. I'd be in traction if I tried that."

"Well, we can't have that," she said, pausing to catch her breath. "It's a virtual half-marathon. A fundraiser for the Mid-Ohio Food Bank."

"Virtual?"

"I run it by myself, when I want. The actual race is next Saturday, in Grove City. But you can run anytime, any-where during the weekend, starting Friday. Virtual races were all the craze during the pandemic. Some places have kept it as an option."

"Sounds like a good cause. Want any company?"

"What do you mean?"

"I could ride my bike with you, if you want?" I'd done the same thing many times when I was dating Anne Coo-per, a serious runner. Even as I said it, I could tell from the look on Alex's face that I'd miscalculated.

"I'm more of a solo runner, if that's okay."

"Of course," I said, retreating quickly even as I glanced over at the picture of her and Kate at the end of a race. "So how does it work? Do you submit your time or something?"

"There's an app that records it. You can follow runners on it," she added, as if to mollify me after her rejection of my offer. "In real time."

"Is it Runnrly?" I thought back to my conversation with Christine Coyle.

"Runnrly? No. It's called RaceDay1. I'll text it to you."

"You don't mind if I, you know, track your progress?"

"Go crazy, Andy."

"Speaking of Runnrly." I went over my conversation with Coyle.

"Yeah, I've got it," she said, tapping her watch, which I realized for the first time sat on her wrist just above a tat-too. "But I only record times with it."

"No running maps?"

"Absolutely not." She straightened back, bent her knees, and went into a series of crunches. "Especially after Mom."

"What do you mean?"

She flipped onto her stomach, braced her elbows on the mat, and held a plank position.

"I don't want anybody knowing where I run, period," she said, gasping a little. "That's all."

"What about RaceDayı? Isn't that tracking you?"

"That's different. It's a one-time thing, and it's not my regular route."

I wasn't sure I saw the difference but held my tongue. Instead, I said, "You know, there's no evidence anyone knew where your mom ran."

"Not true. Plenty of people knew. I mean, she talked about it. Her whole autopilot thing—how she ran the same route every time."

"Everybody like who?"

"I'm sure Billy, for one thing. Since they had the same schedule, they ran together a couple times after work." I thought about the fact that Billy Chowdhury called off the night before, and told Alex what I was thinking.

"That's just a rotten coincidence. I can't see him doing it, all right?"

"Okay. Then who else knew where she ran?"

"Well me, obviously. Natalie, probably. Maybe people in that running group Dr. Coyle's in. She didn't shout it from the rooftops or anything. I'm just saying it wasn't a secret either."

I couldn't help myself. "How about Jamie Thacker?"

She dropped the plank position and glared at me. "I have no idea. But it doesn't matter, remember?"

"I'm sorry. You're right." I took the opportunity to tell her about my call with Dr. Ives the night before.

"Taylor didn't say anything?"

"She didn't make the connection when I called. I'm guessing afterward she did, since I told her father about you."

"Did he say anything? About the actual case? That patient?"

I recalled his forgiving response. *It's hard to fault someone for lashing out under those circumstances.* "Let's just say he didn't want to talk about it, but also made it clear he thought it was hogwash. Which it may well be."

Alex stayed prone a moment longer, then rose to her knees, made a crook of her right leg, and raised it up and down. As she did, I realized the thought was back, the something bugging me from what Riggs said the day I met him in his office. Something to do with Coyle, since her name just came up?

"It probably doesn't matter," Alex said, driving the thought away. "Doug Shortland went over this with me. He didn't buy the idea that any of those people had anything to do with the accident. The whole thing with the yaw marks. Whoever it was tried to stop. And back to Runnrly, Mom didn't use the mapping stuff either. She thought it was creepy."

"Did she ever worry, though, about running? Especially by herself?"

"A little. What woman doesn't? But she said she'd be damned if she'd let that fear stop her from doing what she wanted."

It sounded like the Kate I'd gotten to know in the past few days, not to mention in our one night together. But now I had a more pressing concern.

"So you worry too?"

"Hello. I average one catcall per run. Men are pigs, in case you hadn't noticed. God forbid a girl in shorts and a jogging bra goes out and exercises without being harassed. It's un-American."

"I'm sorry that happens."

"Me too. But trust me, in my case, it's not a problem."

"Why not?"

She stood and walked to the kitchen island. She lifted her running belt, unzipped it, and retrieved what I antici-pated would be her phone. Instead, I found myself staring at a small silver semiautomatic.

"That's why."

"What is that?"

She gave me a look. "It's a gun."

"I can see that. What kind?"

"It's called a KelTec P3AT. It's recommended for jogging. Lightweight, six in the magazine and one in the chamber. Want to see?"

I took it uncertainly, holding it away from Alex. As I'd insinuated to Adam Fawcett that morning, my long-ago point-shaving conviction prevented me from possessing a firearm. I wasn't ignorant about them; I'd hunted with my dad and my uncle plenty of times as a kid. But handguns were a foreign country to me by comparison and I knew hardly anything about them. The ease with which my daughter described it was a little unnerving.

"You have a concealed carry permit?" I said, handing it back handle first.

"I do, even though you don't need one in Ohio anymore. Kind of crazy, if you think about it."

"Have you ever had to use it?"

She set it beside her jogging belt and returned to the yoga mat and her hip flexors. "Not yet," she said. "Is there a problem?" she added, seeing the look on my face.

"No problem. It just took me aback. I never thought about someone running with a gun. But I guess it makes sense."

"My philosophy is it's better to have it and never need it, then to need it and not have it."

"I can't argue with that. How long have you carried it?"

"Since . . . well, since Mom died. I realized I was on my own. I had to look out for myself."

That caught me up. It was irrational, but I found myself feeling guilty about not being there for her. I also realized she'd handed me the opportunity to tell her the other thing on my mind.

"Speaking of your mom."

"Yeah?"

I told her about the breakthrough I'd had regarding Kate. The guys' night out at Damon's. The unexpected book conversation. Me picking her up after her shift ended. From there, I skimmed over the details of our encounter back in my apartment. But she got the gist.

I wasn't sure how I expected her to react. Definitely not by laughing.

"What?"

"That explains so much."

"What do you mean?"

"When I was in high school, Damon's was the big hangout. She never let me go. She never said why." She shook her head. "All the mediocre rib meat and soggy cornbread that I missed, thanks to you."

I laughed as well. For a moment, the tension created by the conversation about the gun eased.

"Do you mind if I ask—your tattoo. Was it for her?"

She colored a little and reflexively touched it. It was simple—the universal symbol of a nurse's cap with a cross above a heart. I realized it matched a magnet on her refrigerator that sat side by side with one of a Columbus police department seal. She followed my eyes.

"Yeah. I hadn't really thought about getting one. Then Jamie found that magnet at Target and got it for me. It was a nice gesture, but it also happened to be the same day I broke up with him. The day I found out about Taylor." She laughed nervously. "I kept the magnet and dumped the guy. I got the tattoo later."

"Sounds like he deserved dumping."

"For what he did with Taylor, no shit. But other reasons too."

"Like what?"

At first I didn't think she was going to reply. Eventually, looking away, she said, "He was a jerk. He could be kind of cutting. And he drank too much. Like, a lot. He passed out on a date once, which wasn't cool. He even told me he was drunk when he hit on Taylor, like that's an excuse."

I waited, afraid to interrupt her. And also because I had drunk too much at that age and hit on other guys' girls when inebriated and had passed out on at least one date myself. Possibly within days of meeting Kate. What was it they said, about girls marrying their fathers? At least Alex wised up.

She continued, "Mom didn't like him and told him so to his face. I knew she was right. I just needed to come to the same realization myself. Obviously, it was the right choice."

I nodded, deciding not to push it, grateful that I'd made even that much progress in her sharing personal details. Even if one did involve a KelTec P3AT.

"I should get going. I need to pick up Joe, and then at some point I need to figure out how to talk to Billy Chowdhury. It's hard with him having the overnight shift."

"Tell me about it. He's probably awake now, though."

"Yeah, but—"

"Why not bring Joe back here? He can hang out with me while you do your thing. We can have dinner and I'll drop him home."

"That's so out of your way."

"Not really. I'm working a Kohl's distribution hub in Obetz this whole month. It's not that far from you. I haven't seen your place anyway. I might take a little nap, though, if it's okay."

"You're sure?"

"I'd like to, actually. Give me and Joe some time to bond. Talk about the old man and stuff."

I felt a little bad about imposing but took her up on the idea in the end. It was unorthodox, but so was this whole case. I texted Joe and his one-word response—**Cool**—relieved most of my concerns. Finished stretching, a glass of Gatorade in her hand, Alex saw me to the door. I told her I'd be back with Joe soon and thanked her again.

On the tip of my tongue as I said goodbye was a question gnawing at me like a fresh splinter, but one which I chose not to pose. Yet I hadn't stopped thinking about it since she explained why she ran with a gun in a jogging holster since her mom died. *I realized I was on my own. I had to look out for myself.*

What I was dying to ask, but realized I couldn't, maybe ever, was: Do you still feel on your own with me in the picture?

18

RIGHT BEFORE six o'clock, Joe safely ensconced at Alex's, I pulled up to Billy Chowdhury's townhome, parking beneath a streetlight that looked like something left over from the set of Mary Poppins. The Grandview Yard development just west of downtown had exploded in recent years and was now one of the hottest zip codes in town. Though the units were pricey, it didn't seem out of place for a single guy on a hospital pharmacist's salary. Any optimism I felt about speaking with him evaporated when no one answered the door after five minutes of bell ringing and knocking.

I backed down the steps leading to Chowdhury's door and thought for a second. He could be anywhere. Then I remembered something Alex told me, that Kate and Billy occasionally ran together after work, although Billy had done so only grudgingly, preferring to head home and sleep, then work out. On a hunch, I walked down the street and stopped in front of a wrought iron sign jutting out of a bed of flowers. "Clubhouse," it said, with an arrow pointing around the corner.

Entry to the glass-walled gym situated on a grassy expanse around back required a keycard, as I feared. I figured I'd have to return another time, or adopt a different approach.

A strange man lurking outside a private gym, especially one that appeared to be filled mainly with a bunch of young women hammering away on treadmills and elliptical machines, would attract the wrong kind of attention quickly. But for once I was in luck. As I approached the entrance, one of those women, finished with her workout, walked out of the gym and held the door open as she spied me.

Inside, the facility seemed bigger than its footprint thanks to a wall of mirrors at the back. The layout consisted of a main room lined with three rows of workout machines, all facing a bank of flatscreen TVs hanging along the wall closest to the entrance, the monitors turned to CNN, Fox News, and ESPN. Around the corner a secondary room held free weights and a few weight machines. To blend in—as much as was possible in my street clothes—I grabbed a towel from an aluminum rack near a water fountain and looked around. No one returned my gaze, so focused was everyone on their workout.

I didn't see anyone fitting Chowdhury's description in the big room and wandered casually around to the weight annex. I saw him almost immediately, exercising his legs on a resistance machine in the corner. I approached with the air of a guy figuring out which workout station to start at first.

"Dr. Chowdhury?"

He looked up, confirming at least that I had the right guy.

"Sorry to bother you. My name's Andy Hayes. I'm a private investigator . . . and also a friend of Alex Rutledge."

He stared at me. "How did you get in here?"

"The door was open."

"How did you know I'd be here?"

I couldn't see any reason to dissemble. "Lucky guess. I knocked on your door, and when no one answered, I came here. Alex told me you and Kate used to work out."

"What do you want?"

"To talk about Kate. It won't take long, I promise."

"If you know Alex, then you know I already told her I'm not interested."

"Did Alex tell you why she hired me?"

He pumped out two repetitions, as if hoping I'd go away. "Only that you're trying to find out what happened to Kate. Even though that's the purview of the police."

"That's what I'm looking into, correct. But it's not why she hired me. The reason is that I'm Alex's father."

He stared at me, unable to hide his surprise.

"What are you talking about?"

"Exactly that. Kate and I had a brief affair but were never really together." Understatement of the year. "Alex didn't know I was her father until after her mom died and she discovered my name in some papers. I didn't know about Alex until recently."

Chowdhury sat up and took a swig from a water bottle. A pair of black, bushy eyebrows rose and fell as he shook his head skeptically. "Kate never said anything about this."

"Does that surprise you? She didn't tell her own daughter."

I could see that that hit home, even though based on Alex's description it was unclear how serious the two had been. I recalled that Kate had had a brief marriage and, in the same moment, remembered the fiercely independent young woman I'd connected with, however briefly. An independent nature obviously passed down from mother to daughter. I briefly weighed my own culpability in fostering Kate's go-it-alone approach as a young mom. If only I'd known, I thought for the umpteenth time since the art museum fiasco.

"All right," Chowdhury said.

He rose from his machine, reluctance etched on his face, and gestured for me to follow. He was fit and lanky, wearing workout shorts, a 2022 CapCity Half-Marathon shirt, and an Apple watch on his left wrist that beeped the progression of the workout I'd interrupted. An Apple watch with the Runnrly app downloaded? A touch of gray flecked his otherwise dark sideburns and hair. He was a good-looking guy; I could see why Kate, or any other woman, would find him attractive.

We walked to the front of the clubhouse and sat on a pair of chairs beside a coffee table covered with workout magazines. I handed him a card with my new phone number handwritten on it. He examined it, then looked me up and down as if examining a pharmacy customer with a fishy prescription.

"No offense, but what evidence is there that you're Alex's father? Your word for it?"

"The opposite, in fact." I told him about Alex's raid on my used tissue at the coffee shop and the DNA test. His face relaxed a little. "That does sound like Alex. She's very driven."

"Yes."

"And you're trying to do what, exactly?"

I explained about the attempted theft of the Bellows, Alex's abrupt introduction afterward, and her request that I look into her mom's death.

"That also sounds like Alex. But what about the police?"

"They're doing all they can, as far as I know."

"Then why not leave it to them?"

"Alex thought I might be able to supplement their efforts. The fact they've got nothing after six months isn't a good sign. It doesn't necessarily reflect on them—sometimes cases just go cold. I'm also not working thirteen other investigations either."

"You've talked to them?"

"Yes. The lead, Doug Shortland, isn't happy about my involvement, but I promised not to get in his way."

I watched as curiosity overtook his suspicion. "Have you found anything?"

"Not really." I told him about Leo Brown, which felt like the only progress I'd made so far. I also mentioned my other conversations, including with Ryan Ives, the overnight ICU physician. I left out Jamie Thacker's unfortunate alibi thanks to Ives's daughter, Taylor.

"I'm not sure I see the point," Chowdhury said when I finished. "You can't possibly think any of them is responsible."

"It's like I told Dr. Coyle. I'm just trying to paint a picture of Kate. Sometimes that helps shake things loose."

"Like what?"

"Like who knows? I didn't think much of Leo Brown until his neighbor told me he disappeared right after the accident. It's probably nothing. But I've developed successful leads from less."

We paused while a man and woman walked out of the fitness room, perspiring from whatever aerobic heaven they were in. Her, cute in a full-body Lycra suit and green hair band; him, hip with a Twenty One Pilots concert tee. They filled their water bottles from a fountain, chatted for a second, and returned for more torture.

Chowdhury said, "What did Ives tell you?"

"Not much." I advanced my flimsy theory about a vengeful anti-vaxxer.

He seemed taken aback by this. "How'd that go over? You know his history, right? About his parents, and his wife? I mean, she can't even drive anymore."

"I'm aware of it, yes."

"So what did he say?"

"He dismissed the idea. Even after I asked him about something I heard, that a patient's family member confronted him in the parking lot, he wouldn't take the bait. He was magnanimous about it, in fact." I thought again about Ives's response to my suggestion. *It's hard to fault someone for lashing out under those circumstances. No one should judge someone for reacting to what he perceived as an affront to his own morality.*

"Is that all?"

"Pretty much. Why? Do you think he knows something?" Chowdhury seemed interested in what Ives had to say, in the same way Patience had been dying for more details about my confrontation with Lillian Melnick in the art museum café.

"I doubt it," Chowdhury said, as if sensing he'd come on a little strong. "I'm not sure I could be that forgiving, after everything. The toll taken on them must be overwhelming."

"Them? Meaning him and his wife?"

"And Taylor, his daughter. Did you talk to her?"

"Briefly, before she passed the phone to her dad. Yeah, I can't imagine. She can't be much older than Alex." I wondered for the first time if the stress of her personal life had triggered the reckless behavior of sleeping with Alex's boyfriend. I'd seen the same behavior in some of my girlfriends, probably having driven them to it.

Instead of replying, Chowdhury looked out the window at the glow of streetlamps. Behind us, weights clinked as metal met metal. "Uptown Funk" blared from someone's phone despite signs warning against disturbing people with your playlist. From the main workout room, the rhythmic thud of running shoes fell on a dozen treadmills. I glanced back and saw the woman with the green hair band on her knees on a yoga mat doing leg lifts while her boyfriend pumped iron.

Chowdhury looked pensive, and I thought he was about to divulge something. Instead, after a few moments, he said, "Was there anything else? I'd like to finish up."

"I'll make it quick. Doug Shortland, at Westerville PD. He talked to you?"

"That's right."

"About Kate? Or about calling in sick that day?"

A long pause while he looked me up and down, doing his best to control his anger. "How do you know about that?"

"Relax. I'm not implying anything." A white lie, which he seemed not to buy. "I'm just curious how that went."

"It was about as fun as you can imagine. I didn't appreciate his implication then and I don't appreciate yours now."

"No one's saying you had anything to do with what happened to Kate. I'm not, certainly. But boyfriends are usually the first in the crosshairs."

"I wasn't her boyfriend at that point."

"Why not?"

"What?"

"Simple question. I'm just curious why you and Kate broke up."

"None of your goddamned business."

"Probably not. I'm still asking."

"You think I had something to do with her death, don't you? Is that the real reason you tracked me down?"

"It's not. But it's an obvious question that I had to ask."

"Just like Shortland," he said angrily. "Wonder if it has anything to do with me being the only brown person in Kate's circle of friends and colleagues."

"I couldn't answer that. I'd hope not. But it'd be negligent of me not to ask about the two of you."

"That's your justification for insinuating I killed Kate? 'Just doing your job'?"

"I'm not justifying anything. But my loyalties are to Alex, not you. And Kate did break up with you shortly before she was killed. It's the kind of thing that gets looked at."

"Wrong," he said, rising and stepping away from me.

"What do you mean? That's what Alex told me."

"Kate didn't break up with me," Chowdhury said, anger filling his eyes. "I broke up with her." And with that he turned and walked away.

19

THE EVENING air was cool as I walked back to my van. I tried to recall what Alex told me about Kate and Billy's breakup. She placed the blame on her mother, but she also said her mom didn't talk to her about such things. Did it matter that Billy—at least according to him—was the one who ended it, shortly before she died? From a motive perspective, I supposed it did, since the aggrieved party was typically the aggressor in domestic situations. But was he telling the truth? Absent a review of their text message history and any other evidence, it was his word against that of a dead woman.

I decided I was overthinking it. Even if Kate hadn't told Alex the reason Billy broke it off, Alex undoubtedly would have known about any acrimony between the two, and others would have as well. Chowdhury might believe, with some fairness, that he was looked at closely because of his skin color, although I hoped not. Of more interest was how sensitive he seemed to be to the question of calling in sick the night before his ex-girlfriend was killed. Was he tired of the query? Or was there more to it than that?

Mulling all this over, I texted Alex to let her know I had spoken to Chowdhury and was heading home. I was opening the door of my van when I heard voices. I looked at the club entrance and saw the couple I'd seen exercising together. Twenty One Pilots and Green Hair Band. Walking in lockstep, working their phones post-workout. In Twenty One Pilots's shoes I would have found it hard to keep my eyes off his companion, let alone my hands, with her too-perfect figure and after-exercise glow. In the iPhone age, randiness isn't what it used to be. I had started the van and pulled onto the street, watching them recede down the sidewalk in my rearview mirror—watching her, to be honest about it—when a pair of headlights blocked my vision. Something about the speed with which the car pulled out just as I did caught my attention. As if the driver had been waiting for me and was timing their departure with mine.

I flashed back to the other day and the tail that followed me from Natalie Mettler's. I might have been imagining things. It was quite possible. Some days I feel one conspiracy theory short of being completely paranoid. To be sure, I slowly worked my way through Grandview Yard and over to Third Avenue, taking two unnecessary turns along the way. No question, I concluded. I was being followed again.

Approaching Riverside Drive, I called Alex and placed her on speaker phone.

"We're just leaving. What's up."

I explained what I had in mind. She agreed to assist without hesitation, as I figured she would. Instead of heading to the highway, I reversed direction and drove back into Grandview Heights proper, maintaining an open line with Alex while I kept an eye on the car that, consistent with my suspicions, remained behind me. That time of night, the trap I was setting wasn't all that difficult. I maneuvered my way down Fifth Avenue to North Star, cut over to Kinnear as I skirted the edge of Upper Arlington, and drove around the Lennox shopping center.

All the while Alex was making good time crossing over the top of Columbus on the I-270 Outerbelt. South of the shopping center I pulled onto 315 with Alex now not more than three minutes behind me. As I exited onto I-70 and headed east toward downtown, she narrowed that to two and then one. Thirty seconds before I reached my house I heard her say, "Got him," accompanied by a hoot from Joe.

"They turned left on Kossuth," Alex reported as she emerged from her car.

"Nice work," I said, examining the photo of a license plate Joe had just texted me. "Now let's see what the heck's going on."

Once inside and on my computer, it took less than five minutes to run the plate, a perk of my PI license. Alex's eyes widened a little as she stared at the result, but I wasn't all that surprised. Motive—now that was another question. We would get there eventually, I figured.

It took me a minute to find his card. I dialed the number but after six rings it went to voicemail. It wasn't surprising. Either my contact info was showing up on caller ID or he had a policy against answering unfamiliar numbers. Regardless, I left a simple enough message.

"It's Andy Hayes," I said to Brian Riggs's phone. "Why the hell are you following me?"

IT DIDN'T surprise me that Riggs was savvy enough to tail me. I thought back to the day in his office, when he went over the positions he held when he was on the job with the Columbus department. *Beat cop, narcotics, traffic, training bureau, vice.* Spend that much time in a cruiser chasing bad guys and conducting a civilian tail would be a piece of cake. The fact I'd busted him was due more to his bad luck than anything else: if a driver hadn't honked as Riggs slipped through the red light after tailing me from Natalie Mettler's, I wouldn't have been alerted to his presence. If I hadn't figured out I had a tail that day, I likely wouldn't have been attuned to him outside Billy Chowdhury's gym. And of course, who knows how many times Riggs followed me without me being aware?

"You don't think he, you know, could have . . . ?" Alex left the question hanging, unable or unwilling to finish it. We were sitting in my living room, reviewing the discovery. I didn't bother trying to keep Joe out of the mix.

"Do I think he had something to do with your mom's death? I find that hard to believe. But something's bugging him enough to want to see what I'm up to."

"Like what?"

"Maybe he doesn't like the fact I'm talking to people he told me not to, and he's gathering evidence to shut me down."

"That seems like a stretch. He could just ask Billy or Natalie."

"You're right. But he's got a bug up his ass about something, pardon my French."

"Yeah," Joe said. "A bug."

"What?" Alex said.

"Maybe he's doing his own investigation into your mom but he's too lazy to do stuff himself," Joe said to his sister. "So he's just following Dad around to see what he's found. Sort of like a whatchamacallit. A kleptoparasite."

"A what?" Alex and I said almost simultaneously.

"Animals that steal from other animals. We read about them in biology. This one spider takes over other spiders' webs once they've woven them. Stealing their work. Like this guy is."

"Allegedly is," I said.

"These spiders—they also eat the other spiders sometimes too. Just so you know."

"Very helpful," I said. "Let's hope Riggs doesn't go that far. It's an admirable theory, that he's doing his own snooping into Kate. But why not do it out in the open?"

"He doesn't trust Shortland?" Alex offered.

"Or he doesn't trust someone at the hospital. Or formerly at the hospital." I reminded them of the various employee departures.

"The problem is, this just takes us back to square one," Alex said. "The evidence is clear it was an accident. Somebody was speeding, tried to stop, hit Mom anyway, and fled the scene. Why would someone at St. Clare want to hurt her? Everyone loved my mom."

Alex's comment reminded me of the last thing Billy Chowdhury said to me, that he was the one who broke things off, not vice versa.

"That's possible," Alex said, after I filled her in. "Like I said, she didn't talk much about stuff like that."

"There wasn't any drama beforehand?"

"Like what?"

"I don't know. Fights, heated arguments. That kind of thing."

"Nothing like that. Billy was a nice guy. Mom was a little gun-shy about relationships, especially after Steve's dad. And you," she said, looking at me pointedly. "It's possible she wasn't ready to commit and he decided to pull the plug. She just didn't tell me about it." Despite the disregard in her voice, I could tell the revelation had stung a little; one more thing her mom kept from her, for which there'd never be an explanation. I was mentally thumbing through a list of platitudes when she surprised me by saying, "This is a dead end, isn't it?"

"I don't have much, I admit. But I've only been working on it four days. Let's give it a little more time. If only to see what Riggs is playing at."

"Part of me is sorry I dragged you into this."

"That's understandable. Is that same part sorry we met?"

I surprised myself with the question, the answer to which I dreaded. Joe looked on with interest.

"Of course not. I don't know if we can ever be friends. But I'm glad we connected. I hate loose ends."

Ever be friends. The words rang cold, a sterile alternative to maintaining a healthy father-daughter relationship. I felt more than ever like a business associate instead of her dad.

After talking for a few more minutes, Alex lay down for her pre-shift nap and Joe settled in with his schoolwork. As for me, I couldn't stop thinking about Riggs and what Joe had called him. A kleptoparasite. I went online and searched Riggs's name. After a few minutes I sat back, troubled by what I'd found. But not entirely sure what it meant either.

On the website of a Columbus driving school off Morse Road called Green Light Goals, Riggs was listed as an instructor. The school offered standard driver's ed classes, brush-up instruction for older drivers, and defensive driving techniques for businesspeople traveling abroad, with a list of testimonials attesting to the school's excellence. The company also offered court-ordered remedial driving courses, something I was familiar with: Mike had taken such a class after a Worthington cop pulled him over doing sixty in a thirty-five zone on the way home from summer practice the previous year.

Looking at Riggs's unsmiling face on the website, I recalled Alex's alarmed question earlier in the evening. *You don't think he, you know, could have . . . ?* I'd told her no. I sat back, trying to decide if that was really true. It seemed improbable, to say the least, starting with the obvious question: What possible motive would Riggs have to kill Kate? It seemed more likely he decided to put his driving prowess to use by following me. Was Joe right, that he was using me to piece together his own investigation? Or did he have another, more unseemly, goal?

Once again I tried to recall what was bothering me from my conversation in his office. Nothing was coming clear. And in the end, the only person who could answer any of these questions wasn't calling me back.

On that note, I tried Riggs again, to no avail. I shut my laptop and was ready to call it a night when my phone buzzed with a text.

Try this lady for Leo Brown

Otto Mulligan, getting back to me about my unsuccessful search for Brown, the witness to Kate's death. He'd included a woman's name, Saundra Wellman, and a number.

I texted my thanks and called her, despite the hour. Alex's comment about dead ends had me eager to make progress of any kind.

"Hello?"

I identified myself and explained I was looking for Brown.

"What's this about?" Wellman's voice was scratchy and tired.

"I was supposed to buy a car from him, and finally got the money. But now I can't find him."

"What kind of car?"

"Chevy Malibu."

"How much you paying him?"

"We settled on three grand. It took me a while to get the cash."

"My boyfriend's got a 2011 Camry he's trying to sell. Could give it to you for $2,500."

"What kind of condition?"

"Runs good—promise."

"I might be interested. Let me see what Leo says first and then can I call you back?"

"I suppose," she said, disappointment in her voice.

"So any idea how I can find him?"

"He's staying over in Dayton, last I heard."

"Do you know where?"

"Someplace by the art museum."

"You have an address?"

"Sorry. That's all I heard. You'll let me know about the Camry?"

"Sure will."

After we disconnected, I searched online for Brown in Dayton but turned up nothing. It wasn't surprising; if he was couch surfing, or keeping a low profile, he likely wouldn't show up anywhere unless he was paying a utility bill. It was a fool's errand driving to Dayton with such limited information. But if anybody knew the value of such errands by now, it was me.

20

SAUNDRA WELLMAN'S best guess for Leo Brown's whereabouts wasn't much to go on. *Someplace by the art museum.* But it was all I had. After dropping off Joe at school the next day and arranging with Alex to pick him up, I headed west. I knocked on my first door shortly after nine, sticking out in the largely all-Black neighborhood worse than a kleptoparasite spider sneaking into a strange web. Undeterred, I kept at it. A lot of people weren't home, a lot more told me to hit the road, and the remaining chunk apparently never heard of Leo Brown or if they had did an admirable job of lying through their teeth.

An hour passed, then two. I was three houses away from calling it a day when I stepped onto the porch of a two-story clapboard with a lawn a month overdue for mowing, two boarded-up upstairs windows, and outer walls shedding green paint like eczema off a dragon's backside. I raised my fist to knock but the door opened first.

"Who are you?"

The guy standing before me was all angles, Black like Leo Brown, with a face tapering to a sharp chin and a chest tapering to his waist like a V. Wiry and tough looking, with eyes full of suspicion. For what felt like the hundredth time that morning, I cast out my line with the same spiel. For the first time, I got a bite.

He studied my business card. "Why do you want to talk to him?"

"So you know him?"

"Didn't say that," he said, though the look on his face suggested otherwise.

"Well, if you do know him, he saw a lady get killed in a hit-skip. I'm working for the lady's family, trying to figure out what happened. It's an insurance thing," I added, hoping maybe the suggestion of money being in play would boost his cooperation. "I don't need more than ten, fifteen minutes of his time."

"Insurance thing. Anything in it for him?"

"I'm sure the family would be grateful for any help they receive." I paused. "Very grateful."

He looked up and down the street. "Thing is, he was staying here. I just ain't seen him for a while."

"Any idea where he is now?"

"Nah, man."

"Any chance you could find out?"

"I don't think he's looking to be found."

"Why not?"

"None of your business, that's why."

"Is he in trouble?"

"Who says he's in trouble?"

"Just a guess. He disappeared fast after he witnessed the accident. Right after he was on the news. That's got me wondering if he needed to lay low for a while."

I could tell from the way his eyes flicked to the street and back that I was onto something. I thought maybe I'd made a strong enough case to at least earn an address. Instead, the man said, "Listen, you probably need to get going."

"I don't disagree. I'm hoping to go to wherever Brown is staying." I retrieved my wallet and removed two twenties. "Just an address. No need to say where I got it from."

He eyed the money. "You ain't gonna tell him it was me?"

"Word of honor."

"I hear different, you and me are gonna have a problem."

"You're not going to hear different."

"All right, then." I gave him the bills and watched them disappear. In return, he recited a house number and a street. I thanked him and without another word walked down the steps, across the lawn and its calf-high growth of clover, got back to my van, and drove around the corner. And parked and pulled out my phone.

Because the thing was, I was pretty sure he was lying. Depending on the kind of trouble Leo Brown was in, his friend in the house with peeling green paint probably had little incentive to give him up. Certainly nothing that a measly forty bucks would compensate for. I wasn't sure I blamed him, though it wasn't making my life any easier. Sure enough, a quick Google Maps search confirmed my suspicion. The address he'd provided was a Family Dollar five streets over.

I weighed my options, which came down to returning home empty-handed, knocking on more doors, or waiting things out for a bit. I went with Door No. 3 on a hunch that Mr. Green House wasn't going to stay put. I put the van in park and drove back to his block.

Bingo. Five minutes later, a blue pickup truck backed out of the house's drive and turned right, the man behind the wheel. I waited until I saw it turn two blocks down and pulled out in pursuit.

I followed the pickup out of the neighborhood and onto side streets that soon gave way to a long commercial strip. After another five minutes, he turned onto Doench Avenue. I pulled over to the curb and watched as he drove farther down the street, finally stopping in front of a light-brown brick bungalow. He left his truck, once again glanced up and down the street, and headed for the house.

After five minutes passed and he didn't appear, I put the van in gear, drove past the house, and noted the address. If Leo Brown wasn't holed up inside, I was a Michigan fan.

THIS LEVEL of subterfuge suggested Brown really didn't want to be found. It also made me think he'd be keeping an eye on his surroundings. I decided to drive around the block a time or two to give the man in the pickup time to deliver his message before I made my approach. I was two blocks away, paused at a stop sign, when my phone rang with a Columbus area code.

"It's Jeff Heaton," a man said when I answered. "You called about my mother."

I blanked for a moment until it came back to me. Jeff Heaton—the son of the patient whose death shook up Kate more than usual. Sherry . . . No. Shirley. Shirley Vanhouten.

"That's right. Thanks for getting back to me. The reason I called is—"

"That's what I'd like to know. A private detective? Why would you be calling about my mother? After we've already been through so much?"

"Well, I—"

"You're a hell of a hard guy to get ahold of, by the way. Your number was disconnected. I had to google you and then call some lawyer you work for to get this number. Is that how you operate? Leave a message and then ditch your phone?"

"I'm sorry about that. I really appreciate you making the effort to track me down."

"You should. So what's this all about?"

I eased through the intersection and parked on the next block. Taking the phone off speaker, I explained my mission, starting with the discovery of my connection to Alex and continuing with the investigation she asked me to undertake. Striking an apologetic tone, I said I'd been trying to wrap up loose ends by reaching out to some of Kate's patients.

"Liar."

"What? No, I assure you I'm telling the truth."

"Not you," Heaton said. "That nurse, Kate. And the doctor—Ives? All of them. They lied about my mother. They said she had COVID, which is bullshit since there's no such thing. She had a bad cold is all, and they made it worse, giving her propofol and all this other painkiller crap, sticking her on a ventilator, and then she died. I should sue them is what I should do. And you too, for that matter. Spreading more lies."

"I'm not—"

"And another thing. The mask they made me wear when I was up there? I haven't been the same since. It affected my oxygen. There's another thing to sue over."

"Listen," I said, riled up. "Nobody there was trying to hurt your mom. Especially Kate. She cared for her—I know she did. She was upset when she passed. Very upset."

"Really? That's why she said it, then?"

"Said what?"

"You should get your story straight before you call and harass people, buddy."

"I'm not trying to harass you. What did Kate say?"

"She said, 'Another one,' all right? Satisfied?"

"Another one?"

"I didn't actually hear it, okay? But my daughter did. Your precious Kate came down the hall, and when she found out my mom died, she laughed it off. 'Another one.' Like she was glad she was gone."

"I'm sure she wouldn't have said that—or said it like that. Kate cared."

"Like hell she cared," Heaton said, and cut the connection.

I stared at my phone. I realized I was having trouble breathing. The vitriol flowing from Jeff Heaton was almost palpable, his anger red-hot. And so misguided. *There's no* such thing. How many arguments had I had with my father along the same lines? The only reason he was vaccinated was that my mother laid down an ultimatum: no shots, no supper. My father's inability to even boil water did him in and he was forced to relent, kicking and screaming all the way about Bill Gates and microchips and 5G mind control. But at least he didn't end up dead.

Another one. What was that supposed to mean? I couldn't imagine Kate saying such a thing in malice. It seemed more likely she meant another unvaccinated person dying of COVID, another preventable death. Now I had a million more questions—for Natalie Mettler, for Billy Chowdhury, for Dr. Ives, even for Brian Riggs—especially Riggs. Was Jeff Heaton the one who followed Ives into the parking lot? Of course, the one person who could have solved the puzzle, the one I'd give anything to quiz, was the only individual I had no chance of asking. She died three days after Shirley Vanhouten.

21

DESPITE THE loop that Heaton's call threw me for, I knew I had to stay focused on the mission at hand. After collecting myself, I drove around the block again and parked three houses up from the bungalow I'd seen Brown's buddy walk into. The truck was gone and the coast was clear. I settled in to watch my surroundings before making my approach.

Five minutes in, an older woman strolled past walking a small white dog. Five minutes after that a mail carrier parked a van across the street and began her faithful delivery of what no doubt consisted mostly of junk mail and envelopes stuffed with coupons. A couple of young guys in hoodies strolled past a few minutes later smoking what appeared to be a non-tobacco product, studiously ignoring me as they walked. I gave it another minute, retrieved a clipboard—the universal badge of authority—and walked up to the bungalow's front door.

I knocked and stepped back. Nothing. I waited thirty seconds and tried again. Still no response. Looking up and down the street, I reached forward and tried the door. Locked, as I suspected. I pondered what to do next. I thought briefly of returning to my van and grabbing the Louisville Slugger I kept there for protection or in case the

Toledo Mud Hens ever called me up, but thought better of it. Nothing blows a cover faster than trespassing with a baseball bat in hand.

Instead, tapping my clipboard like an impatient meter reader, I walked down the steps and around to the right of the house, opened the gate on the chain-link fence, and stepped into the yard, a mosaic of shorn brown-and-green grass, patches of weeds, and dirt. I looked for tell-tale signs of a guard dog but saw nothing. Making sure my clipboard was visible to any and all neighborhood sightseers, I mounted the small set of concrete steps at the back door, opened the screen, and tried the knob. It turned. Taking a breath, I pushed the door open and stepped inside.

"Hello?"

No response. I stepped farther inside. "Hello?"

I thought I heard a sound someplace deeper within but couldn't be sure. I stepped all the way into the kitchen—leaving the door open behind me—and tapped my phone in my pocket, reassuring myself with its presence.

"Hello?"

There. A sound for sure this time. Around the corner.

"Hello?"

I took two more steps and peered around the doorjamb—and dove back around as I caught sight of a gun in the hands of a man in a shooting stance on the far side of the room.

Bam. Bam. Bam.

Shit. Shit. Shit.

"Don't shoot!" I yelled.

I didn't wait for a response but ran for the back door, crouched low. I nearly made it out when I heard footsteps behind me and a voice say, "Don't move."

I froze, my back to the gunman.

"Don't shoot," I said. "Unarmed. Private eye. Just had some questions."

Silence.

"Show me your hands."

I dropped the clipboard and raised my arms like a man doing the world's slowest wave.

"Turn around. Real slow."

I obeyed. And found myself staring into the eyes of Leo Brown.

"The fuck are you?"

"Happy to explain," I said, unsuccessfully trying to calm my pounding heart. "Possible to lower the gun first?"

"No. Answer the question."

I swallowed. Now or never. As much as I tried to keep an even keel, it came out in a rush of words.

"My name's Andy Hayes, I'm a private investigator from Columbus, I want to talk to you about the hit-skip death of Kate Rutledge last May."

Brown stared at me as if I'd announced my arrival from Alpha Centauri.

"The fuck are you talking about?"

"I just told you."

"I heard what you said. But I don't know shit about that."

"You were there, though, right?" Nothing emboldens you like the sight of a gun and the sense there's nothing to lose.

"So?"

"So I just have some questions. That's all. I'm not trying to cause you any problems."

"You're already causing me problems. That train has left the station. And like I told you, I don't know shit about Kate whoever. You hear me?"

"I do, believe me." I swallowed and took the plunge. "The thing is, the reason I'm here is that after Kate died, I discovered that she and I shared a daughter I never knew existed. Her name is Alex. Alex Rutledge. She wants to know who killed her mother. It's been almost five months and the cops don't have anything. Since you were sitting in the drive-through at McDonald's, it's pretty obvious you weren't the one who killed Kate. That's not why I'm here. I don't care about anything you're into. I just want to find out who killed my daughter's mother. I was hoping you could help me with that. That's all."

The drip-drip-drip of the kitchen faucet boomed as silence settled over the room.

"Prove it."

"Prove what?"

"Prove you're a private eye."

"License," I said, without moving. "In my wallet."

He didn't speak for a moment, staring hard at me. Finally, he said, "Take it out. No funny business."

I did as I was instructed. I showed him the wallet first, then extracted the license, and extended it toward him. He took it with his free hand, examined it, and handed it back.

As I took it, I heard a siren in the distance.

"Shit," Brown said. "Now look what you've done."

Discretion being the better part of valor, I decided against pointing out that his gunshots were the thing that attracted someone's attention.

Instead, I said, "Anything you remember."

"I ain't seen nothing. Heard the crash is all."

"I don't believe you."

"Listen, bitch—"

"Don't bitch me. If you didn't see anything, why'd you run right after giving that TV interview? Yeah, I know all about that," I added, seeing the surprise on his face.

"I didn't run."

"Okay. Relocated with great haste."

"None of your business."

"Actually, it is. This is the mother of my daughter we're talking about. I'm not looking to jam you up here." I nodded at the window over the kitchen sink, indicating the sound of the siren, even louder now. "I just want to know what happened that morning."

"Not jam me up? Now the cops are coming, thanks to you. I oughta drop you where you're standing."

"Don't be . . . ridiculous." I stopped myself from saying "stupid" at the last second. "People know I'm here. They know I'm looking for you. That will just compound your problems."

"You're my only problem at this point."

"I'm your solution, trust me. We can work this out, as long as you tell me what's going on. Anything you saw that morning with Kate. I promise."

"Why in the hell should I trust you?"

"Because I'm trying to do the right thing by my daughter. It's not about you. It's about her."

"Not my problem."

My bowels loosened as he sighted the gun at a point between my eyes. A moment later I relaxed as he pulled the weapon back. Despair replaced fear as, just for a second, I thought he was raising the gun to kill himself. Instead, he jammed it into his waistband, stepped around me, and walked to the back door. I figured he was going to leave without speaking, but then he stopped.

"That car," he said.

"What car?"

"The one that killed that lady."

"What about it?"

"I saw it."

"I know you did—"

"I saw it before," he interrupted. "I always stopped at that McDonald's on the way to work. It was there the morning before the accident. The day before, I mean. Someone was inside, sitting there, watching that lady cross the street on her run." And with that, he turned and fled.

22

I DIDN'T bother giving chase. Pursuing unarmed art thieves is one thing; following guys with guns who aren't afraid to use them is another. Besides, I was too stunned by what he'd just said.

If Leo Brown was telling the truth, Kate's death hadn't been an accident. Someone targeted her. But who? And why?

I didn't have time to figure that out now. I had to act, and fast, and do things in the right order. The sound of additional sirens filled the air. The cops would be here any second.

First, I called the Westerville Police Department and asked to speak to Doug Shortland on an urgent matter. Instead, naturally, I ended up with the traffic investigator's voicemail. I left a detailed message about what Brown told me, that according to his account the driver who killed Kate had been conducting reconnaissance on that intersection for at least a day before the accident. I gave him my new number, then told him to call Dayton police to confirm my whereabouts and the circumstances under which I'd gained this information.

Next, I called Burke Cunningham. His cell went to the office number, where LaTasha apologized, saying he was at a BBA meeting, but she'd get a message to him immediately.

Burke had either chaired or sat on the Black Bar Association's board nearly as long as I'd known him. I thanked her and said it was fine.

Finally, I had my pointer finger poised to call Alex. I never got the chance. The cavalry showed up. And they had a lot more guns than Leo Brown.

THE OFFICERS who questioned me were about as pleased as you'd expect to come across an out-of-town private eye sitting in a house on their turf spinning an objectively iffy story about being shot at by a man who was nowhere to be found. I wasn't surprised when ten minutes after their arrival I was cuffed and sitting in the back of a cruiser. What a fun day this had turned out to be.

Fortunately, I was spared the indignity of pleading for a bathroom break by Doug Shortland, who got my message, called the Dayton cops, and after being passed around from number to number, confirmed to a supervisor the story of Leo Brown witnessing Kate Rutledge's death and the fact that, though he wasn't happy about it, he was aware I'd been looking into her killing.

That gave me enough purchase to call up the video clip of Brown's brief interview with Suzanne Gregory of Channel 7 on the day of Kate's death, though I left out my connection with Suzanne and what she'd said about how nervous Brown seemed in the portion of the clip that didn't make the news.

A call right after that from Burke Cunningham acknowledged my occasional stint for him as an investigator, and based on that, the cops finally checked on my credentials with the state and discovered I was in good standing.

Nevertheless, despite all this positive intervention, it wasn't until nearly six o'clock that evening that I found myself headed back east on I-70, balancing the conflicting feelings of success at finding Brown and learning what he had to say, and despair at the fact there was a good chance

Kate was murdered, not the victim of a random hit-and-run after all.

Soon enough, an afternoon of drinking too much police department coffee caught up with me and I stopped at the last rest station before greater Columbus to relieve myself. Back in the van, I texted Alex and Joe with my ETA. I was doing a quick sweep through my email when a call from an unfamiliar number came in.

"Mr. Hayes?"

I paused, recognizing the voice immediately. "Billy?"

His turn to pause. "That's right. Is this a convenient moment?"

I started my Odyssey and headed back onto the highway. "For sure. What's up?" To say the least, my surprise at hearing from Chowdhury almost put the day's events out of my mind.

"I've been thinking about our conversation. At the gym."

"Okay. Me too, if that matters."

"I overreacted. You took me by surprise, showing up like that."

"I apologize. My techniques aren't always the most subtle."

"The thing is . . ."

I waited, letting silence well up between us.

"I'm afraid I left the wrong impression. I mean, about Kate. Well, yes and no. Not what I said to you. I was the one who broke up with her. I was sorry about it. I liked her. I just couldn't . . ."

Another pause.

"I couldn't be present to her the way she needed me to be. I had a lot on my mind. In trying to express that to you, it came out the wrong way."

"I understand."

"I appreciate the fact you're trying to find answers. I didn't make that clear, last night. As far as I can tell, the police have done nothing except question me for what I thought was the most ridiculous but to their minds most obvious reason. I assumed . . . well, I assumed you were drawing the same conclusion."

"What changed your mind?"

"I made some calls. I know you're talking to a lot of people."

I went quiet again, not sure what I had to add to Chowdhury's odd confessional call.

"May I ask you something, Mr. Hayes?"

"Of course. And feel free to call me Andy."

"All right. Andy. As a private investigator, do you have to, you know, follow confidentiality rules? Like a lawyer?"

"Not exactly. My conversations are privileged, but unlike a doctor or a psychiatrist, I can be compelled to testify in court."

"I see."

I could hear the disappointment in his voice. "It's rare," I added quickly.

"All right."

"Perhaps you could give me an outline of what you're getting at? We could consider parameters of a conversation?"

"Parameters?"

"Sort of a conversation about the conversation."

"I suppose." A pause that lasted so long I thought he might have disconnected. "Well, you know about me calling off sick the night before . . . before Kate was killed."

"Yes."

"This raised a lot of questions. From the police, from Doug Shortland, I mean. Especially because . . ."

I waited.

"Because I wasn't at home that morning. At the time Kate died, I mean."

"Where were you?" Recalling Chowdhury's handsome face and fit physique, I had a feeling I knew where this was going. But his next words surprised me.

"I was on my way to Cincinnati. I had an eight o'clock meeting with a lawyer. I called off to be sure I could be there in time."

"A meeting about what?"

Another long pause. On my left, tractor-trailers filled the passing lane as they plowed toward the multiple Columbus distribution centers that would facilitate the delivery of multiple boxes of crap to the greater world. In the interim, my phone flashed with an incoming call from Burke Cunningham. I sent it to voicemail.

"Dr. Chowdhury? A meeting about what?"

After another few seconds, he finally responded.

"About possible Medicare fraud at St. Clare."

23

I STAYED in the driver's lane, keeping comfortably back from the cars and trucks ahead of me.

"Go on."

"For starters, how much do you know about that kind of thing?"

"Just enough to be dangerous." I explained that I occasionally investigated alleged workers' comp fraud cases, which mostly amounted to documenting guys with debilitating on-the-job back injuries who were mysteriously able to play games of weekend hoops or frame two-story houses with no visible sign of pain.

"This is more subtle than that."

"In what way?"

"Well, a physician might bill for something that wasn't medically necessary—maybe a blood test or something. Or they might upcode—like billing for a procedure more expensive than one that was actually done. You also see unbundling—a doctor might bill parts of one procedure separately. That kind of thing."

"Got it. That was going on at St. Clare?"

He paused. "Based on some things I saw, I had my suspicions. About one doctor in particular."

Crap, I thought. "Don't tell me—Ryan Ives?"

Chowdhury sounded surprised. "No. Why would you think that?"

I backpedaled. "No reason, I guess. Just that, as you know, I've talked to him about Kate." I reminded him of my anti-vaxxer theory, backed up by the allegation that someone threatened Ives.

"No, it wasn't Ives. It might be easier if it was, honestly."

"What's that supposed to mean?"

"Nothing."

"Who is it, then?"

Yet another pause. "David Coyle."

It took me a second. "Christine Coyle's husband?"

"That's right."

"The hospital administrator's husband was committing Medicare fraud?"

"Allegedly."

Before I could stop myself, I blurted out, "Did Kate know?"

"No," Chowdhury said, emphasizing the word. "At least, not from me. I decided to keep this to myself until, well, until I was sure."

"You're not sure?"

"I'm sure something wasn't exactly right. That's why I consulted with a lawyer."

"I'm not following."

"The problem with Medicare fraud is if you know what you're doing, it's difficult to detect. The ones who get caught are typically the greediest—it becomes so blatant they might as well put it in lights. Triple-billing for back braces, that kind of thing. Ambulance rides that never happened. Upcoding and unbundling are much more discreet. It goes on a lot more than anyone cares to admit, but if done right, it's hard to trace."

Again, before I could stop myself, I said, "Is this the reason you broke up with Kate?"

Silence again. I waited as more distribution hub trucks rolled past me.

"Like I said, I'd become distracted. I decided it was better if we took a break while I figured out what was going on. I didn't want to compromise her in any way. I knew she occasionally worked with Dr. Coyle, with David. But . . ."

"But what?"

"It turns out Kate wasn't a 'take a break' kind of person. It was all or nothing with her. So that was that." Another pause. "To my everlasting regret."

I thought back to the all-or-nothing decision Kate made about me after our one night together. "All right," I said. "Things ended between you. What happened with David Coyle?"

"Everything kind of stopped for a while. After Kate was killed, I mean. Eventually, as far as I know, there was an internal investigation. He was cleared, although there was some remediation required."

"Remediation?"

"He was faulted for paperwork. Some kind of agreement was reached."

"About what?"

"About him staying at St. Clare, at least for the time being, instead of following Christine to 21st Century Care."

Something occurred to me. "Wasn't he one of her investors?"

"I'm not sure. It wouldn't surprise me if he was. Why?"

"I'm just wondering how much of an investigation was really done. It wouldn't have looked good having an investor charged with Medicare fraud. Especially the husband of the new clinic director."

AFTER CHOWDHURY hung up, I gripped the steering wheel, afraid I might lose control as I wrestled with our conversation. Despite his insistence that he kept Kate walled off from the information, the question remained whether she knew of the allegations against David Coyle. If she did, had stumbling across that information cost Kate her life? Could that awful possibility be the reason Riggs was tailing me? Was he worried I'd learned something that he, as the hospital security director, would rather the wider world not know about? That in the course of looking for answers to one mystery, I'd uncovered another? Or—back to a motive for Kate's death—could the two things be related?

If they were, were we back to Alex's question from the other day: Did Riggs have something to do with Kate's death?

I reminded myself he had an alibi—the alarm he'd come in early to address. An alibi as strong as Alex's now ex-boyfriend, if not quite as slimy. Ditto for Christine Coyle, assuming she hadn't tied her watch to her dog to fake a Runnrly post that morning. But that just meant neither was personally involved. It proved nothing about them hiring out the job. Thinking about Riggs, I reminded myself there was something still bothering me about my conversation in his office that day. Could that be connected to this development?

As I went over all this, I remembered that Burke Cunningham had called in the midst of my conversation with Chowdhury. I called the lawyer back and after three rings heard Cunningham's baritone voice.

"You've had an interesting day."

"Variety is the spice of life?"

"In your case, plain vanilla might suit you better. Are you all right?"

I told him I was, and reviewed the incident at Brown's house, concluding with his stunning allegation about Kate's killer conducting reconnaissance the day before.

"If that's true, why didn't he tell police that morning?" Cunningham said.

It was a good question, one that had begun to bother me as the day wore on. "It's possible he didn't remember it just then. He also doesn't strike me as someone who wanted to get involved, especially with the police."

"He cared enough to call 911."

"To tell the kid at the McDonald's to call," I corrected.

"And stayed long enough to be questioned."

"True. But it's also possible he had no choice. Traffic stopped pretty fast after the accident. He might have been stuck."

"In any case, it's an interesting revelation," Cunningham said. "I hope it was worth what you went through."

"Given that I'm speaking to you instead of the alternative, the answer's yes."

"I'm just glad you're okay. Now, if you have time for another matter?"

"Of course."

"It's regarding the art museum. By any chance have you been out campaigning on your behalf?"

"What do you mean?"

"Two different trustees called me. They heard I was representing you and were concerned about how the museum handled the situation."

I explained the connection some of them had to my derring-do at the fireworks show a few years earlier.

"It's always something with you, isn't it?"

"Some would call it a gift. Is that all you needed? Nothing new on your end, with the FBI, I mean?"

"Nothing so far. Which isn't surprising. It could be days or weeks before we hear."

"Dangling me over the fire?"

"That, or just good old-fashioned bureau bureaucracy. Art theft's pretty far down on their priority list these days, and art theft in Ohio is even lower. My guess is they saw a window to rattle your cage in case you were involved and had something to hide, and now it's hurry-up-and-wait time."

"Rattling my cage or not, they still needed probable cause for that search warrant." I related what Suzanne Gregory told me, about my internet search history.

"That's fascinating, considering the warrant and the affidavit behind it are sealed. Either way, I'm guessing they've got a CHS."

"A which?"

"Confidential human source. A rat, in other words. Though I take it you weren't researching art theft in your spare time?"

"My neighbor has a sweet *Dogs Playing Poker* I've got my eye on. Other than that, no. Well, wait a minute." I told him about Patience's habit of taking my phone to look up artists.

"It's possible someone misconstrued that, though it seems like a stretch. More likely someone at the museum has it out for you and fabricated something for the FBI to chase."

I thought about my small circle of co-workers at the museum, including Patience, but settled quickly on the face of Lillian Melnick. "There's something I should probably tell you."

"That doesn't sound good."

I went over my trip to the museum where I confronted Melnick in the art museum café.

"You really did not do that," he said, his baritone deepening with more than a hint of irritation. Cunningham was famously slow to anger, but when he did, it wasn't a good idea to be close by.

"My emotions got the better of me," I lied, knowing perfectly well it had been a calculated move. "But as long as I'm out of the running for client of the year, there was something that struck me."

"Which was?"

"Right at the end. She seemed nervous. Not because I was there, or not totally because of that. It was more like, I don't know, she was in trouble somehow." I reviewed her *Please just leave* request.

"Seems like an understandable reaction," Cunningham said. "I know Eleanor Seward. You don't want to get on her bad side."

"That's my impression too. But it seemed unusual coming from Melnick. Let's just say she doesn't have a reputation for showing fear."

"I think you're barking up several wrong trees, but I'll keep it in mind. As long as you promise not to pull a stunt like that again."

I agreed and, for a change, didn't have my fingers crossed.

24

STILL THINKING about the possibility raised by Cunningham of an art museum rat, I called Patience to see if I could pry loose anything she might be hiding, either to protect me or herself. She didn't pick up, and I ended up leaving a noncommittal message about her gallery opening.

Next, I tried Brian Riggs, also with no luck. His lack of communication seemed childish, the equivalent of a toddler pulling a blanket over his head to keep from being found. If I can't see you, you can't see me. Eventually, though, he was going to have to come clean.

I INSTRUCTED Alex to buy takeout after retrieving Joe, so I was surprised to arrive home to the odor of cooking filling the house. I came inside, greeted Hopalong, and walked into the kitchen, where Alex was supervising Joe over a large pot.

"That smells delicious."

"Sautéed garlic shrimp with tomato and onions in angel hair pasta," Alex said matter-of-factly. "I had to talk Joe into the shrimp."

"Amazing."

I grabbed a Black Label from the fridge, seeing as I did that Alex was working on one of her own.

"Hope it's okay I took one," she said.

"Of course."

"No offense, but you do know how many good micro-breweries Columbus has now, right?"

"'Sometimes you just need a cold one.' Remember?"

"Not every day though."

"You drink in your church, I'll drink in mine."

I waited until we were seated and enjoying the first few bites of dinner before I told Alex and Joe about my day in Dayton. I figured the evening would be ruined regardless and there was probably no good time. Joe took the news with his usual calm, showing no more reaction than if I'd given him a blow-by-blow description of filling my gas tank. Alex, by contrast, grew still, even as her eyes brightened. What she said when she finally spoke, though, surprised me.

"You could have been killed."

"Possibly. Brown's on the run from something, and it was a boneheaded move on my part to sneak in like that. But, and I'm not sure exactly how to say this, he didn't seem like a bad guy."

"You're kidding."

"Evil guy, is maybe what I mean. He seemed like a guy being squeezed from all sides just trying to survive. The fact he stopped and told me about the SUV says a lot."

"What did Shortland say?"

"I haven't heard back directly. But he should realize this puts things on a whole other level."

"But what about the accident scene? The yaw marks? That shows the person tried to brake. That's the whole reason we've assumed it was a hit-skip and the jerk was just too cowardly to stop."

"Maybe he got cold feet, right at the last second. Or reflexes kicked in—it would take nerves of steel not to hit the brakes—"

"Or maybe it was staged," Joe said.

Alex and I both stared at him. "What do you mean?" his sister said.

"It's just something I've been thinking about."

That was Joe. Always thinking. I recalled his comment about Brian Riggs, likening him to an animal that piggybacks on the work of others. A klepto-whatchamacallit.

"Go on," I said.

"Maybe the point was to make it look like an accident. I saw something like that on this one video game. Like, some Venezuelan dude ordered a hit on this Russian dude and paid this other Venezuelan dude to take him out as he was crossing a bridge in London or someplace, but to make it look like an accident. In that one, he went up on the sidewalk and back and then hit the brakes on purpose—"

Alex suppressed a sob.

"Joe," I said.

"It's okay," Alex said. She sniffed and rubbed her face with her hands, composing herself. When she was finished, a hard expression replaced her momentary sorrow. "It's a lot to take in. But I think Joe's right. It's the perfect explanation. But why? Why would someone want to kill my mom?"

AFTER ALL that, I didn't have the heart to go over my conversation with Jeff Heaton, not to mention Billy Chowdhury's revelation about Dr. David Coyle. After dinner, Alex lay down for a nap ahead of her shift. While Joe did his homework, I washed the dishes and tried to make sense of the day's bombshell, with the supposition added by Joe—however insensitively—that not only had someone been stalking Kate; they might have deliberately staged the killing to make it look like an accident. But fundamentally, it all came back to Alex's teary question: Who would want to kill Kate? To keep from going crazy—crazier—I went through the short list I'd formed so far.

Jamie Thacker, Alex's boozy ex-boyfriend, pissed that Kate didn't like him and wasn't afraid to say so. Despite his "unfortunate alibi," I still was wary of him.

Brian Riggs, whose face swam into my crosshairs only because I knew he'd been following me. He had the driving skills to pull off a fake braking job ahead of impact thanks to his work as a police training instructor and later his part-time job at Green Light Goals. But, like Thacker, he had an alibi. The malfunctioning alarm wasn't the kind of story you made up: security cameras would no doubt back him up, along with multiple colleagues. Unwilling to let the theory go, I spent another few minutes researching Riggs's vehicle ownership history with the state BMV. There was nothing there. Riggs hadn't owned anything close to a dark SUV. And so what if he did? What fool trying to disguise his or her tracks would use a vehicle so easily traceable to them? Now that we knew Kate's killing was premeditated, it stood to reason the vehicle was stolen or at the very least untrackable in one way or another.

Then there was Christine Coyle, who might have millions of reasons for keeping secret the fact her cardiologist husband had been committing Medicare fraud and thus jeopardizing his role as one of her investors. But if that was true, why wasn't the target of Christine's ire Billy Chowdhury himself, who knew the alleged details?

Thacker, Riggs, Christine Coyle. All intriguing, yet any evidence linking them to Kate's death was like exhaust from a tailpipe: it lingered in the imagination, never entirely dissipating, but impossible to contain in any measurable way.

Once again, I considered the possibility, thanks to Jeff Heaton, that a once-laughable suggestion—an aggrieved anti-vaxxer—now belonged at the top of my suspect list.

There was no question that in the COVID era, antiscience rage was real and red-hot. If it could affect my own father, a certified pain in the ass but not generally a malicious person, who's to say what that anger could spur in a less-balanced person? And Heaton had definitely come across as off-kilter.

I realized that the calculus came down to this: Would a family member mourning the loss of Shirley Vanhouten have the emotional wherewithal to turn around a murder plot a few days later? Related to this, there was something else I couldn't ignore. Heaton's story of Kate saying, "Another one," in the moments after his mother's death.

I dismissed outright Heaton's suggestion that Kate was making light of Shirley Vanhouten's death. Thinking about it, a new possibility occurred to me. Maybe Heaton misheard. What if it hadn't been a statement, but a question: "Another one?"

If that was the case, Kate's query implied a pattern that superseded a normal cluster. That even after the height of a COVID surge, something nefarious might be going on. A dark thought indeed. And also one that begged the question of what Kate did after Vanhouten's death. Did she find Dr. Ives and tell him of her concern? Or someone else—Christine Coyle, for example? If that were the case, what would Ives or Coyle have done with the information? Maybe that was the trigger I was looking for. Having ducked a scandal with her husband, Coyle couldn't have been happy about another potentially damning St. Clare disgrace. How far would she have gone to keep that particular truth from emerging?

I checked the time. Just past 8 p.m. At least three hours before Alex had to leave for work. I made my decision. I had to get to Brian Riggs sooner rather than later. But before that, it was time to follow this "Another one" thread to the only person besides Kate who might know enough to shed light on what that meant.

"Joe—I need to go out for a while. You'll be okay?"

"What?"

I gestured for him to remove his earbuds and repeated my statement. He nodded distractedly.

"The two Kevins are right next door if you need anything."

He gave me a thumbs-up. My across-the-alley neighbors had bailed me out with babysitting duties before, both for Joe and for Hopalong, simultaneously amused by and interested in the quirk of living by a private eye.

"Also, can you let the dog out in a while?"

Another thumbs-up, the boy already engrossed in his multitasking universe.

Satisfied the house was more likely to survive my brief absence than not, I grabbed my keys and headed out the door to my van, and an evening visit to Dr. Ryan Ives.

25

IVES LIVED at the end of a cul-de-sac in a subdivision south of Hoover Reservoir in a big but not ostentatious split-level with a two-car garage. I parked behind a white SUV sitting in the drive and looked around. Absent streetlights, the only illumination came from lampposts in yards and lights over doorways. But even in that enveloping darkness, I could tell that Ives's yard was probably the most in need of landscaping love. Another casualty of his wife's illness, I guessed, reminding myself to tread carefully.

A long minute after I rang the bell, the door opened a crack and I found myself looking at a young woman with worried eyes in sweatpants and a *Cars* Disney movie T-shirt under an oversized flannel shirt. Taylor Ives, I guessed. This could be interesting.

"Andy Hayes," I said, handing her my card. "Sorry to drop by unannounced. I need to speak to Dr. Ives. It's important."

Her eyes, dark with exhaustion, widened in panic. You could almost see the synapses firing as she made the connection between me and Alex.

"Hang on," she said with a squeak and shut the door in my face.

This time nearly three minutes passed before footsteps approached inside. Once again the door opened and I found myself staring into another pair of deeply fatigued eyes.

"What can I do for you?" Ryan Ives said, the weariness in his voice audible even through his medical mask.

"I need your help," I said.

WE SAT in a large, carpeted living room that would have felt luxurious but for the clutter—baskets of unfolded laundry tucked to the side, unread copies of the *Wall Street Journal* piled atop a glass-topped coffee table, cardboard boxes piled in the corner, some opened, some sealed tight, marked "medical supplies." I recognized a stack of Klonopin packages from my grandmother's last weeks when doctors attempted to level out her uneven sleep as cancer ravaged her.

"I'm sorry about the mess," Ives said. "I think I mentioned about my wife, on the phone . . ."

"Please don't worry about it. I live with a teenage boy," I said, unsuccessfully trying to break the tension. The doctor's eyes gave nothing away. Taylor, sitting in a recliner in the corner, did her best not to stare. She'd put a mask on since answering the door, as had I, at Dr. Ives's request. Her presence made me wonder yet again if her father knew about her and Jamie Thacker. She had an unhealthy pallor about her that I attributed to the stress of her situation. She was also heavier than I imagined for a person who Alex said had run in Coyle's group from time to time. With everything she was going through, jogging probably was low on her priority list, for good reason.

Silence descended over the room, interrupted only by Ives jiggling his keys in his pocket. As nervous tics went, it seemed forgivable given his circumstances. As if underscoring the point, I heard what sounded like the click and mechanical aspiration of an oxygen machine coming from upstairs. I imagined Mrs. Ives prone on a bed, struggling with breath as she fought the effects of long-haul COVID.

Natalie Mettler's description of the illness's impact on Mrs. Ives came back to me. *It left her nearly disabled—couldn't drive anymore, couldn't be in front of a screen.* Simultaneously, I heard the red-hot fury of Jeff Heaton over the phone. *She had a bad cold is all, and they made it worse.* Not sure where else to start, I related my conversation with Heaton, concluding with Heaton's anger at what he saw as Kate's insensitive dismissal of his mother's death.

Ives rubbed thick fingers into his forehead. "You're saying this person might have taken his anger out on Kate because of what happened to his mother?" He had the fleshy face of someone paused in the transition of either gaining or losing weight, with brown eyes flitting between resignation and resentment at my presence in his living room.

"I'm not ready to go that far. But he was angry—very angry. It made me wonder if he's the same person who followed you into the parking lot. That might be good to know for starters."

"You must know this doctor can't talk about patients or their families."

"I understand that. But maybe you could tell me if he's someone I should be taking a closer look at. In the interest of justice for Kate."

Ives didn't respond right away. Taylor snuck a glance at him, as if curious herself what he might say. When she saw me looking at her, she quickly dropped her gaze.

"Heaton followed me," Ives said with a sigh. "He was upset. It was inappropriate, but he needed to have his say."

"Did he threaten you? Or Kate?"

"Nothing like that. Mostly the usual gibberish about COVID, denying that's what his mother had, accusing us of misdiagnosing her, of not treating her properly. Of, well, being responsible for her death. All very irrational. She would have died two days earlier if not for the ventilator. But it's like I told you over the phone. It's difficult to blame someone for lashing out under those conditions. He had his perspective."

"Even if it was completely dumbass," Taylor whispered.

"Taylor," her father said. "In any case, it didn't last long. One of the guards came by and separated us."

"Did you hear from Heaton again?"

"I didn't, no. I'm not sure about the hospital. He threatened legal action, but I don't think he followed through. At least not yet."

"Legal action? On what grounds?"

"This medical professional couldn't say. Doctors and hospitals are sued a lot."

"Malpractice suits, you mean."

He shook his head, his distaste at the phrase obvious. "That's right. It's an occupational hazard."

I tried to imagine what such a lawsuit would look like. An opinion founded in misinformation and hate up against scientific and medical reality. No doubt a judge would dismiss it as frivolous, but it would still take time and exert a toll on people like Ives. I wondered if Jeff Heaton knew that too and might be counting on it.

"Did Heaton say anything directly about Kate, that morning?"

"Not that I recall. He was mostly focused on the doctor."

I puzzled at that for a second before realizing he meant himself. Ives had an odd—or was it simply affected?—way of referring to himself in the third person. How'd the old joke go? "Who's that arrogant guy trying to cut in line?" "That's God. He thinks he's a doctor."

I dismissed the thought and returned to the "Another one" comment—or was it "Another one?"—that had Heaton so fired up. "Did he say anything to you about that?"

"'Another one'?"

"That's right."

"I don't believe so. Honestly, though, it was several months ago now, at the end of a long shift. He wasn't the first emotional family member I've spoken with in my career. And especially in the past year. Just because someone's misguided doesn't mean their feelings aren't valid."

I thought about the way Ives finished a version of that thought on the phone the other day. *No one should judge someone for reacting to what he perceived as an affront to his own morality.*

"Your restraint is admirable."

"That's kind of you to say, I suppose. But it's not how this doctor sees it. It's easier just to roll with things sometimes."

The clicking of the oxygen upstairs distracted me again. Ives saw me react to the sound. Feeling bad that he noticed, I said, "If I may ask, how is your wife doing?"

Ives looked at Taylor.

"She's not well. That's about all I can say."

"I'm sorry to hear that."

"So are we," Taylor said, unable to contain herself.

I sat back and folded my hands across my right knee. I wasn't sure what else there was to discuss. I considered bringing up Billy Chowdhury's allegations about David Coyle but rejected the idea immediately. This wasn't the time, whether or not Ives might know something about it. And especially not with his daughter sitting there. In fact, I was questioning my decision to pay this visit at all. I was no closer to determining whether Jeff Heaton was crazed enough to take his anger out over his mother's death by running down Kate than when I first came across his name. If anything, he seemed more likely to attack Ives, the attending physician.

"Just one other thing with Heaton," I said. "If I may."

"Yes?" Dr. Ives said wearily.

"His mother, Shirley Vanhouten."

"What about her?"

"Kate seemed to take her death particularly hard. Or so I'm told."

Ives seemed to think about this. "I wouldn't know. Kate was a resilient person. In some ways perfectly suited for what we see on the ICU. But we were dealing with a lot of deaths then. I'm not sure what about Mrs. Vanhouten would have been different than any of the others."

"Something must have stood out, though." I reminded him of Kate's "Another one" comment, at least as reported by Jeff Heaton.

"Unless she was reacting in the moment to yet another loss. Everyone reaches his breaking point at one time or another. It's just hard to predict how and when that will happen."

And that was that. Once again, silence filled the room with the exception of the mechanical sounds coming from upstairs. I glanced at Taylor, who was staring at the floor, and stood up.

"I'm sorry to have bothered you at home."

"Good luck with the investigation," Dr. Ives said. "We all miss Kate. I hope you turn something up."

I was at my van, pausing to admire the stars in a night sky unsullied by streetlights, when I heard the door to the house open.

"Mr. Hayes."

Taylor approached, gingerly stepping across the cobblestone drive in slippers, hugging herself in the brisk October evening.

"Um . . ."

I waited, saying nothing.

"I wondered if Alex was doing okay?"

"Alex?" I said, surprised.

She made a face. "I'm guessing you know about, well, what happened?"

"Between you and Jamie, you mean?" I said it as gently as I could. Though the episode angered me as Alex's father, it would have been hypocritical to come down all that hard on her. As a young man, I'd played the role of Thacker in the same scenario, and more than once.

She nodded.

"I'm aware, yes. It's also none of my business. As for Alex, she's doing all right."

"Just all right?"

"For now, yes."

She shivered and her eyes went dull. "I'm so sorry," she whispered.

I resisted telling her that it was okay, because despite my own history I knew it wasn't. Instead, I stayed silent, studying the SUV parked in front of their garage as I waited for the rest of this awkward scene to unfold. At last she said, "Can I ask you something?"

"Of course."

She didn't speak for a moment, composing herself. To break the silence, I said, "That was my son's favorite movie for a while. Alex's brother, Mike."

"Sorry?"

"*Cars.*" I gestured at her shirt. "He'd watch it over and over." Sticking discs into video machines and pressing play: what passed for my parenting in those days.

She glanced down. "Oh, yeah. Me too," she said, and quickly wrapped herself in the flannel shirt, a hint of embarrassment in her eyes. It was hard to blame her for seeking comfort in a familiar childhood memory given the straits her family was in. With that thought, the obvious occurred to me.

Thanks to COVID, Taylor had had to grow up fast. In short order, she lost her paternal grandparents and then, for all intents and purposes, her mom. She might even have felt like she lost her dad as he became subsumed with caring for the tsunami of coronavirus patients. The result, it appeared, was that she'd been thrust into the unwelcome roles of both caretaker and gatekeeper. I recalled how she answered the phone the night I first called the house. How she answered the door tonight, not her father. And how she stuck around for her father's and my conversation in the living room, a meeting that had to be a serious trigger. No wonder, given all these unexpected obligations, she flipped out and had a fling with Jamie Thacker. It might not be forgivable. But it was understandable.

When I didn't say anything, Taylor took a breath and said, "Do you think that guy, the one who threatened my dad, could have, you know, killed Alex's mom?"

"I really don't know," I said, relieved that we'd moved away from her transgression with Alex's boyfriend. I thought about Leo Brown's revelation, that someone apparently targeted Kate. But it was nothing I could tell Taylor, just as it wasn't anything I could have revealed to her father. "I'm just looking at all the angles for now."

"You have to understand something," she said, glancing back at the house. Her voice finally rose above a whisper. "These people were crazy. My dad's like super forgiving. But I don't trust any of them. I mean, these are the same type that went to that doctor's house with guns. You know what I'm talking about, right?"

I told her I did. A few months into the pandemic, armed protesters showed up outside the house of the then–state health director. She resigned the position not long afterward, a decision hard to second-guess under the circumstances.

"There's no telling what they might do," Taylor said. "That's why I was a little freaked out when the doorbell rang. We can't be too careful."

"Have there been more threats? Against your dad, I mean?"

"Not lately. Things have calmed down a lot. But we're still wary."

"I'm sorry he went through that."

"I guess what I'm asking is, Will you tell us if, you know, you find out something? About this guy, I mean?"

"Sure," I said, though I knew my first call would be to Doug Shortland at the Westerville Police Department.

"Thanks. Also . . ."

Once again I waited for her to finish a sentence.

"I was just wondering, if Alex would ever . . ."

She went quiet again. After a moment, I said, "Listen. What happened with Jamie is between the two of you. I honestly can't say whether she wants to see you, talk to you, whatever. But my advice in these situations is just to try. Otherwise, you won't ever know." To say the least, it felt odd brokering some kind of engagement between Alex and the girl who'd stolen her place in bed. But in a strange way, I figured I owed her as much after showing up at her house unannounced.

Also, as weird as it sounded, maybe they could bond over a shared loss. Though Taylor's mother wasn't dead, it sounded like she might never recover, never work or drive or go out alone again. Another obvious thought: Taylor and Alex both had to grow up fast in the past few months.

"Thanks," she said, brushing her right slipper over her left. "I'll think about it."

"Sure. You should get inside. It's a cold night," I added. "I'll let you know if I turn up anything else."

"Okay."

"Good luck with your mom. I know it's been hard."

She didn't reply, but only nodded before turning and walking back to the front door. She turned once, pausing as she saw me watching her, then disappeared inside, head bowed.

26

ALEX WAS still asleep when I returned home. Joe and I watched the end of *American Ninja Warrior* before I directed him to bed. When Alex got up and was dressed for work, I briefed her on my conversation with Ryan and Taylor Ives.

"She really asked that? About me?"

"She did." I kept my voice neutral.

"Such a bitch."

I studied Hopalong's food bowl.

"You know, she broke up with him like two weeks later."

"Okay."

"Which tells you what kind of person she is."

"I'm just the messenger here, though I'm not saying I disagree. For what it's worth, which is probably nothing, she seemed remorseful. She also seems like she's under a lot of stress. With her mom, I mean. Stress can make people do stupid things. Take it from someone who knows."

"Like that's an excuse."

"I said it was probably worth nothing."

She sighed. "Fine. So that happened. Which is just perfect. What about her dad?"

"What about him?"

"Well, he either thinks Jeff Heaton was angry enough to go after my mom and he doesn't want to admit it, or he doesn't know or doesn't care. Either way, we're no farther along than we were."

"We're a lot farther than we were yesterday. As far as Dr. Ives goes, it's like I said about Taylor. I think he's got a lot on his plate."

"So do I."

Shortly after eleven I walked Alex to her car, parked a block and a half up on Mohawk. As much as I wanted to, I resisted the urge to hug her and instead said goodbye and told her to be careful.

"Of what?"

"Space aliens. Invading Russians. Another virus. Everything."

"Get a grip, Andy," she said, and climbed into her car.

I AWOKE the next morning remembering that Patience's exhibit opened that night. Accompanying that thought was the realization I'd have the house to myself since Joe would be up north, assuming Crystal and Bob had gotten their act together. Maybe a silver lining lay ahead following what had been a supremely stressful week.

After dropping Joe at school, I returned home, settled on my couch with coffee, and looked up the *Dayton Daily News* online. There was no mention of me or Leo Brown. No surprise there. "Report of shots fired" hadn't merited a second glance from whatever reporters still monitored the police scanner or perused the daily blotter. I was reviewing the encounter with Brown and trying to figure out what was keeping him on the run when my phone rang.

"Andy? It's Detective Shortland."

"I'm glad you called. I was—"

"You've been busy," he interrupted.

Just doing my job, I thought, but kept it to myself. "Brown was a loose end, and to be honest, my only loose end. Trust me when I say I didn't expect things to turn out the way they did."

"I need you to come to the station and give a statement. About what he told you."

"Okay."

"As soon as possible."

I suppressed a twinge of frustration, thinking about how I'd put my life on the line to gain the information Shortland now wanted. I was also in no position to argue, and we both knew it.

TRYING TO make nice, I arrived at the Westerville police station with two coffees I'd picked up at Northstar Café only for Shortland to inform me he was a tea drinker. I sat in the same conference room as before and wrote out a statement.

"How are the kids?" I said, handing him the completed document.

"Busy. Like me." And that was that.

"You realize how reckless this was?" he said a minute later, finished reading.

"Yes."

"You could have been killed."

"Alex said the same thing."

"Brown didn't say why he left this out the first time we talked to him?"

I related the theory I'd given Burke Cunningham when he asked the same question, that Brown wasn't someone who wanted anything to do with the police but that morning was forced to because he was literally stuck there.

"He seemed happy enough to talk to that Channel 7 reporter."

"I'm not sure that's true." I reminded him of Brown's laconic responses to Suzanne in the short interview. I also explained—leaving out my personal connection to Suzanne—that she, though perhaps not ambushing Brown, hadn't given him much choice when she showed up at his apartment.

"I guess that's plausible given his situation."

"His situation?"

Instead of responding, Shortland surprised me by saying, "Any thoughts on who that might have been? Scoping out the intersection, I mean?"

"Plenty."

"Care to share?"

I went over my original suspicions, from Brian Riggs based on him tailing me, to Jamie Thacker despite his icky alibi, and finally to Jeff Heaton. Then, because I couldn't think of a reason not to, I told him—without revealing my source—about the Medicare fraud allegations against David Coyle and the motive I thought that gave his wife.

"Wow," Shortland said finally.

"Wow what?"

"Wow in that I don't know where to start."

"My sentiments exactly. How about this: Did you know about the Medicare stuff?"

He looked to be on the cusp of another "No comment" but in the end just shook his head. "That one's news to me. But . . ."

"But?"

"Unless Kate also knew about it, I'm not sure what bearing it has. And you say she didn't?"

"As far as I know."

"I won't lie: I wish I'd known at the time. But I'm still not sure it moves the needle. As for the other people, I just don't think there's anything there."

"Really?"

"Well, accusing Riggs is insulting, plus he has an alibi. Thacker's also off the table. That leaves Heaton, or someone like him, which seems far-fetched."

"It does, on the surface. But he was also really angry about his mother's death, and he seemed to think Kate showed insensitivity over her passing."

Shortland scribbled in a notepad. He looked up. "Anything else?"

"I guess that's enough for now. How about you?"

"Me?"

"I just gave you a lot, including Leo Brown's big reveal. What can you tell me?"

"Nothing. It's your word there's a suspect. We can't confirm it until we talk to Brown ourselves."

"Give me a break."

"Save it. You know I can't get into stuff with you. We're doing everything we can, which is what I keep telling Alex. In case you were wondering, it's not making my life any easier having the father of the victim's daughter running his own investigation."

"We went over all that before. I'll have you know my first call in Dayton was to you."

"Don't pat yourself on the back for doing the right thing." Before I could object, he added, "I can tell you we're taking this thing with Brown seriously. I've already been on the phone to the gas station this morning telling them we need the previous week's footage, not that I'm sure how much it will show. But it's a start—a big one."

"Since you're being so forthcoming, any idea what Brown was running from? Or who? Or what that 'situation' is you mentioned?"

Shortland didn't speak for a full count of ten. I watched as a struggle played out on his face between his law enforcement obligations and what I hoped was a desire to play fair. He couldn't have been any more conflicted had a cartoon devil and angel been sitting on his shoulders whispering into each ear. Finally, uncrossing his arms again, he said, "I'll be honest and say I don't have all the facts yet. Brown was into some penny-ante shit, marijuana possession, receiving stolen property, stuff like that, that apparently got him crossways with someone a lot more hardcore."

"Like who?"

"I can't say. Suffice to say, he had a good reason to disappear after his mug showed up on TV that night talking about Kate. That reporter blew his cover big-time, apparently."

Try as I might, I couldn't get anything more out of the detective. Bonding over kids hadn't worked, that's for sure. Not that I was surprised. He was a married father of six. I was a guy still trying to clean up two and a half decades of botched relationships. So be it. Meanwhile, it was at least clear that Brown's revelation had kickstarted a cold investigation into high gear. I had no doubt that Shortland would now be looking hard at who might have a motive and also access to a dark SUV. He might even reinterview Christine Coyle. But he wouldn't acknowledge any of that. Our interview was over.

As I walked out of the station, I thought more about what the detective said about Brown. Into some penny-ante shit that placed him crossways with someone worse. But who? That list was lengthy and growing longer every day. As the quiet Columbus of my college days morphed into a booming midwestern metropolis, with cranes rising seemingly on every corner, the shiny new buildings were casting the predictable long shadows of accompanying crime and malfeasance. Homicides had gone through the roof, especially during the pandemic. No wonder Leo Brown was scared. Suzanne Gregory had unintentionally flushed him into the open at the worst possible moment.

I was almost back to my van when I was interrupted by a call from Alex.

"You're up early. Everything all right?"

"Yes and no."

"What's wrong?"

"I was wondering . . ."

I waited.

"Do you think I could come down? To your house, I mean."

SICK TO DEATH

"Of course. I'm just wrapping things up. I'm actually not far." I told her about my conversation with Shortland.

"The thing is . . . could I, like, stay?"

"Sure. I may be in and out but—"

"I mean, like, for a few days. The couch would be fine."

"No problem at all. Is everything okay?"

"I just need to get out of here. This whole thing with Leo Brown, it's got me a little freaked out. Knowing there's someone out there, someone who did this intentionally. That's why I couldn't sleep, after my shift. I don't mean to sound like a wuss—"

"Stop right there. It's fine. I'll be home in thirty minutes tops."

"Don't rush. I have something to do first. But I appreciate it."

"My pleasure. Plus Joe will get a kick out of it. Just text me when you're on the way."

"Thanks, Andy," she said, and disconnected.

27

I TURNED over my conversation with Alex nearly the whole drive home, feeling worse about it with every second. I didn't regret telling her about Leo Brown's revelation—not that I had any choice in the matter. But that it made Alex so uncomfortable—that weighed on me. In hindsight, given everything she'd gone through, the discomfort was inevitable. Yet it still bothered me. Both because of what she was feeling and the thought that, in fact, she could theoretically be in danger somehow. But why? Someone had wanted Kate dead, not her.

I was nearly home when a second, semi-terrible thought crashed down on me. In the drama involving the FBI search of my house, followed by my narrow escape in Dayton, I had completely forgotten about the fact I still hadn't told my sister or my parents about Alex. Jesus, what an oversight. That would be legitimate grounds for a tongue lashing from Shelley involving some choice—and well-deserved—comments about my lack of consideration for others. I promised myself that as soon as Alex showed up, we'd make arrangements for the big reveal.

Once inside and settled, I opened my laptop and was reviewing notes when I started thinking more about Alex's impending move-in, however temporary it might be. Which led me back to the only person so far who was guilty of a hospital-grounds confrontation: Jeff Heaton, the son of Shirley Vanhouten.

To satisfy my curiosity, I looked up Vanhouten's obituary again. She had passed away on May 17, a Saturday. Just three days before Kate's death, on May 20. Leo Brown said he remembered seeing the SUV the previous morning, the nineteenth. That left Sunday, May 18, as the day when something could have happened to trigger the murderer's reconnaissance at the intersection the following morning. Jeff Heaton had previously confronted Dr. Ives and was furious after the "Another one" or "Another one?" comment the night his mother died. The timing seemed to fit.

I recalled my previous thought that, if posed as a question, the comment no longer came off as a snide remark about an anti-vaxxer's death—as Heaton believed—but instead suggested a trend, perhaps one with insidious undertones. I decided to take a closer look.

Finding additional St. Clare obituaries was about as difficult as I expected. For starters, there were a lot of St. Clare hospitals. I had to refine my search several times, then wade through online obituaries and try to nail down the day of someone's death. Eventually, after about an hour I came up with three additional names of people who died at St. Clare–North in the days or weeks before Kate's death:

Clarence Kamer, age seventy-nine.

Carol Radcliff, age forty-six.

Stanley Elliot, age sixty-two.

Even as I typed Elliot's name on a document I'd titled "St. Clare's Deaths," a wave of discouragement swept over me. What the hell had I accomplished? Three people who died on a busy big city hospital ICU in the same month during COVID? Four, if you counted Shirley Vanhouten? People died in hospitals all the time, even more so when they refused a simple measure against a deadly virus—if indeed that was the case with these other deaths. This was like congratulating myself for figuring out that apples dropped from trees in an orchard.

After a moment, I realized what was happening. I'd let the adrenaline rush of Leo Brown's story contaminate other aspects of this investigation, if you could even call it that. I wanted Heaton's story of what Kate said to mean more than it did. I was looking at a sky only slightly less cloudy than the day I met Alex and was trying to fill it with stars.

An hour later, I was still trying to make sense of any of it when Alex knocked on the door.

"Sorry to hit you with this first thing," I said as I carried one of her bags to the spare bedroom. I explained about needing to introduce her ASAP to my sister and my parents.

"You mean like today?"

"I'm thinking maybe we could set up a call with Shelley later on. Maybe go out to my parents' tomorrow?"

"That works. I took the whole weekend off because of the half-marathon."

"Perfect."

I told her to sleep in Joe's room for at least the next two nights. While she settled herself, I texted Shelley and asked if she was free for a video call later that day.

I tamped down annoyance at her abrupt reply. Skepticism was fair under these circumstances; it's not like I'd ever made such a request.

It's a surprise. It'll be worth it, promise

She eventually agreed on five o'clock. That settled, I refilled my coffee cup and spent the next couple of minutes firing off texts to Kym, Crystal, and my mom to set things up for the next day. My mother, a veteran of my shortcomings when they came to family, asked right away what the occasion was.

> Boys miss you

With luck, she'd buy the white lie. Mike, apparently on a break between classes, once again asked if his girlfriend could come. I mentioned the request aloud, shaking my head.

"Let her, Andy," Alex said.

"What?"

"Let her come. Last time I checked, a high school guy who asks to bring his girlfriend to his grandparents' is doing something right. Besides, I need to check this girl out." She smacked her right fist into her left palm. "Make sure I approve."

"You might scare her off. Big bad cop sister."

"She might as well get used to it."

While I finished the arrangements, Alex rummaged for food, securing a box of raisin bran, a bowl, and some milk. I had just finished texting my mom the plan when Alex spoke, her mouth full of cereal.

"Can I tell you something?"

"Of course."

"You know that thing I said I had to do? Before I came down here?"

"Yeah?"

"It was coffee."

"That's nice."

"With Taylor Ives."

I looked at her. "Really?"

"She texted me this morning. I don't think she realizes I work nights, but it didn't matter in this case since I was already awake."

"Wow."

"She asked if we could meet. I wasn't going to at first. Then I thought about what you said, about the stress they're under. It doesn't make me forgive her. And I told her that. But honestly, we'd actually never talked about what happened. I figured, what the hell."

"And?"

"She apologized like crazy. After a while, I told her to stop. I think that made her a little mad, but I couldn't take it anymore."

"Anything else?"

"It was pretty awkward. But I have to say, I think mainly she's lonely. And, like you said, stressed. Actually, she asked a lot of questions about you. She seemed fascinated by the idea of me finding you out of the blue. She said it'd be weird to get a dad like that."

"What'd you tell her?"

"That I agreed with her. It is weird, no offense."

"None taken."

"She also talked about her mom. How hard things have been. She talked a lot about her, in fact. How it was a good thing she and her dad are both in the medical field, because they weren't sure she'd survive otherwise."

"She's carrying a lot."

"I know. It doesn't make any of it any easier. But I guess I'm glad I went. She talked about wanting to do something sometime. Go running or something. And she was definitely interested in how you're doing with finding out who the driver was that killed Mom."

"You think you will? Go running?"

"I suggested she run the half-marathon with me Sunday. She took a pass."

I recalled Taylor's pasty face and obvious weight gain.

"That was cold."

"Was it?"

"Since she reached out to you, sure. There's no way she could do something like that right now. And you know it."

"Leave it. This was a big step for me. From wanting to throttle her to having a latte together. Just because I met her doesn't mean I'm still not pissed as hell. She said she'd watch me on that app instead. Satisfied?"

"I guess. I'm impressed you had the stomach to sit down with her. I'm not sure I could have done that."

"Good thing you're not me." She ate a spoonful of cereal, clearly ready to change the subject. She wasn't the only one.

After a moment, she said, "What's this?"

"What?"

"Sorry, I didn't mean to be nosy. I just saw the thing on your computer. Those names."

I explained the internet searches I'd done on other deaths that appeared to happen on St. Clare–North's ICU.

"You're saying . . ."

"I'm not saying anything. I went down a rabbit hole, is all."

"Do you have the dates? That they died, I mean?"

"No, but I can get them." I spent a couple minutes online, found the dates, and added them to the document. Alex pulled out her phone and did a search of her own.

"That's not good."

"What?"

"Mom was on each of those days."

"How do you know?"

"I kept track of her schedule. Between my overnights and her work hours, things could get a little crazy, so I liked to know her shifts. Now it makes a lot more sense."

"What does?"

"What Jeff Heaton claimed she said."

"Which was?"

"'Another one'? It absolutely was."

28

WE STUDIED the obituaries, trying to see if anything linked the four.

"It could easily be a coincidence," I said. "A lot of people died at St. Clare around that time."

"Except for 'Another one?' I might believe you."

"That could still mean anything."

"But remember how upset Mom was about Mrs. Vanhouten? If there were three others before that, related somehow, it makes sense her saying that."

"How did you find out she was upset?"

Alex finished her cereal and thought for a moment. "I don't think I heard about that lady until later the next day. So Sunday. I got up late because of my shift, and Mom was gone, and she hadn't left a note. I remember thinking that was strange. She came back in the early afternoon. I asked her where she'd been and she just said errands. I could tell something was bugging her, and eventually she told me about Mrs. Vanhouten."

"What did she say?"

"Just that she'd had a patient die the night before and she was upset. We talked about it a little, and someplace along the way she mentioned her name. One of the reasons I remembered the name was that it was a little out of character for her."

"What do you mean?"

"It's not that she never talked about work. But she was careful not to say a lot about her patients because of confidentiality stuff. Plus, she had this thing about trying not to be my best friend or anything."

"Really?"

"Keep in mind she was only twenty when she had me," Alex said, avoiding my gaze. "For a long time, until she met Steve's dad, we only had each other. One time, a few months before she died, I found this book she'd left in the bathroom by mistake. The title was something like *Be a Parent, Not a Friend!* I didn't say anything about it, and the next morning it was gone. But it was kind of eye-opening."

"I bet." I realized I still had no idea what kind of relationship I was supposed to have with Alex, now or in the future. Although the fact she kept calling me Andy was a clue, I was guessing.

"So, this is some serious shit," Alex said.

"What is?"

"These names. Three people die on the ICU on nights my mom worked. Then Mrs. Vanhouten dies. My mom's the thread connecting them." She looked at me. "What if she had something to do with that?"

"What are you saying?"

"Do I have to spell it out? Maybe their deaths weren't, you know, natural."

"Now hang on a second."

"We have to consider it," she said, her voice firm.

"Maybe. Except that first off, that doesn't fit with what you and everyone else have told me about your mom. Hard-working, compassionate, devoted to her patients even when they were spouting crazy shit. Second, if Jeff Heaton is telling the truth, why would she say, 'Another one?' if she had something to do with it? It sounds more like she's *reacting* to a trend, not responsible for it."

"I suppose." Though Alex's tone was neutral, I could see relief in her eyes. "But now it's a little harder to ignore the obvious."

"Which is?"

"She was killed three days after remarking on what potentially was a fourth death on her watch."

We sat without speaking for a minute. It felt as if, while on a walk across a nondescript field on an ordinary day, we'd suddenly found ourselves inches from a deadly precipice.

I had decided to follow my gut and was about to tell her about David Coyle and the Medicare fraud, regardless of how it fit into the puzzle, when Alex said, "We should call some of these people."

"Which people?"

She pointed at my laptop. "The relatives of these patients. See what they know. See if anything was suspicious about the way they died. Did Mrs. Vanhouten's son say anything along those lines?"

"Only that the hospital made things worse." I told her about Heaton's anger over the propofol and the ventilator.

"Makes you wonder," Alex said.

"Well, you know the saying 'Just because you're paranoid doesn't mean they're not out to get you'?"

"Sure."

"What if there was something to what Heaton said."

"Like what? That COVID's not real? C'mon."

"No, not that. About the propofol. One thing we know about drugs like that is they're deadly under the wrong circumstances. Just ask Michael Jackson." I also knew this from professional experience: more than one of my missing person cases in recent years had ended with me staring at a corpse in a hotel room with a needle in their arm.

"Okay," Alex said. "But what's your point?"

"My point is, I'm wondering what exactly these folks died of."

We looked at each other again, the implication hitting home.

"We should see if they have Mrs. Vanhouten's records," Alex said. "Or can get them. Or if there was an autopsy. And ask relatives of these other people the same thing."

I reached for my coffee cup. "That could get tricky."

"How so?"

"They hear from a private detective that something might have been off about their mom or dad's death, their first call is either to the hospital or a lawyer. Either way, we're suddenly looking at a wall of silence. Not to mention the grief we're going to pile on just when they're getting over the loss."

Alex pushed a hand through her hair. After a moment, she said, "That's why I should do it."

"How do you mean?"

"Think about it. 'The grieving daughter of a beloved St. Clare's ICU nurse,'" she said, forming air quotes. "I tell them I'm just now recovering from the shock of what happened and trying to learn a little bit about my mom and her work. She spoke fondly of her patients, especially Mr. or Mrs. Fill-in-the-Blank. Honestly, that's more than half true, except for her telling me the names."

"What if she didn't provide care for those particular patients?"

"Only one way to find out."

I WAS wary about the endeavor, but one thing I was learning about Alex was that once she smelled even the trace of blood, there was no holding her back. I felt momentarily proud, then remembered that the same trait in her old man was one of the reasons I was still single. Before I could say more she started googling phone numbers.

"Don't you want to sleep?"

"Not now. I can sleep when I'm dead."

"That's morbid."

"Forget it. I'm too hyped."

I moved into the kitchen rather than leave the impression of watching over her shoulder. Even so, I heard her leave a message for someone regarding the first name, Clarence Kamer, marveling at the ease with which she walked the line, in an earnest and forthright tone, right up to the edge of prevarication. I snooped long enough to hear her reach a live human the second time, and then opened cupboard doors to assess the grocery situation. As the minutes passed, I escorted Hopalong out to water the back fence while I studied the leaves in the yard. Yup, they definitely needed raking.

"Hey."

I turned. Alex stood at the back door, arms crossed.

"How'd it go?"

She had a funny look on her face. "I had to leave a message at the first number. I got the son-in-law of the third person, Stanley Elliot, and he said he'd tell his wife I called. But Carol Radcliff's son talked to me. Briefly, anyway."

"And?"

"Short version, it's the same story as Mrs. Vanhouten. She obviously had COVID. She could barely breathe when they brought her in. My guess is they waited too long because they were in denial. Mom said they saw a lot of that. It broke her heart, but what could they do? I got an earful from this guy about quack doctors and the 'plandemic' and microchips. The usual crap. But here's the interesting thing."

"Yes?"

"He says she stabilized after she arrived and went on a ventilator. They never had the impression she was in immediate danger of dying. And get this—propofol was one of the drugs she was given while she was intubated."

I watched as Hopalong nosed a piece of mulch out of the far corner of the yard and methodically munched it. "Did he know an actual cause of death? Or have any records?"

"They were told it was acute respiratory distress."

"Who told them that?"

"Dr. Ives. The same physician on for Mrs. Vanhouten."

Once again we stopped and looked at one another.

"It could be nothing," I said at last. "We're still talking about a busy ICU during COVID when most victims weren't vaccinated."

"True. But two people in a row who were anti-vaxxer types, with propofol in the mix?"

"That's a little weird, I'll give you that. I just don't think we should jump to any conclusions yet. Any luck on seeing his mom's records?"

"I never got around to asking. You were right about it being tricky. I couldn't figure out how to broach it without all kinds of red flags going up."

"That's okay. I'm amazed at what you did get. You're a natural, I have to tell you."

She shook her head a little at that, and I recalled her compliment-averse nature. Before I could say more, she pointed at her phone as it buzzed with a call. I nodded as she rose and answered. A moment later she stepped back into the house.

When she didn't immediately reappear, I settled into the better off of my two rickety Adirondacks and checked my messages. My email inbox was the usual combination of spam, shopping discount offers, news alerts from local media that weren't really news alerts—"New brewpub to offer mix of German wheat beers"—library borrowing updates, and links to hometown news from my mom. It had been a few days since I'd hacked the thicket of mail down to manageable levels, and so I nearly missed the one truly oddball message, from none other than Lillian Melnick.

Possible you could call me? I've tried your cell but it says
voicemail is full. I tried texting too.

Weird. Why in the world would the closest person I
had at the moment to a mortal enemy want me to call her,
especially after the accusations I threw her way over lunch
in the art museum café? Was she having second thoughts
about firing me? Maybe the pressure had grown too
great from those library trustees whose kids and grandkids I saved from a downtown fireball a couple summers
ago. Not to mention heat over the theft from the dowager countess—board chairwoman Eleanor Seward. That
seemed the most logical explanation for Melnick's request.
Whether I wanted to take her up on it, especially with the
FBI breathing down my neck, was a different question. I
programmed her number into my new phone and made a
note to ask Patience about the request tonight but didn't
bother to call. Melnick wasn't getting off that easy.

I was exchanging texts with my mom about tomorrow's
visit when Alex stepped back into the yard. Hopalong approached her and was rewarded with a biscuit that Alex
had snagged from the bowl in the kitchen. I was about to
tease her about spoiling him when the look on her face
stopped me.

"What?"

"That was Stanley Elliot's daughter, calling me back. She
was actually the most suspicious, which is kind of ironic."

"Why?"

"She fully admitted her dad had COVID and that he
was in denial about it. Apparently it was a real bone of con-
tention between them. She said he'd been a normal guy,
conservative but not a wacko, until he hurt his back at
work and was off for a few weeks and started watching a lot
of Fox News and going on the internet. Before she knew
it he was down a coronavirus rabbit hole. He couldn't
be convinced it was anything but a massive government

conspiracy. Unvaccinated, swearing he'd die before he'd take it."

"And then he got sick."

"Right. He was overweight, and things got so bad he had to be rushed to the ER, barely able to breathe. Before I could even say anything she apologized for the way he treated the staff once he was on the ICU and stabilized. And that's the key. On a ventilator, but stabilized. They never dreamed he was in danger of dying. She was adamant about that. She said it was a shock when he told them he had passed."

"He who?"

"Dr. Ives."

29

TWO MINUTES later we were seated at my kitchen table. I typed notes under the names of the people whose relatives Alex talked to that morning—Stanley Elliot and Carol Radcliff—while she dictated.

"One other thing," she said when I was finished.

"Yes?"

"Susie—that's Mr. Elliot's daughter—also said her dad was given propofol."

"Hoo boy."

"They asked Ives about it, because everybody knows about Michael Jackson. He assured them it was standard protocol."

"Maybe. But it raises an obvious question."

"Is that what killed him? And the others?"

"Exactly."

"How would we find that out? Asking the families could really raise suspicions. And it's not like we can *Mission Impossible* our way inside St. Clare and peek at medical records."

"No," I said, something occurring to me. "But maybe someone could help us. Someone who might have a vested interest."

"Like who?"

"Like Billy Chowdhury."

"You think he'd do it?"

"To quote you: 'Only one way to find out.'" Before we got off track again, I told Alex about Chowdhury's allegations of Medicare fraud, the reasons he said he broke up with Kate, and where he'd been that morning.

"Shit," she said. "Does that make Christine Coyle a suspect?"

"I'm not sure yet. At best, it means we need to keep an eye on her and maybe Brian Riggs. This"—I gestured at the list of names—"is our top priority right now."

"Okay. But we're going to have to be careful. We're accusing a doctor of purposely killing people."

"Are we?"

"We're starting to see a pattern, right?" Alex said. "Three people, same story with each. Abusive COVID deniers sick with the coronavirus. It's a bad combination, especially—"

"Especially with someone like Ives with his personal situation. Pre-vaccine, his parents die and his wife becomes a coronavirus long-hauler. She quits work, stops driving, the whole enchilada. Imagine his reaction to folks who mock what could have helped her."

"Taylor," Alex said.

"What about her?"

"Could she have known what her dad was up to?"

"Allegedly up to. Remember, we're skipping a bunch of steps, starting with the Hippocratic oath. We're also dealing with a small sample—four potential victims over the course of a month, when we know a lot of people were still dying, nearly all of them unvaccinated."

"I suppose," she said, not sounding convinced.

I thought about Ives, who struck me as both compassionate and understanding. *It's hard to fault someone for lashing out under those circumstances.* "I think it's good to keep an open mind. But also to be careful. It feels like we don't have all the facts yet."

"Meaning what?"

"Well, look at what we know. Mrs. Vanhouten dies three days before your mom is killed. Your mom says, 'Another one?' after she passed. Her son took it as a slight, like she was twirling her finger at her head about another anti-COVID patient. Maybe even celebrating. Now it looks like she was reacting to something else altogether. Seeing a pattern. Expressing a concern. The question is, What did she do with that information? Like, did she confront Dr. Ives?"

"Maybe," Alex said. "It was near the end of her shift, as I recall. She was pretty methodical, which makes me think she wouldn't have rushed to judgment that way. But maybe the next morning? Remember, I told you she was gone when I woke up?"

"That's right. Maybe that's where she was. Meeting with Ives?" Even as I said it, it didn't sound right. "Actually, wouldn't she go to hospital officials first? Tell them of her suspicions? Or would she have confided in someone else even before that?"

"Like who?"

"Natalie Mettler, maybe? Or Billy?"

"If Natalie had known, she would have said something, I'm sure. Especially after the accident."

"Point taken. Plus, I didn't get the impression Natalie was hiding some big secret when I met with her."

"As far as Mom and Billy?" Alex said. "They weren't a thing by then. And trust me, once Mom was done with someone, no matter who broke things off, she was done." She met my glance briefly then dropped her eyes.

"Point taken again," I said, torturing myself with yet another "What if" flashback before returning to the moment.

"What about someone else at the hospital?" Alex continued. "Like maybe Dr. Coyle? She seems like the obvious choice."

"Now that you mention it, yes." I recalled my visit to 21st Century Care, such a far cry from the hugger-mugger of daily life at St. Clare–North. Natalie Mettler's comment about the investors it needed. *You don't launch something like that on a shoestring.* Then something else occurred to me.

"What?" Alex said, seeing my face.

"I don't know. It's a little nuts."

"This whole thing is."

"Well, it's obvious Coyle had a lot riding on 21st Century Care. That's a big deal, going out on your own like that. And she'd already put out one potentially huge fire related to her husband and the fraud allegations."

"And?"

"Another complication was the absolutely last thing she'd want to deal with."

"Complication like what?"

"How about headlines proclaiming mysterious deaths of anti-vaxxer COVID patients at her hospital?"

Alex went a little pale. "You're saying she killed my mom to keep what Ives was doing quiet?"

"I don't know—it sounds crazy hearing it out loud like that. And she didn't, you know, strike me as the killer type." Even as I said it, though, I knew the observation was meaningless. In my experience, killers rarely struck you as the type, until they did.

Alex walked into the kitchen and poured herself a cup of coffee. "Assuming any of this is true, why would she agree to meet with you like she did? You'd think she'd want nothing to do with someone asking questions."

"It's a good point," I said, grabbing a fresh cup of my own. "She may have figured it was better to play along. Nothing invites suspicion faster than a 'No comment.' She strikes me as a smart cookie, no matter what."

"I suppose. Back to my mom. What if Coyle's the one she told?"

"Yeah. It's hard to believe Coyle would sit on that kind of allegation, scandal or not."

"Maybe she went straight to Ives, confronted him, and he killed my mom."

"One step at a time. We're going out on a lot of limbs here. I'm not saying it isn't possible. But I feel like we're jumping to conclusions."

"Maybe. It also feels like the answers we're looking for lie either with Ryan Ives or Christine Coyle."

I was about to reply when I stopped, thinking about something. Finally. The thing that had been bugging me since my visit to Riggs in his office. He'd been talking about the impact of Kate's death on the staff at St. Clare–North. *Dr. Ives was devastated, as was Christine.*

Not Dr. Coyle. Who didn't reciprocate when I told her to call me by my first name.

Christine.

I thought about the obvious tensions that David Coyle's actions—alleged actions—might have created in his marriage. Then I thought about the debonair Riggs, as eager as anyone to keep me from talking to current St. Clare employees about Kate. *People have only now started to heal. You'd be picking at a painful scab.* Was that his real concern, the impact on employees' emotional well-being? Or did he have another reason to shut me out, not to mention tail me? Something Coyle put him up to?

"What?" Alex said.

I explained what I was thinking. Then I added, "We need to talk to Billy ASAP."

"Not Coyle? Or Ives?"

"Them too, of course. But we need to see those medical records first. Identify causes of death. See if our theory holds up. Then we can decide our next move."

Alex took a drink of coffee. "Should we at least tell Shortland?"

"About these patients?"

"Yeah."

"I'm thinking not yet."

"Why not? You told him about Leo Brown."

"That was actionable information. Brown saw some-one, presumably the killer, conducting surveillance ahead of time. That's the first anybody heard of it. This stuff about Ives killing patients is still a theory. I'd rather hand Shortland confirmed evidence, like the car that hit Kate, than get bawled out for treading on his turf again based on speculation."

Alex nodded but didn't respond. It was clear my little speech had triggered something.

"What is it?"

"Nothing."

"Really? Your body language suggests otherwise."

"I was just thinking. The cop in me says it's better to leave this to the professionals. That's what they're there for. But the Andy's daughter part of me agrees with what you just said."

"You did hire me to find out what happened."

"And you kept going even after I told you to stop."

"What can I say? I'm a lousy listener. Which is probably why I sleep alone."

"TMI, Andy."

"Sorry. I hope none of this is affecting your decision. About becoming a police officer, I mean."

"Just the opposite, in fact."

"Oh?"

"Hanging out with you hasn't made me want to be a private eye, in case you were wondering."

"Thank God for that. What then?"

"It's made me want to be a better cop."

30

BILLY CHOWDHURY yawned as he opened the door to my knock at his townhouse two hours later.

"Thanks for agreeing to see me. I know this is first thing for you."

"It's fine. I figured it was important when I saw your text. Come in."

I entered to the smell of coffee and the sound of jazz. We settled in a comfortable living room heavy on Scandinavian-style furniture, plants in decorative planters fired with swirls of color, and framed photos of market scenes in a variety of faraway settings. A shelf beside a modestly sized flatscreen TV held not books but what looked to be hundreds of record albums. Light poured into the room from windows overlooking a grassy inner courtyard. It was a comfortable, inviting space. I wondered how often Kate had been here to appreciate it.

He poured me a cup of coffee from a French press and refilled his own. "So what's up?"

I pulled myself out of my reverie, handed him a printout of the four patients' names and their obituaries, and explained the connections Alex and I had made. His eyes widened as he read.

"Who else knows about this?"

"No one. Just me and Alex."

"Not the police?"

"Not yet."

"Why not?"

"I'm not sure what we'd be telling them. It's a theory, and a thin one at that."

"Then why tell me?"

"We need your help."

"How?"

I explained the necessity of looking at internal medical records. "There's evidence that at least three of these patients of Dr. Ives who died were administered propofol at some point. We need cause of death."

"Propofol's a standard sedative for intubation. Plus, these are four random patients. What would that prove?"

"That's the thing, though—they're not random. Three of them at least were anti-vaxxers, and two for sure were assholes about it. They or their family members put the staff—including Kate—through hell. One of their sons confronted Dr. Ives in the parking lot."

Down the hall, the sound of a toilet flushing. Looking in that direction, I watched a dark-haired woman wrapped in a bathrobe emerge from the bathroom and retreat around the corner.

"I'm sorry," I said. "I didn't realize . . ."

"It's all right. I'd introduce you, but—"

"But nothing. I'll try to make this quick." I set aside the surreal feeling I was experiencing, my heart aching ever so slightly that Kate Rutledge, a woman I'd spent exactly one night with a quarter century ago, wasn't here instead of Chowdhury's apparent new girlfriend.

"What is it you want me to do, exactly?"

I brought myself back into the moment. "Check their records. We need to know all the medications they were on and the exact cause of death."

"That would be a highly irregular request, especially this many months later."

"Don't you have access to electronic files or something?"

"I'm not saying it's not possible. I'm just saying I'd have to be careful. And assuming I could find the information, what would you do with it?"

"It depends on what it shows."

He leaned back and took a sip of his coffee. I followed suit. It was between seven and nine Kenyan coffee plantations above the quality of my standard Kroger brew. He said, "There's one problem with this theory."

"Which is?"

"The patients were presumably on medically appropriate amounts of propofol. A bigger dose, like a fatal bolus, would be tough to pull off."

"A which?"

"A bolus. It's a large dose of something given all at once, instead of dispersed slowly on a drip. When someone's receiving something like propofol, the pump is literally locked in a box on the IV pole. You need a key to access it." He shook his head. "Plus, it would be hard to cover up the fact it was administered."

Something occurred to me. I reviewed what Natalie Mettler told me, about Kate's frustration over the pumps' software not always talking to the back-end recording system.

Chowdhury looked thoughtful for a moment. "The Medication Administration Record. I hadn't thought about that. It's possible it could be missed. Unlikely, but possible."

"Tell you what. You're raising all the objections to this theory I hoped you would. Let's stick with what we can learn from the records, and go from there. And, I suppose it goes without saying, be careful."

"Obviously."

"I mean it." I explained about Brian Riggs tailing me.

"What? When?"

"He was outside the night I came to the gym to see you. And at least one other time."

"Why?"

"I'm not sure. He won't return my calls."

"So you have no idea?"

Dr. Ives was devastated, as was Christine.

"Not exactly. I think he thinks he's looking out for the hospital by seeing what I'm up to. I won't know until I talk to him."

He glanced at the list of names. "You're not saying he knows about this? Which might mean that . . ."

"That Christine Coyle knew? I'm not saying that. But I don't know. We think Kate told someone her suspicions the day after Shirley Vanhouten died. Maybe Ives, maybe Coyle. Maybe someone else. I assume not you?"

"Nope," Chowdhury said. "We weren't really talking at that point. But even before we broke up, I knew something was on her mind."

"Like what?"

"I'm not sure. In hindsight, maybe she was seeing a pattern with Ives but was afraid to say anything."

"You never asked?"

He glared at me. "I tried, of course. But Kate could be very insular. She threw up stop signs fast. It was clear she didn't want to talk about it."

"Anyway," I said. "What about these records?"

He looked down the hall at the bedroom door the woman had disappeared behind. "Once I'm at work it won't take long. I can't access them remotely. Everything's stored on the hospital intranet. I could go in early but it might raise suspicions. Otherwise, I'm on again at eleven tonight. I can check then."

I tried not to let my disappointment show. I'd felt my pulse quicken this morning when Alex and I began putting pieces together and the fever of the hunt took over. But I also understood the dangers of rushing.

"That's fine. Let us know whenever you can. It's possible it's nothing. But—"

"I'll do my best, Andy. I promise. Especially if it gets us any closer to what happened to Kate."

"That's all that matters at this point."

He walked me to the door. As I was about to leave, he said, "Andy?"

I looked at him, alarmed at his stricken expression.

"What?"

"I just wish, now, that . . ."

"That what?"

"That I'd pushed Kate. About what was on her mind. What if she'd told me of her suspicions? If she had—"

"Don't," I said. But it was too late.

"If she had, maybe she'd still be alive."

31

THE HOUSE was quiet when I returned. I read a text from Alex as I walked inside saying she'd gone for an easy run ahead of Sunday's virtual half-marathon, the one that raised money for the food bank. The one she didn't want company on. That one.

I opened my laptop but couldn't concentrate. I was haunted by what Billy said. The big "what if?"

What if Kate's "Another one?" was a demonstration that she suspected Dr. Ives was up to something deadly? What if, instead of trying to protect Kate by breaking things off, Chowdhury had had an open and frank conversation with her? If that had happened, maybe she would have been someplace entirely different the morning she was killed. Helping authorities as they investigated what could be a Jack Kevorkian–style scandal, except these patients didn't want to die.

This brought to mind my suspicion, unproven but tantalizing, that something might be going on between Christine Coyle and Brian Riggs. Something more than collusion over hiding suspicious deaths. Something . . . personal. Or maybe both. That, regardless of what their relationship was, he might be trying to protect her professional fortunes.

I spent the next couple of minutes combining Riggs's and Coyle's names in internet searches. At first, it proved a dead end. Two or three times they showed up together in online PDFs of St. Clare's newsletters, and in a couple other innocuous links about St. Clare–North where they both happened to be mentioned, along with several other administrators. If they were a thing, they'd done a good job of masking it. Unlike many straying spouses I investigated who thought they were being oh so clever keeping their lover a secret except for that pesky little matter of the too-cozy Instagram selfie.

I was about to give up when I saw a familiar weblink among the latest batch of search combinations. I clicked on it and a moment later found myself staring at the list of testimonials posted on the website of none other than Green Light Goals, the driving school where Riggs had been an instructor. One bit of kudos stood out.

"Thorough and professional."
Christine C.

Christ, I thought. That couldn't be a coincidence. Then an even darker thought occurred to me.

Riggs had an alibi for the morning Kate was killed. The breached-door alarm that had been going off.

But did Christine Coyle, other than her own account of jogging?

I spent the next few minutes on a wild goose chase as I looked as deeply as I could into Coyle's vehicle owner history. As with Riggs, it was difficult to fathom Coyle as a killer. But other than the revelation that Leo Brown had dropped in my lap, the Green Light Goals discovery was bothering me more than anything. There could be a zillion reasons why Coyle—assuming that was her—had taken classes at a driving school where Riggs was an instructor. But given his background training cops in precision driving, what did that make her capable of? Especially if Coyle knew of Kate's suspicions about Ives and wanted to bury them, even more so after dodging the bullet with her husband's alleged fraud indiscretions?

Soon enough, any hope for a gotcha moment faded as I examined the list of vehicles Coyle and her husband had owned, all high-end models in keeping with a pair of successful physicians. Nothing close to a dark, older model SUV. Of course, that by itself didn't mean much. It's not as if a killer intent on staging a fatal hit-and-run would expose themselves like that. The vehicular weapon of choice was far more likely to be borrowed or stolen and, once used for the crime, sitting at the bottom of a lake or in a long-term airport parking lot. Talk about a needle in a haystack. And as I'd previously surmised, there was nothing preventing someone wanting to get rid of Kate from hiring out the job, though that entailed loose ends that could complicate matters down the road.

I sat back, frustrated. Based on everything we knew so far, I had a possible motive: the chance that Kate knew something was wrong on the ICU, that Coyle wanted it covered up, and that she was willing to go to any lengths to do so. That in and of itself seemed like thin gruel, made thinner by the lack of any obvious vehicle in Coyle's ownership history. Beyond that: pure speculation. It seemed no more likely than my original, half-baked theory that an anti-vaxxer was the murderer.

I checked the time. It had grown late. It was a long shot, but I was guessing that Riggs was off work by now. As I'd made surprise visits a hallmark of this investigation, or whatever it was, I figured I might as well keep going. In any case, I still had a couple of hours until Patience's gallery opening. I looked up Riggs's address, left a note for Alex telling her what I was up to—without providing all the details—and asked her to let the dog out. Five minutes later, I was out the door once again.

LIKE DR. Ives, Riggs also lived in Westerville, but in a slightly more prosaic subdivision with houses closer together and streets that much narrower. The neighborhood, off Sunbury Road, was a confusing jumble of "Courts" and "Drives" and "Boulevards," the streets curving here and there like a Google Maps version of a fever dream. Eventually I found it, a robin's-egg blue split-level with attached garage and the kind of perfectly manicured, crosshatched front yard you'd expect from a detail-prone cop, currently on the force or not.

I parked half a block down and examined the house. In my experience, it always paid to build in a minute or two of surveillance before making an approach, especially when my presence at the door wasn't likely to receive the same warm greeting as a Girl Scout pulling a wagon piled high with boxes of Thin Mints. Always better to have a sense of the bear's den first. Nine times out of ten the pause did nothing but delay the inevitable. Today, the technique paid dividends.

Just as I was about to disembark and stride up the sidewalk, Riggs's garage door slowly rose. I prepared to restart my van and do some tailing of my own when I took a closer look and realized it wasn't Riggs at the wheel of the blue Lexus backing down his drive. The driver continued smoothly onto the street without waiting to watch the garage door close, expertly cranked the wheel to the left, avoided two parked cars by inches, and drove up the street past me.

Seated behind the wheel, wearing the universally recognized smile of a satisfied lover, was Dr. Christine Coyle.

To judge by the way Riggs's face fell when he opened the door two minutes later, it was obvious he'd been half-expecting to see Coyle, perhaps having forgotten something in her haste to leave undetected, and that in her stead I was the absolute last person he wanted on his threshold.

"What are you doing here?"

"Wrapping up some unfinished business. May I come in?"

"No. What's this about?"

"It will only take a second."

"I said no. I have nothing to say to you, anyway."

"Perhaps you'd like to say something to Dr. Coyle's husband instead? Maybe explain what she was doing here on a Friday afternoon instead of wrapping up paperwork at the office? Or I can fill him in if you're busy. Clever, by the way, giving her a garage door opener. Makes the in and out so much easier. So to speak."

He stared at me, slowly shaking his head. He was barefoot, wearing an inside-out T-shirt and a pair of cargo shorts with the belt having missed one loop.

"It's not what it looks like."

"It never is."

"Did she . . ." He looked up the street. "Did she see you?"

"I think she had other things on her mind."

He shook his head again. "Jesus Christ, all right. Five minutes."

WE RETREATED to a pair of chairs at his kitchen table in front of a large glass window overlooking a yard that could easily have served as a backdrop for an L.L.Bean photo shoot.

"You followed me from Natalie Mettler's house, and again from Billy Chowdhury's. Why?"

"None of your business."

"Good one. Why didn't you return my calls?"

"I've been busy."

"That's obvious."

He looked up at the ceiling and down at the floor. "I wanted to see what you were up to, all right?"

"You could have just asked."

"Would you have told me?"

"I already did, in case you've forgotten. I'm trying to figure out who killed Kate Rutledge. I literally spelled out my game plan to you."

"I had to be sure. There's a lot at stake right now."

"What's that supposed to mean? I'm looking into the hit-and-run death of one of your employees. Does that have something to do with St. Clare?" I wasn't ready yet to reveal our suspicions regarding Dr. Ives.

"Like I'm going to tell you anything."

"'A lot at stake right now.' Does that mean you know something about Kate's death?"

"No."

"Do you know who killed her?"

"No."

"You sure about that?"

"I'm sure. I want her death solved as much as anyone."

"Then what's so important you need to follow me around?"

"Like I told you, it's—"

I decided to go for it. "Is it to find out if I know about Christine's husband and the Medicare fraud?"

His face lost most of its color. "I have no idea what you're talking about."

"Don't worry, because I do." Now I had to proceed carefully. "What I'm really wondering is, Is there anything else, besides that, that Christine is worried about me finding out? Other than the fact she's shagging you behind her husband's back, I mean."

He bunched his hands into fists. Just for a moment I wondered if I needed to worry about my safety. I'm a big guy in decent shape. But Riggs was younger, fitter, and looked more than capable of handling himself—and me.

Instead of attacking, however, he took a breath and said, "I needed to know who you were talking to. Christine—Dr. Coyle—has a lot invested in 21st Century Care. Not just financially, but personally. It's an evolution in health care, and she's worked hard to be at the forefront."

"In other words, she doesn't need any negative publicity."

"Sure. Whatever. A private eye talking to current and former employees made her nervous, is all. Especially after . . . Anyway, maybe she overreacted."

"I take it she's the one who put you up to this?"

His stone face was as good as a yes.

"In that case, I can see her point," I said. "Running a for-profit emergency room that doesn't take Medicaid in the area's swankiest zip code? There's millions of reasons why she wouldn't want bad publicity."

"Don't be ignorant, Hayes. At least she's accomplished something with her life."

"Sticks and stones. Why did she take your driving course. At Green Light Goals?"

"How do you know about that?"

"It's called detecting. Answer the question."

"None of your business. Ask her, if you're so interested."

"I will. Since she seems to have above-average driving skills for a hospital administrator."

"I'm not sure what the hell you're getting at."

"Someone with those kind of skills killed Kate Rutledge. Braked to make it look like an accident. You don't learn that on your own."

"Good God. Are you implying what I think you are?"

"Just stating a fact."

His face reddened in anger. "Get out. Now."

I wasn't giving up that easily. "What are you in this scenario, anyway, besides the rent-a-cop sent to do her bidding? The salve to her conscience? She takes pride in keeping one last connection to the world of community health by sleeping with the little people's protector? I bet she's the same girl who fucked the country club pool guy when she was home from college right before leaving for her boyfriend's lake house. How's that make you feel?"

This time I really thought he was going to hit me. Instead, face white with fury, he rose and pointed toward the front door. "Get out."

I stood up too, careful to keep an arm's-length distance. "What would current and former St. Clare employees have to tell me that would make Coyle nervous?"

"Out."

I thought of Jeff Heaton and the other relatives of the dead patients. "Are we talking lawsuits? Maybe somebody knows something that doesn't look good?"

"Out."

I could practically feel the rage pulsing from him now like heat from a radiator and decided to take the hint. I followed him into the foyer where he flung open the front door.

"You pull a stunt like this again and I'm not responsible for what happens. Stay away from me and stay away from Chris—from Dr. Coyle. I mean it."

I stepped through the door, turned, and looked at him.

"Your shirt's on backwards," I said, and retreated to my van.

32

NATURE MORTE, the gallery exhibiting Patience's watercolors, occupied a small storefront on Pearl Street in the Short North, a block off High. I arrived later than I wanted after struggling to find parking in the bustling arts and entertainment district. The Short North had come a long way from its gang-infested roots three decades earlier, a time no one missed. Except for how much easier it was to park in those days.

"Andy," Patience said a few minutes after I entered, extracting herself from a conversation with a man wearing all black and sporting a fashionable three-day spread of stubble that despite my best efforts I never seemed able to pull off. "Thank you so much for coming." She kissed me on the cheek and gave my arm a promising squeeze. She looked every bit the artist tonight in a long-sleeved rose-and-evergreen-patterned floral blouse over gray leggings and zip-up red leather boots.

"Wouldn't have missed it."

"Have some wine," she said, steering me to a table in the back.

"Nice turnout."

"You never know these days," she said, though I could tell she was pleased.

"Don't let me distract you. Especially from buying customers."

"You're not a distraction, my friend." She linked her left arm in my right and walked me around the brightly lit exhibit, the color of her paintings popping off the gallery's matte white walls. We were standing before her largest work, a representation of the old Columbus train station gates now standing guard in the city's Arena District when she said, "Oh boy. Time to sit up straight." I looked over to see an older couple entering the gallery. Him I didn't know, but the woman, wearing a gray lambswool overcoat accented by an olive patterned scarf, was familiar for all the wrong reasons. Eleanor Seward, the art museum board chairwoman. The last person, other than Lillian Melnick, who I wanted to see tonight. Well, good for Patience that she'd deigned to grace her opening.

"Best behavior now," I said.

"No shit, Sherlock. Grab a drink afterward?"

"I could probably manage it."

I watched Patience move across the room, admiring the sight, and then masked up before Seward could spy me. No point taking chances with my health or my identity. I moved on to the next painting, a smaller work that I recognized as an Impressionist likeness of the Umbrella Girl statue in Schiller Park, down the street from my house. I wasn't sure Patience's craft was my style, but it was obvious she had talent, if only to judge by the size of tonight's crowd. Seward's presence was also a good sign, I had to imagine. While the offer of a post-showing drink was a positive omen, I also figured it would be a few hours before Patience closed up. I retrieved my phone and checked my messages.

Alex had texted, asking if there was anything she should pick up before tomorrow's trip to my parents'. I told her not to worry about it, without mentioning the obvious: she was the only thing that would matter after the first thirty seconds of our arrival. My sister, Shelley, had basically said the same thing during our video chat after I returned home from my confrontation with Brian Riggs: "A new grandchild at their age. And one who can wipe her own nose. They'll be over the moon."

"Har har," Alex said, though I could tell she liked my Cleveland sister's brand of humor.

Studying my phone, I went through the rest of my messages. Kym had also texted, wondering what time I'd be back with Mike and his girlfriend tomorrow, as had my mom, inquiring about beverage choices for the boys. After answering both, I checked my email and was surprised to see another message from Lillian Melnick.

Still hoping you could call.

Stranger and stranger. Glancing across the gallery, I saw Patience deep in conversation with Seward and her husband. As I watched, Patience pulled her phone from a hidden pocket and held the display up so Seward could see whatever she was showing her. I observed the interaction with interest. I looked on for almost a minute as they discussed the contents on the phone, so long I was afraid Seward might see me. At last, I gave up my vigil, removed my mask, and stepped outside.

"Hello?"

"It's Andy Hayes."

"Andy," Melnick said after a pause. "Thank you so much for calling. You're a hard person to get ahold of."

"The FBI took my phone after they searched my house. A favor I have you to thank for, I believe. This is a replacement."

I heard what sounded like a deep sigh. When she didn't speak, I said, "I'm a little busy tonight. What can I do for you?"

Another sigh.

"Lillian?"

240

"The reason I was trying to reach you is . . ."

I waited.

". . . is, I need your help."

My turn to pause. "You've got to be kidding me."

"I wish I were."

"You fired me and then sicced the FBI on me. Despite being the hero in this situation, I'm in serious trouble thanks to you."

"I'm sorry about that. I fired you because, well, I had no choice. I realize now that was a mistake. But as I told you the other day at the museum, I had nothing to do with the FBI and you. I promise."

I stepped to my right as another couple arrived for the exhibit and entered the gallery. I looked through the window and saw Patience showing Seward's husband a painting she'd done of the Columbus skyline.

"What kind of help?"

"It'd be better if we could speak in person."

"Maybe for you."

"I could meet you right now, wherever you want. If it's convenient."

I looked through the gallery window again. "It's not."

"Are you sure? It's, well, it's rather important."

I reviewed the scene a few minutes earlier that caught my attention, when Patience whipped out her phone to show something to Eleanor Seward. I said, "Where do you live?"

"Upper Arlington."

I thought for a second. "Do you know the Rusty Bucket?"

"I can't say I've ever been there, but I know where it is."

I glanced through the window at the growing throng of people arriving for the showing.

"I can meet you there in thirty minutes."

"Any place less public?"

"Take it or leave it."

"All right then," she said. "I'll see you there."

I disconnected without responding. I sure as hell

didn't want to meet up with Lillian Melnick of all people on a Friday night. But I'd also soured on my plans for the evening. A nightcap with Patience, and whatever might follow, had lost its appeal. I sent an apologetic text and walked up the sidewalk to my van. Less than a minute later, Patience responded.

> Have a good night, my friend.
> Another time

I wondered if that would be the case, although I didn't put it in writing.

MELNICK WAS at the bar when I arrived, an untouched glass of white wine in front of her. From the look on her face it might have been a dose of strychnine she was summoning the courage to down in a single gulp.

"Andy. Thank you so much for meeting me."

"I don't have long." I slid onto the stool beside her. I ordered a draft Rhinegeist Truth and glanced at the baseball playoff game on TV. "Shoot," I said. "Clock's ticking."

She took a breath. "First off, I owe you an apology."

"You don't say."

"I didn't handle things well that day. The day of the theft, I mean. I was nonplussed, to say the least."

"There's a word you don't hear every day."

"I was under a lot of stress," she continued, ignoring the dig. "The Bellows—it was a big investment for the museum." She lowered her voice to a whisper. "Very big. The hope was it would boost attendance. Revenue took a serious hit during the pandemic. We still haven't recovered."

"It didn't, I take it?"

"Not as much as people expected. And that's the irony."

My beer arrived and I lowered it by a lock or two.

"Meaning?"

"Meaning that since the theft the crowds have been

huge. People are lining up to see the painting. Memberships have grown by 15 percent."

"Seems a little, I don't know, morbid."

"I agree, though it's happened before. After *The Scream* was stolen in Oslo and then recovered, people lined up three deep. Hell, even missing paintings are worth something."

I suppressed a smile at the profanity, the effect coming from the buttoned-up Melnick like the *pssst* of a beer can opening at a fine wine tasting.

"What's that supposed to mean?"

"You're familiar with the Isabella Stewart Gardner Museum theft in 1990? In Boston?"

"Vaguely. Mobsters or something?"

"Those were the supposed culprits. The actual artworks have never been recovered. But people still pay to stare at the empty spaces on the wall where those paintings hung."

"So stolen paintings, especially ones that are recovered, have an unintended and positive consequence. All's well that ends well?" The lesson in the seamier side of art museum finances was interesting, but I was feeling even more confused as to the reason for this meeting.

Melnick took a sip of wine. "Obviously you know the FBI is investigating the possibility it was an inside job."

"That's my impression," I said dryly.

"I can't hold that against them. I studied art theft in graduate school. A lot of robberies are carried out by insiders or are at least assisted by guards who know the routines and are happy to take some extra money to pass the information on."

"Listen, if you're implying that I—"

"Not at all," she said, waving away my protest. "But something happened recently to make me think the chances are good this theft wasn't just an inside job. It had a specific purpose."

"Which was?"

"I think someone at the museum arranged the theft to

help boost revenues."

AROUND US, conversations buzzed, servers rushed back
and forth with trays of food, and bartenders shook ice-
filled tumblers. An ordinary Friday night, with a conspiracy theory on tap.

"Explain," I said, letting the enormity of that accusation sink in.

"It took me a while to put the pieces together. It started
that day. No sooner had I finished talking with you outside
than I had a call from Eleanor Seward."

"Okay."

"She said she'd heard about the theft and wanted to
know all the details. At the time, I was so flustered I didn't
consider how strange it was that she knew so quickly. I
mean, we hadn't even talked to the detective yet and she's
on the line."

"Maybe someone else at the museum called her?"

"That's what I assumed. At the time it didn't matter. I
was too stunned by her request."

"Request?"

"That I fire you. On the spot. Don't get me wrong—
suspending you was my call. There are protocols. It seemed
to me we should at least review what happened. But she
was adamant. I had no choice. I'm sorry."

"Not as sorry as me. Though I appreciate you telling me
this, I guess. Not that it matters."

"That's the thing, Andy. It does. It matters more than
you know."

"Matters how?"

She looked around the bar, then reached over and lifted
a tablet out of her purse. She shifted on the stool so I could
see as she activated the screen.

"You're familiar with the security video from the
galleries."

"Sure. That's how they corroborated my story."

"Exactly. The problem is, not all the footage was checked."

"Meaning?"

Without responding, she clicked on a folder, and a folder within that folder, and a folder within that folder, and then brought up a video whose frozen first image showed several people sitting at a large banquet table in a room I recognized as an upstairs museum event hall.

"I've been over the security video from the gallery where The Boulevard was displayed multiple times since that day," Melnick said. "As far as I can tell, the thieves started scoping things out ten days earlier. First the man of the couple you heard arguing, then the woman. Back and forth. It's pretty obvious what they were up to."

"All right. So why look at this?" I pointed at the video in front of me.

"I'm getting to that," she said. "Three days ago, Mrs. Seward was at the museum having lunch with the director. Afterward, they stopped by my office to say hello. Of course we were talking about the theft and the business it had generated. As we talked, I happened to mention your visit to the café."

"Good of you."

"Let me finish, please. I pleaded your case. I told Eleanor the painting would be in the wind if it hadn't been for you. She frowned and said something like, 'It doesn't matter what he did. Imagine the consequences if the painting had been dropped, or torn, while he's trying to play the hero like he's back on the gridiron.' I realized it was a lost cause at that point and stood down. I was about to say something about just being glad we got it back. But when she saw me start to speak, she said, and I quote, 'We're not paying good money to ex-jocks to stick their noses where they don't belong. I mean, what if that couple hadn't been part of this whole thing and really were in divorce court?'"

"Weird that she'd defend the people who helped steal the painting."

"No, Andy," Melnick said impatiently. "That's not it."

"What then?"

"How did she know about the divorce court remark?"

I thought for a moment. "Did Patience hear it?"

"She was one room behind at that point. It's on the cameras."

"I don't know, witnesses who got interviewed?"

"There weren't that many people around you. Trust me, I've watched the video enough times."

The truth of what she was trying to tell me began to come clear. "So, you're saying . . ."

"I'm saying that Eleanor's comment got me thinking. I decided to look at all the security footage we have, not just from the galleries. From the café and the event spaces too. And that's when I found it."

"Found what?"

"Watch." She started the video on her tablet. She let it play a few seconds, then fast-forwarded ten minutes or so. "There."

"What?"

"Eleanor Seward, sitting beside her husband."

"You don't think he—"

"Not him. Him." She pointed at a black-clad caterer leaning close to Seward as he refilled her water glass.

"Jesus Christ."

Sunglasses or not, and even without his COVID mask on, it was plain as day. Serving Seward, with a black watch on his hand—the same one he'd checked repeatedly in the gallery that day—was the male half of the couple whose arguing lured me away from the Bellows and toward one of the biggest messes of my career.

33

I MADE Melnick play the clip again. And a third time. "That can't be a coincidence," I said at last.

"Obviously not."

"Have you shown this to the FBI?"

"Not yet."

"Why in God's name not?"

"First, I wanted to tell you the real reason I was forced to fire you. Or at least the reason I think I was."

"Which was?"

"Because you'd foiled Seward's plan, and she needed you out of the picture fast."

"Her plan?"

"Don't you get it? Seward arranged the theft. It was the ultimate inside job."

"You've got to be kidding me. Why in the world would she do that?"

"Because of what I've been trying to tell you. She set the whole thing up as a publicity stunt to boost the museum's fortunes."

My second beer arrived. I took a perhaps overly aggressive gulp.

"You can't be serious."

"I wish I weren't. But it's all so clear. If I had to guess, a week or two would have passed, the police would have received an anonymous tip, and the painting would have been found someplace safe. It wouldn't be the first time stolen artwork was recovered like that."

"It's a lot of effort to generate some extra income."

"You don't understand. The museum may have purchased that painting, but Eleanor Seward championed it. That whole thing about her grandfather having known Bellows? She made it her personal mission to acquire The Boulevard as a pièce de résistance in the museum's collection to honor that legacy. The fact it had all the impact on museum revenue as a fart in a hurricane did not sit well for her, or the rest of the board. Especially the board."

Despite the gravity of the situation, I once again fought a smile at her analogy. It was so un-Melnick-ish.

"In that case," I said, "how far up does this go?" I reminded her she'd said that Seward was having lunch with the director the day Lillian caught on to the significance of the "divorce court" remark.

"The director's as clueless as I was. As far as I know, Mrs. Seward acted on her own."

I had my doubts about that. But what I said was "All right. You've spilled the beans, which I appreciate. Now do you go to the FBI?"

"Soon. First, like I said, I need your help."

"What kind of help?"

"Proving all this." The excitement in her eyes was unmistakable, and I realized I was seeing Melnick in an all-new light that had me intrigued.

I pointed at the tablet. "That video's pretty convincing."

"I think so too. But you have to understand something. Eleanor Seward has the governor on speed dial, along with both of Ohio's U.S. senators and a clutch of Fortune 500 CEOs from here to London. If a bomb blew up on the day of her annual birthday bash, it would take out a who's who of movers and shakers."

"You're saying she's connected."

"I'm saying if she goes down, there's a better than even chance she'll take the museum with her."

"That sounds unlikely."

"I don't mean literally. But the fallout would damage the institution for years. It's a good place, Andy. We've gained a national reputation, a well-deserved one." Pride shone in her eyes as she spoke. "All that goes out the window if this plays out in the wrong way. We need to have ironclad proof. As it is, she could easily argue she had no idea who that caterer was."

"They seemed pretty cozy to me."

"A toady currying favor with a brazen compliment of her necklace. I see it all the time."

"Tough crowd. So what are you asking for?"

"I need the evidence to be unshakable. That's why I want to hire you."

"To do what?"

"To come up with absolute proof of what I've been telling you."

I stared at her. This was a bad idea in every way possible. Poking at a police cold case like the death of Kate Rutledge was one thing—it was the bread and butter of many investigators, including me, even when it didn't involve a newly found family member. Conducting a parallel investigation with an FBI case was something else altogether. My instinct told me to run away as quickly as possible.

Before I could respond, my phone buzzed with a text. Alex, letting me know she was lying down for a nap before her overnight shift. I thought of the left turn the evening had taken, from a possible tryst with the curvaceous Patience to drinks with a desperate Lillian Melnick. I responded to Alex by saying I'd try to be home before she left. I needed to unpack all the details of my visit with Riggs; she'd only received the SparkNotes version before I left for the exhibit.

"I need to get going," I said.

Melnick paid the tab, disappointment on her face, and I walked her to her car.

"Will you at least consider my request?" she said, standing beside a red Audi. I wouldn't have predicted this for her vehicle—a sensible Toyota product came to mind—but I was realizing there was more to Lillian Melnick than met the eye.

"Against my better instincts, yes."

"Really?" she said, surprised.

"I don't think it's a great idea. But I'll do what I can."

"Thank you, Andy. I truly—"

"This isn't charity, though. I'm going to send you a contract."

She pursed her thin lips like a woman on the verge of spitting out a piece of gum. "Is that a good idea? A paper trail, like that?"

"I'll keep the details vague. But it benefits both of us to have an official arrangement."

"Benefits us how?"

"It will help with our defense if we're ever indicted."

BACK HOME, Alex and I went over what I'd learned about Brian Riggs and Christine Coyle's affair.

"What difference does it make, though?" she said. "He could be protecting her interests without wanting to hurt my mom."

"True. But what about Coyle?" I explained how easily she backed out of Riggs's garage and zipped onto the street. For better or worse, she had some driving chops.

"Doesn't she have an alibi, though?"

"She was supposedly running. But can anyone prove that?"

"Wouldn't it be on Runnrly?"

"That's a good point. But only if she activated it that morning. Right?"

"Yeah. Or you can pause it too."

"What do you mean?"

"Well, she could have jogged to a car, paused her run, driven the car to where Mom . . . I don't know. It seems too crazy."

I had to agree with her, even though I still had my suspicions about Coyle. The whole running app world made me think not so much about the creepiness of people tracking you but the ways in which the information could be manipulated.

"So where were you?" Alex interrupted.

"When?"

"After visiting Riggs."

"Oh. That. Yeah, that's interesting." I explained about Patience's exhibit, followed by my meeting with Melnick.

"You're going to do it?"

I told her I was. "I need the money, frankly." Even as I said it, though, I wondered who would be paying me. Was Melnick footing this out of her own pocket? I decided not to worry about it, partly after watching her drive off in her newer model Audi.

"Do you need any help?"

"Help with what?"

"With the job. I've got time most days before I go to work. I'm off tomorrow and on Sunday the race shouldn't take that long."

"The race?"

"The virtual half-marathon. The food bank thing."

"Right. I appreciate the offer. But I think we've got more important things to focus on." I reminded her of the information we were waiting on from Billy Chowdhury about the medical records of Dr. Ives's alleged victims. What I didn't tell her was that a plan for securing the evidence against Eleanor Seward that Melnick needed was starting to take shape in my head. And it was nothing I cared to share with my police officer–in–training daughter. It wasn't exactly illegal. But I didn't want my penchant for gray areas to jeopardize her budding law enforcement career. Not yet, anyway.

34

AFTER ALEX left for work, I dozed on the couch, intermittently waking to check my phone for any messages from Billy Chowdhury. When nothing appeared by 1 a.m., I called it a night and crawled into bed.

I was deep in a dream involving watercolors, jogging, and a red Audi driven not by Lillian Melnick but by Dr. Christine Coyle when a sound slowly and painfully dragged me awake. My phone, or more specifically, my current eighties ringtone, Tom Petty's "I Won't Back Down." My heart raced as I gained consciousness, thinking of Alex.

"Andy?"

"Billy," I said, relieved. I checked the time: just past 7.

"Sorry if I woke you. I just got home and wanted to call as soon as I could."

"It's fine. Talk to me."

"It's not good news, I'm afraid."

"Go on."

"The short version is that you and Alex were right about the propofol. Each of the four patients you identified was on a propofol drip."

"So that's it. Our smoking gun?"

"Not exactly. Like I told you before, propofol use is pretty common with intubated patients."

"Shoot. Back to square one, then?"

"Not exactly. For starters, the patients shared a few other things in common."

"Such as?"

"Well, they were all unvaccinated, but you already knew that. I found notes in three of their charts that indicated combativeness by them or their family members. I have to say, in my experience, that's rare. And I can tell you that St. Clare–North treated a lot of unvaccinated COVID patients. Very few showed hostility toward staff. For the most part, they were more confused than angry."

"Understood. Back to these patients—what about Dr. Ives?"

"The attending physician each time."

"Is that our smoking gun?"

"Yes and no."

"Now I'm confused."

"You should be. Because I was too, at first."

I glanced at Hopalong. He lay at the foot of my bed, snoring like a lumberjack sleeping one off.

"Meaning?"

"I told you that three of the files mentioned combativeness. Then I saw that four of the five also had a strange notation about Ives."

"Five?"

"Yes, sorry. You missed one. The Tuesday before Mrs. Vanhouten. A young man, mid-thirties. His wife was extremely rude to Ives, according to the chart."

"What about this notation?"

"What it boils down to is in four of those cases, Ives was seen leaving the patient's room right before they coded."

"How's that unusual? Seems like that's where a doctor would be."

Chowdhury scoffed. "Just the opposite. An ICU ward that busy? It's the nurses running the show. A doctor's rarely in the room except for rounds, and then never alone."

"I'm still not sure what any of this means."

"I wasn't either, although it seemed damned suspicious. Then I came across a note in the file of the young man whose death you and Alex missed."

"Okay."

"The nurse who responded to the code noted the propofol drip was set to fifty micrograms an hour."

"Is that a lot?"

"Normally, not at all. But that's not the situation here."

I felt myself running out of patience, on top of which Hopalong was beginning to stir.

"So what is?"

"Remember we talked before about the Medication Administration Record? Because of something Natalie Mettler told you about the software pumps?"

It took me a second. "Right. Kate complained about an occasional communication problem. What about it?"

"A MAR record is completed electronically for every drug that's given. The problem in this case is the pump showed an 800 microgram bolus had been administered. That'd almost certainly be lethal."

Bolus—a large dose of something given all at once. Which didn't sound good.

"Lethal how?"

"Hypotension most probably. A dose that big would cause fatally low blood pressure."

I thought about it. "So the patient was supposed to be getting a basic sedative supply but this pump showed a huge dose?"

"Correct."

"How's that possible?"

"Best guess is someone manually adjusted the pump's infusion rate to administer the bolus. If not for data validation, I don't know that we would've ever known about the bolus to begin with."

"Data validation?"

"Sorry. I know it's jargony. What I mean is the amount of drug given per the pump did not match the amount manually recorded in the MAR."

"For that patient, or all of them?"

"Initially, just that one. But I dug a little deeper. There's discrepancies between the pump doses and recorded doses in the MAR for all five patients. Which means, as far as I can tell, someone was going into the pump, adjusting the pump settings to deliver a lethal dose of propofol, then resetting the pump back to the original infusion rate to disguise the bolus."

Another thought occurred to me. "Didn't you tell me the pump is locked in a box? And you need a key to open it?"

"That's right."

"And?"

"Someone must have had a key. Sorry, did have a key."

"What do you mean?"

"I checked some records and a key went missing a few weeks before. Whoever was doing this, it's pretty likely they had that key."

"Any guesses who?" I asked, realizing I already knew the answer. I recalled Ryan Ives nervously jingling his keys in his pocket the night I visited. And something Brian Riggs told me when we first met. *After twenty years of shootings and stabbings, helping a panicked doc find his keys is a nice change of pace.*

A long pause.

"Billy?"

"It's obvious, isn't it? Someone like a doctor seen emerging from these patients' rooms every time."

DESPITE THE gravity of what Chowdhury just told me, I had to excuse myself and make a run for the back door to let Hopalong out.

As I watched the Lab water the begonia pot, I rubbed my unshaven face and considered Chowdhury's revelation. Despite the facts before us, I was having a hard time reconciling the distraught look in Ives's eyes the night I visited him at home—exhausted and distracted from caring for his wife—with the notion that he was a killer. After all, what was it he said the first time we spoke that I kept coming back to? *It's hard to fault someone for lashing out under those circumstances.*

Suddenly, Chowdhury's words echoing in my mind, I heard the sentence differently for the first time. I remembered the quirk I noticed about Ives, the way he sometimes referred to himself in the third person. *It's not how this doctor sees it.* What was the rest of Ives's "lashing out" comment? *No one should judge someone for reacting to what he perceived as an affront to his own morality.*

I nearly shouted in frustration at myself. How could I have misunderstood Ives so badly? He hadn't been speaking with compassion about an anti-vaxxer's temper tantrum. He'd been talking about *himself.* He, who'd dealt with unimaginable loss thanks to a deadly virus whose worst effects by now were preventable yet who was reviled by people taunting the very person trying to help them. That's the morality that had been affronted.

"I'm back," I said, retrieving my phone.

"No problem. So what now?"

I held off telling Chowdhury my revelation about Ives, and instead asked, "Wouldn't that MAR thing have detected these fatal doses?"

"I thought about it. Then I remembered what we talked about before, that the pump software wasn't always talking to the MAR. A nurse enters the amount of drug administered during her shift into the MAR."

"Meaning?"

"Meaning you'd have to look for discrepancies between the pump records and the MAR." He paused. "Like I did."

"I'm surprised the nursing staff didn't catch this issue of Ives being present each time."

"Remember, we had a lot of travel nurses. The post-vaccine COVID surge may have let up, but St. Clare still was short-handed, like a lot of places. New people were always rotating in and out."

I adjusted a pillow and scooted against the wall. "Okay. One other thing. These patient notes. Did Kate write any of them?"

"One second. Yes. For someone named Clarence Kamer. He died on April 26."

"Did she catch the thing about Ives being in the room?"

"That's the irony. That's the one with no mention of it."

I was momentarily deflated. Then I remembered the by-now familiar two-word phrase thrown in my face by Jeff Heaton: "Another one?"

I told Chowdhury what I was thinking. "What are the chances Kate checked the records herself after Mrs. Vanhouten died?"

"Knowing Kate? Pretty good."

"And if she found this same pattern . . ."

"It would have been enough to tell someone," he said, finishing my thought.

Tell someone. But who? Christine Coyle? Ryan Ives?

All signs, I decided, were pointing toward Coyle. Who had more to lose should knowledge of a killer doc become public? The green fields of 21st Century Care would turn brown quickly if that news got out and spooked Coyle's investors, not to mention the clinic's patients.

I recalled what Alex told me, that her mother had gone someplace after work two mornings before she died, breaking her usual routine. Gone to Coyle to report her suspicions? And if so, had Coyle gone directly to Ives?

The fact that Ives still worked at St. Clare–North spoke of some kind of pact, an agreement he and Coyle might have reached. A deal the basis of which was now taking form at the back of my brain. I was guessing the last thing Ives could bear was a prison sentence tearing him apart from his wife and daughter, leaving Taylor on her own to care for her ailing mother. Is that what won his silence? A threat by Coyle to expose him if he didn't stop his deadly behavior? It wasn't hard to imagine her desperation at that point, having dodged the scandal that her husband barely avoided.

"You there?" Chowdhury said.

"Yes. Listen. We need to move fast."

"What do you mean?"

"I need you to compile something we can take to the cops. Can you write up summaries of each of the five cases, with copies of whatever medical forms back up what happened?"

"Sure. How soon do you need it?"

"As soon as possible. And—"

"Yes?"

"It goes without saying. Don't tell anyone."

"Of course not—"

"I mean it. There's a killer still out there. We can't take any chances."

I WAS making case notes of my own an hour later when Alex arrived home from work. Once she was changed and settled, I explained about Chowdhury's call. Her face fell as I outlined the potential motive for her mother's killing.

"You really think Coyle was—that she's responsible?"

"I can't say with 100 percent certainty. But let's look at the facts. She had the most to lose if Ives's actions came to light. We know she was a good driver—she took Riggs's class at Green Light Goals. She had motive and ability."

"But in that case, why aren't we also looking at Riggs? Even as an accomplice?"

"His alibi's ironclad, remember? He came in early to deal with that alarm."

"He could have put her up to it."

"It's possible, sure, if he saw himself riding her coattails to a cushier life at 21st Century Care at some point. On the other hand, it's also possible she kept him close to keep him out of the loop. It's not the craziest reason I ever heard for an affair."

"Except they're still together according to you."

"Good point. Maybe she's using him now to keep tabs on me to see what I know, without telling him what's really at stake."

"That's creepy. So what now?"

I thought about the day ahead of us. There was no bigger priority than dinner at my parents'. Even Shelley was going to be there, insisting as soon as we broke the news the day before over FaceTime.

"You need to get some sleep before we head to my parents'. Plus you've got your race tomorrow."

"I can skip that. It doesn't matter at this point."

"Didn't you say it was a fundraiser? Did you raise money?"

"Well, yeah."

"How much?"

"Um, about $2,000."

"That's amazing. Is it too late to contribute?"

"I guess not."

"All right then. Let's get through today with my folks and your race tomorrow, and we'll see what happens."

She rose and headed toward my bedroom, Hopalong click-clicking down the hall behind her, always happy for a nap companion.

"Andy?" She stopped, facing me.

"Yes?"

"Thanks."

"For what?"

"For everything you found out. It's not easy to hear. But at least you're getting answers."

"You're welcome. Now get some sleep."

"The way this guy farts?" she said, pointing at Hopalong. "Good luck with that."

35

ONCE UPON a time, the newspapers dubbed me "the Farm Boy Phenom," despite the fact that no matter how hard I tried to explain, I didn't grow up on an actual farm. My parents' modest two-story white house, shaded by an enormous, spreading maple tree, sat on an acre and a half in the village of Homer with a cornfield behind it, though not theirs. I suppose that fact, combined with the large garage my father and uncle built for the family cars, and the small pole barn behind that where my father stored his riding mower and various gardening tools, made the place just agricultural enough for your average undiscerning city sportswriter. So "Farm Boy Phenom" it was. Until it morphed into "Farm Boy Felon" after my arrest for point-shaving and I gave up trying to set the record straight.

Joe sat up front with me on the drive to Homer that afternoon while Alex took the back seat and grilled Mike's girlfriend, Hannah, on everything from her classes to her high school soccer practices. I didn't know Hannah that well, other than the fact she fit Mike's girlfriend criteria of being pretty, smart, and athletic. But Kym vouched for her, especially since neither of their grades suffered as a result of the time they spent together, which was good enough for me.

As we pulled into my parents' driveway, I rehearsed the introduction that I'd prepared one last time. I took a breath, my stomach flip-flopping in nervous anticipation. Give me game-day jitters instead, any day. As it turned out—just like at the pizza place with my boys—none of my preparation mattered. My mother opened the door, Shelley right behind her, and stepped onto the porch, intercepting us as we headed up the steps. She seemed about to speak, to greet the arriving horde, but instead stopped and stared, first at Alex, then at me. Then, without a word, she approached Alex and looked at her as if she'd seen a ghost. Time crawled to a stop.

"What's your name, dear?" she said to Alex.

To my surprise, Alex said softly, "It's Alexandra. Alexandra Rutledge. But most people call me Alex."

"And you're . . ."

She looked over her shoulder at me. "I'm Andy's daughter."

"Of course you are," my mother said. "You're his absolute spit'n image. You'd have to be blind not to see it."

Naturally, my mathematician mother had deduced the truth immediately. Why had I even bothered readying an explanation?

"I have a lot to tell you," I said, stepping forward and giving her an awkward hug. She returned the embrace, released it after a second, and took Alex's hand.

"No shit," she said.

THE NEXT few hours passed in a jumble of conversation, laughter, and a few tears. In typical fashion, it took my father the longest to come around. Eventually, though, he was brought on board by what turned out to be Alex's encyclopedic knowledge of Indiana University basketball, an institution that she skillfully compared to Ohio State football, which soon had them chatting about my bygone playing days, with my dad telling stories that were mostly true. After Mike and Joe took Hannah and Alex and Shelley's boys outside to explore the property, I told my parents everything I knew about Kate Rutledge, up to and including her death. For now I left out the possible conspiracy we had stumbled upon.

"It's so tragic," my mother said.

"And so typical," my father said with a grunt. I let it pass. My dad and I had reached a détente of sorts in recent years, part of which involved me granting him permission from time to time to lament my wasted youth without protest.

"I would have been there for her, if I'd known. I swear."

"At least you're there for her now," my mother said. "Or are you?"

"I am." Though I wondered if that were really true.

THE RIDE home was quiet, with the boys and Hannah hunched over their phones, watching videos together. Alex rode in front this time, glancing once or twice at her own phone but for most of the trip looking out the window as farmland slowly transitioned to suburbia while the autumn shadows deepened.

"You okay?"

"Fine."

I left it at that. We both knew it was a lie but acknowledging it aloud would accomplish nothing.

"Hannah's a good kid, by the way," Alex said as we pulled away from Kym's house an hour later, both boys now back with their respective moms. "Mike better not screw this up."

"You are aware that he's a teenage boy? And my son?"

"Yup. But your mom also told me that Joe and Mike are apples that fell far from the horse's ass."

"Beautiful."

"Just repeating what she said. So what now?"

"You mean with the case?"

She nodded.

"We wait for Billy to compile the information, I guess."

"But aren't we still at square one?"

"Meaning?"

"Meaning, if Mom did put the pieces together, who did she tell?"

"It had to be Dr. Coyle."

Alex was silent for a moment. Then she said, "That's what Hannah thinks."

I put my left blinker on as we approached the entrance to 315 off Dublin-Granville Road. "Sorry, what?"

"Hannah said it's super likely Mom would have gone straight to Coyle. Bypassed her supervisor in case she was somehow in on it."

"You told Hannah about our theory?" I tried unsuccessfully to keep my voice down. "No offense, but what the hell were you thinking?"

"Whoa, calm down. I'm not stupid, Andy. Joe let it slip when they were walking around. She asked me about it later. Both her parents are doctors, by the way. Makes sense she'd be interested."

"At least tell me you swore her to secrecy." I shuddered at the implications of the allegation getting out.

"Don't take me for an idiot. Of course I did. The fact is, though, it's a confirmation of what we're thinking."

"That that's where your mom went that morning you got up and she wasn't there? To see Coyle?"

"Right. Two days before she died."

I came up to speed on the highway but kept to the driving lane on the right. I started to relax, though was still torn between wanting to hug Joe and throttle him.

"Okay," I said. "Your mom tells Dr. Coyle. The question is, What does Coyle do then?"

Alex thought about it. "Best guess, she wigs out, facing the possibility of her cushy new clinic going up in flames if the truth is revealed, and she confronts Ives."

"Confronts, or threatens?"

"Does it matter?"

"Remember, there's no evidence these deaths continued after your mom was killed. And Ives is obviously still working. The only conclusion is that if Coyle went to see him, she told him to knock it off under threat of some kind of retaliation."

"Like losing his job?"

"Maybe. And if he lost his job, Taylor would probably lose hers. That would be a serious blow given the care Mrs. Ives needs."

"So now both sides lose if the killings are discovered."

"Right," I said. "Mutually assured destruction."

"Just like in the Cold War."

I wasn't surprised Alex knew her USSR-US history. Her mom, after all, had been the one reading a Stephen Jay Gould book at age nineteen for pleasure.

Alex said, "The big question is, Did Coyle let slip to Ives how she knew what was happening?"

"Meaning, did Ives know your mom knew?"

"Correct. Otherwise, how else did Dr. Ives know who to kill?"

"If it was Ives. And not Coyle herself."

"You think Coyle could pull that off?"

Reluctantly, I reminded her of my theory about Coyle's driving skills, gleaned through tutelage from Brian Riggs— with or without his knowledge of what she was up to. On that front I was undecided.

"You said you couldn't find any cars owned by Coyle or her husband that fit the description of the one that killed my mom."

"True. But that just means she didn't use one of theirs. Desperation fuels innovation. If it was her, I'm guessing she found a way. Even if we can't prove it, it's probably worth including that in our report."

Alex glanced over at the Ohio State medical complex on our left. "So what do we do now?"

"We get some sleep. You run your race. We toast your accomplishment with a cold one or two. And then first thing Monday morning, we go see Doug Shortland."

36

BUT THAT wasn't entirely true. I'd left a little something out.

The forecast for Sunday called for temperatures no
higher than the low fifties, perfect for running 13.1 miles. It
also meant Alex could sleep in for a change since it would
be cool all day. By eleven o'clock she was up, breakfasted,
and doing last-minute stretching.

"Good luck."

"Thanks, Andy. I'm kind of looking forward to it. I feel,
I don't know, like a burden's been lifted."

"It's progress, anyway. See you on RaceDay1."

"Right," she said, and with a wave was out the door and off.

Five minutes later I was in my Odyssey and on the way
to Christine Coyle's house.

Twenty-five minutes after that, I was standing on the
threshold of her Westerville home, being stared at by her
clearly annoyed husband, David.

"She's not here," he said, fingering my card as if I'd
handed him something a dog left in his front yard. He
wasn't nearly as fit-looking as his runner wife, with a stocky
build and receding, gray-streaked hair.

"Any idea when she'll be back?"

"No."

"Any idea where she went?"

"What's this about, anyway?"

Where to start? The alleged Medicare fraud? His investments in 21st Century Care? His wife's discovery of a second potential scandal in the form of Dr. Ives's murderous actions? The affair with Brian Riggs?

I decided to leave it lie. I had to guess that with his wife off someplace on a Sunday morning, combined with a private eye showing up at his doorstep, he might be making a few unpleasant connections all by himself.

"Would you let her know I stopped by?"

"If you tell me why you want to see her."

"I think she knows."

THE NEXT stop was obvious: Riggs's house. I gave the odds fifty-fifty that Coyle was there, either enjoying another rendezvous or huddled with him as they figured out what to do about the questions I was asking. I headed that way, but was barely out of the Coyles' subdivision when my phone rang showing an unexpected number. I recognized the voice right away, though.

"Dr. Ives?"

"I'm not sure what you and your daughter are playing at, but it's gone too far."

"I'm sorry?"

"We received a call this morning from someone who says he's the son of a patient I treated. He made a lot of alarming allegations about the treatment his mother received. I asked him where he was getting his information, and he said it was your daughter."

"Alex?"

"That's right. That's the name he had."

"Who was it?"

"Ben Radcliff. His mother was Carol Radcliff."

I tried to remember the names of the patients we compiled. A moment later the details came back to me. Radcliff and her family were combative toward staff, accusing them of being part of a grand conspiracy. A documentary they'd seen online, full of misinformation and lies about the virus, was mentioned frequently.

"I'm not sure why he'd be calling you."

"He's calling me because he thinks I killed his mother, based on questions your daughter was asking him."

"Did you?"

"I beg your pardon?"

"Did you kill his mother?"

"How dare you."

"It's just a question."

"An inflammatory one in keeping with what I see now as your true motives. I thought you were trying to find answers to Kate's death. We both did. That's clearly not the case."

"We?"

"Taylor and I. She's more upset by Radcliff's call than I am. She thought your daughter was a friend. It appears she stabbed her in the back instead."

That was rich, I thought, realizing his comment confirmed that Ives didn't know about Taylor and Jamie Thacker.

"You need to leave Alex out of this. It's my case—"

"If that's true, why weren't you the one calling these family members? If the goal was to fill their heads with nonsense, why not do it yourself? Why put your daughter up to it? Is that the kind of man you are? Someone who—"

"Who what?"

"Who lets others act in his stead."

"Like you did with Christine Coyle?"

"Christine? What are you talking about?"

"I think you know."

"I think you're going to be hearing from my attorney and the hospital's in short order."

And with that he was gone.

I kicked myself mentally the rest of the way to Riggs's house. I realized now what a colossal mistake I'd made contacting those family members. Or rather, as Ives said in his righteous anger, letting Alex do it. I should have known that, given the hostility they'd already shown hospital staff, they might not sit quietly by once they pieced things together based on the questions Alex was asking. My biggest mistake was assuming they'd hire lawyers. It never occurred to me they'd tip our hand by going straight to the source themselves.

Of lesser concern, but still nagging at me, was the thought that the undertaking had inadvertently destroyed whatever odd friendship Taylor and Alex were fostering. I'd wondered privately whether it was a bond, however bizarre, that Taylor might need if the revelations against her father were proven. But there was little chance of that relationship continuing now.

Before Ives's call, I'd been bracing myself for a confrontation with Brian Riggs that I knew could be our ugliest yet. My fears were confirmed when he answered the door and I saw the anger in his eyes.

"Get the hell off my property."

"I'm looking for Christine Coyle. Is she here?"

"I said get off. Now."

"Is she? Because—"

I didn't finish the sentence. Instead, I stopped as I found myself staring at Riggs's shirt. It appeared to be the same one I'd caught him in the last time I was here, on backwards on that occasion. But not today.

"What is that?"

"What? I just said—"

"Your shirt. What is that?"

He looked down. "Green Light Goals," read the words emblazoned in large letters across the chest. Below that, a smiling car giving an anthropomorphic thumbs-up.

"It's a giveaway. From a class. Now for the last time—"

"What class?"

"What does it matter, what class? It's just a shirt, from a thing I did. A freebie. Now would you please . . . are you all right?"

Under any other circumstances, the note of concern in Riggs's voice juxtaposed with the tone he'd been taking just a minute earlier would have been comical, the verbal equivalent of a vaudevillian spit take. But there was nothing funny going on now. Because I'd seen this shirt before. Not necessarily this one, but one very similar.

Taylor Ives had been wearing it the night I stopped by the Ives's house unexpectedly. I'd commented on it as she hugged herself in the evening chill after following me when I thought our conversation inside had ended. At the time I mistook the automobile for something from the cartoon film *Cars*. Now I saw my error. It was a cheap rip-off, one that might not survive a copyright challenge. But it wasn't from a Disney movie. It was the mascot of a driving school.

"Did Taylor Ives take this class?"

"What are you talking about?"

"Answer the question. Please."

Maybe he took note of my obsequious tone. Or maybe he just wanted to get this crazy guy off his stoop. Either way, Riggs said, "Yes. Along with a few others from St. Clare. I was able to get them a discount."

"Defensive driving?"

"I think so, yes. She'd gotten in two fender benders. One more and she would have lost her license. Listen, what's all this about?"

"When?"

"When what?"

"When did Taylor Ives take the class? Recently?"

The alarm in Riggs's eyes made it clear he thought I'd gone around the bend. "Over a year ago. I don't work there anymore. It was just a part-time thing anyway."

Without responding I pulled out my phone, went to recent calls, and pressed the number of the last person I'd spoken with.

"What now?" Ryan Ives demanded, picking up.

"You said Taylor was upset by the call you received. From Ben Radcliff."

"We were both upset."

"But she knew, correct?"

"Knew what?"

"She knew that Alex was the one making the calls to the family members?"

"Yes, dammit. Taylor was especially upset because of what she thought was her and Alex's—"

"Is she there?"

"Who?"

"Is Taylor there?"

A short pause. "No."

"Where is she?"

"She went out. Right before I called you. I told you, she was very upset."

"I need to talk to her. I need her number."

"No, Mr. Hayes. I'm not going to do that. There's no reason."

"Then call her. For me. Tell her it's an emergency. Tell her to stop what she's doing and come home. Please."

"I just told you—"

"Please," I said, and disconnected.

"Hayes," Riggs said. "What the hell is going on? What's wrong with you?"

"Is Christine here?"

"What?"

"Christine. Dr. Coyle. Your mistress. Whatever. Is she here?"

"What business is it of yours if she is?"

"How about it's life or death? Yes or no."

"Yes," he said at last, nearly spitting out the word. "Now for the last time—"

I didn't wait for him to finish. I was already running to my van.

37

IT TOOK an agonizingly long sixty seconds for me to open the RaceDay1 app tracking Alex's virtual half-marathon, find her event, and type in her name, all while Riggs stood in his driveway and glared at me. I ignored him and, to my relief, finally spied a virtual icon of a runner bearing Alex's name inching across my screen. I looked closer and saw she was headed south on the Alum Creek activity trail. I relaxed for a moment, realizing she was on a protected path. Then I noticed she was almost exactly three miles from where the path crossed the busy intersection of Livingston Avenue.

What was it Alex said, relating her and Taylor's awkward coffee shop conversation? *She said she'd watch me on that app instead. Satisfied?*

I went back to the nighttime visit I paid to Ryan Ives. Recalled the fact they had a two-car garage and yet, in a household with just two drivers, one car still had to be parked outside.

So what was parked inside that garage?

At that moment, the thing Natalie Mettler told me about Mrs. Ives's long-haul COVID came back to me: *It left her nearly disabled—couldn't drive anymore . . .*

I pushed it to ninety once I was on the highway, keeping an eye out for cruisers as I weaved in and out of traffic, cursing my stupidity as I drove. Yes, Christine Coyle had a lot to lose if it emerged that Ryan Ives was euthanizing patients on the ICU on her watch. But Taylor Ives had just as much to lose, if not more. And was it any surprise that a young woman forced by circumstances beyond her control into a gatekeeper role at home had heard—or overheard—Coyle's threats to her father? That she had learned what her father had been doing, and what its revelation might cost her?

Because if her father went down, was arrested or jailed, what would that mean for their mother?

Taylor, as much as anyone, had reason to be sure the allegations facing her father based on Kate's discovery went no further. And now she knew that Kate's daughter was tracking the same information . . .

I slowed down briefly when I remembered the crux of the issue with Taylor, that she'd been with Jamie Thacker the morning Kate died. He had a rock-solid alibi, after all, as scummy as it was.

Now, a sinister possibility struck me. Something we'd all overlooked. It wasn't that Taylor Ives was Jamie Thacker's alibi.

Thacker was Taylor Ives's alibi.

I thought back to his public intoxication and DUI arrests. The fact Alex said he was a heavy drinker, even passing out on a date once. I remembered the boxes of Klonopin in the Ives's living room, meant to ease Mrs. Ives's troubled sleep as she battled long-term COVID. How hard would it have been for Taylor, after a round of sex or two, to doctor a drink to make sure Jamie slept soundly all night and into the morning?

It was a stretch, I knew. But could I afford to ignore my gut?

Alex wasn't answering her phone, which was maddening but made sense. It was either on silent mode or she was too wrapped up in her effort to detect a buzz or ring. Meanwhile, the virtual figure that was my daughter grew closer and closer to Livingston Avenue.

Alex was in good shape. She was a lifelong athlete, with years of running and basketball under her belt. She'd told me she thought she could hold an eight-minute pace the entire way. That meant twenty-four minutes from the time I spied her until she reached the path's intersection with Livingston. I arrived twenty-two and a half minutes after leaving Brian Riggs's neighborhood. I pulled over a car's length from the path and glanced around. The light was red and traffic was stopped. I didn't see anyone in the cars next to me or on the other side who looked like Taylor Ives. But what science was there in that?

The light changed and a driver behind me honked their horn. I stayed put. The honking continued. I rolled my window down and waved for them to go around. That won an even more strident blast. I held my ground and the driver finally went past, laying on their horn the whole way. I threw on my flashers and kept my eyes glued on the app and my virtual daughter. In another few seconds the light changed back. Runners and bikers now had the right-of-way across the intersection. According to the app she was almost there.

I looked in desperation for Alex but saw only a peloton of five bikers cross the intersection. I wondered whether I'd miscalculated, or whether the app, like any virtual tool, suffered from a lag of anywhere from seconds to minutes. Had I let my imagination run wild? Were my suspicions about Taylor nothing more than the fantasy of a man at the end of his rope? Was I permitting my anger at what she'd done to Alex by sleeping with Jamie outweigh common sense? Then I glanced across the street and saw a dark SUV paused on the opposite side. Behind the wheel sat Taylor Ives.

At almost precisely that moment, I looked over and saw Alex approaching the intersection, moving fast, stride strong, arms loose and relaxed.

The SUV started moving, ready to run the red light. Right into the path of the oncoming Alex.

I gunned my engine, blasted my horn, and lurched forward just as Taylor entered the crosswalk and less than two seconds before Alex would have run into the same space. We collided head-on and everything went black as my airbag exploded and slammed me against the back of my seat. The smell of gas and burnt rubber filled the air.

What felt like an eternity but was probably only a few seconds at most passed. I came to, somehow managed to open my door, and hauled myself out.

"Alex," I gasped.

No response. I called her name again, then lost the struggle to stay upright as I stumbled and fell. Trying unsuccessfully to right myself, I heard the sound of metal grinding and managed through the pain in my neck and the spots clouding my eyes to see the dark SUV backing up and then heading toward me. I made a half-hearted effort to roll to my right, out of the way, but I knew in my heart it wasn't going to be enough. I wasn't going to make it. I only hoped it would be over quick.

It was. A series of loud reports filled the air, followed almost simultaneously by the splinter of breaking glass and the crunch of metal. I heard screams and the squeal of brakes and more honking horns. Confused, I struggled to my knees and looked around. Where was Alex? I didn't see her at first, my view blocked by what was left of my Odyssey. Jesus—where was she? Had Taylor Ives gotten her anyway? I half stood, and then Alex came into view. I stared, dumbfounded.

Alex stood in the middle of the intersection, both hands grasping her KelTec P3AT, as she examined the inside of the blue SUV.

"Taylor?" she said. "Taylor? Talk to me. Stay with me now."

I collapsed onto the asphalt, unable to hold myself up any longer.

38

"SORRY I'VE been incommunicado. It's been an interesting few days."

"No apologies, Andy," Lillian Melnick said. "I watch the news. I'm just glad you and Alex are okay."

"That remains to be seen. But thanks."

Three days had passed. Alex and I spent most of them answering multiple questions from both Columbus and Westerville police detectives. Dr. Ives had been suspended from St. Clare–North, where a full-bore investigation was underway into both suspicious patient deaths and Medicare fraud. Mrs. Ives had been moved to an assisted living facility while her future was sorted out. Meanwhile, Christine Coyle had announced that 21st Century Care was suspending operations indefinitely. Alex's status for the January police academy class was changed to provisional while a separate investigation determined her fate.

Taylor was at Grant Hospital, severely wounded but expected to live. She'd been rushed to the Level 1 trauma center after paramedics pulled her from what was left of her mother's dark blue SUV—the one hidden in the garage where it had sat after long-haul COVID forced Mrs. Ives to stop driving. And which Taylor had retrieved nearly five months earlier after tiptoeing out of Jamie Thacker's apartment early one morning as he lay unconscious, sated by booze, sex, and sleeping pills.

Leo Brown was still in the wind, but that wasn't my problem anymore. With the number of agencies looking for him, I figured he'd be found sooner rather than later.

With the dust finally clearing and Alex in Westerville to clean out her mom's apartment, I'd taken a moment to call Melnick about the other job on my plate. Fortunately, thanks to an airbag—and Alex—my injuries from the crash were mostly superficial.

"Interesting timing," Melnick said. "I was talking to Eleanor Seward just now."

"What did she want?"

"She claims she was checking on security for an event on Friday. But I'm guessing she's still nervous about the FBI."

"As she should be. She'd better hope they don't find the people she hired."

"That has to be her fear, for sure. But I'm guessing that's not why you called."

"Yes and no. You said Seward championed the painting's purchase. It's her baby, start to finish."

"That's right."

"And she obviously took pains to protect it during this counterfeit theft."

"That's why she was so upset with your interference. I'm sure whoever those people were, they had strict instructions to keep the painting safe at all costs. They thought they had the 'no pursuit' rule on their side. Good thing they didn't, in hindsight. Thanks to you."

"Backhanded compliment accepted. But let me ask you this: What if the painting wasn't worth protecting?"

"What do you mean?"

"What if the painting were a fake?"

From the intake of breath I detected over the phone, it was clear I'd hit a nerve.

"It's not a fake, Andy. I reviewed the provenance personally. I'm a leading expert in early twentieth-century American paintings." Some of the stodgier Melnick crept back into her voice.

"Of course it's not a fake. Obviously, you would know," I said, recognizing an ego that needed stroking if I'd ever seen one. "But what if Seward thought it was? That she found out she strong-armed the museum to buy the artistic equivalent of, I don't know, Hitler's diaries or the Shroud of Turin?"

"She'd be ruined, or her reputation would, anyway. Along with that of the entire museum. And me, personally," she said, unable to disguise the trepidation in her voice. "I'd never work in the field again."

"Precisely. But humor me for a second. What if she found out you had suspicions about its origins?"

"Suggest it's a fake, you mean?"

"Correct. But not to her."

"What are you talking about?"

"I'm talking about setting a trap."

"How?"

"By moving the painting out of the museum for a pretend authentication. If she learned of that, how do you think she'd react?"

"Assuming she thinks no one suspects her involvement in the theft, I believe she'd consider it better if the painting permanently disappeared than be declared a fake."

"Then that's what we need to do."

"What?"

"We need to arrange for The Boulevard to be stolen. Again."

39

WE SET the move for Sunday at midnight.

Any earlier in the day and there still existed the possibility of too much pedestrian traffic. As it was, we ran the risk of night owl Columbus College of Art and Design students strolling down Gay Street on the way back from a studio, or a bar—or both. But we had no other choice.

Lillian and I split up the tasks. She purchased an equivalent-sized frame as the one holding *The Boulevard* and packaged it accordingly, wrapped smartly in canvas. I rented a white panel van and pulled it up to the loading dock. Together, we sat in her office for ten minutes until, based on what we were seeing on the outside security cameras, we were sure. We both wore dark clothing, but Lillian looked a bit more put together in green corduroys and a ginger-brown riding jacket over a dark blouse.

"All right," I said, glancing at the monitor. "It's time."

"You're sure this is going to work?"

"We're about to find out."

We walked through the loading dock bay without speaking and toward the heavy gray doors leading to the dock's apron. Patience, who we'd positioned there twenty minutes earlier, nodded at us and carefully pushed the door open, leaving room for me to pass. I caught the faintest whiff of her fragrance and summoned up a tantalizing image of how things could be. I stepped onto the apron and breathed in the cool evening air. Lillian and Patience proceeded around me and down the concrete steps to the van. Lillian opened the sliding rear side door and stepped back as I walked to the edge of the apron and carefully handed the frame to Patience.

As I did, I took a moment to collect my thoughts and find my bearings. The night was quieter than expected, and the street facing me was clear of the pedestrian traffic I had worried about. In fact, the only people moving around at that moment besides our hardy little band of art patrons were the two masked figures in all-black pants and long-sleeve turtlenecks who emerged from around the back of the van and stopped just behind Lillian.

"We'll take it from here," the taller of the two said, grabbing the right side of the painting.

"What is the meaning of this?" Lillian said in the half-haughty, half-fearful tone we rehearsed.

"Nice and quiet and nothing happens to it," the second man said.

Feigning outrage, Lillian paused for a long three seconds—another part of the rehearsal—and stepped away without a word. Patience looked on in shock.

"Smart choice," the first man said, backing up. "Now listen carefully. Any sign of a pursuit, any hint there's someone following us, this goes out the window, understood? It won't matter what speed we're going."

"Understood," I said.

"Smart man," he said, as they turned to go.

"See you soon," I added, giving a little wave.

"Right," he said, as both disappeared behind the van in the direction of Gay.

An eternity of five seconds elapsed before my parting words came true. The pair emerged first, backing up slowly with both sets of hands in the air, followed by a trio of men. On the left and right loomed two bounty hunters I'd only ever known as Buck and Big Dog, each aiming shotguns at the two wannabe ninjas. In the middle stood Otto Mulligan with the frame in his hands.

"On your knees, both of you," he instructed, in a voice that didn't leave room for negotiation. Once they complied, he said, "You too."

A brief interlude of silence overtook us, but sound soon filled the void. The sawing of crickets in the museum's sculpture garden. Laughter from a couple of blocks away. Slightly farther in the distance, the rush of traffic on the 670 expressway.

"I said, you too." Otto gestured at Patience.

"What?"

"Do it," Lillian said, steel in her voice.

"Andy," Patience said, turning to me with confusion in her eyes. "What's going on?"

"What's going on is you'd better listen to my friend. He's had a lot of practice apprehending criminals."

"Criminals? Andy—"

I glanced at Lillian, who had stepped to the side and had her phone to her ear, talking to a 911 dispatcher.

"You were the only one who knew what was happening tonight," I said. "The only person who could have tipped them off."

"That's not true," Patience protested. "Mrs. Seward knew. You told her—you said you outlined the whole thing."

"That's what we told you, you're correct. But that conversation never happened. We only told you. You were the only person who heard our plan. You tipped her off, not us."

"No—this is crazy."

"As crazy as setting up the heist in exchange for what?" Melnick said, lowering her phone for a moment. "Mrs. Seward footing the bill for your gallery opening? Was it worth it?"

The stricken look on Patience's face suggested it might not have been. "If I can just explain—"

"Down," Otto said.

Patience glanced at me and at Melnick, searching unsuccessfully for a hint of mercy. Finding none, the look on her face slowly hardened from affliction to indignation, and she did as instructed at last. Satisfied, Otto looked up at me, raising the frame in his hands.

"Believe you misplaced something, Woody?"

"WELL, THIS is me," Lillian said two hours later as she directed me into the driveway of her house on Edington Road in Upper Arlington. "You really didn't have to do this."

"It's easier all around." I reminded her of the plan for me to drop the van off at the rental office the next morning to save her the bother.

"I have to tell you, I'm wide awake after all that. I don't suppose I could interest you in a nightcap? Or no, you probably need to get going."

"Why not? It's fun being out past my bedtime."

The past few days had revealed a new side to Lillian Melnick, to say the least, but nothing about the home I toured a few moments later surprised me. Sculptures, paintings, and fine art photographs filled every room and nearly every wall. The lone exception came in the living room, where the display of art was interrupted by floor-to-ceiling shelves housing volume after volume of art history doorstops, many of them with creased spines that suggested frequent consultation.

"No beer, I'm afraid. It gives me gas," Lillian said, returning from the kitchen and joining me in front of the bookcase. "But I've got a nice chardonnay I picked up from the Twisted Vine." She handed me a glass filled with a generous pour.

"To a night to remember," she said after we settled ourselves on a tufted white sofa with an arched wooden back that might have been delivered straight from a Gilded Age period drama.

"*A Night to Remember.* Isn't that the book about the Ti-tanic?" I said as we clinked glass.

"If it is, that pretty much sums up how I feel."

We chatted a bit about the evening's events. Patience and the two black-clad conspirators were in custody. I felt a little bad—but only a little—when I awakened FBI agent Adam Fawcett at 1:30 in the morning to inform him of the development and to tell him he'd be hearing from my lawyer bright and early. I wasn't sure he fully grasped what I told him, that the art theft searches they found were done not by me but by Patience when she borrowed my phone time after time on the pretense of art instruction.

I didn't bother to explain how the sight of her pulling her own phone out so easily at her Nature Morte opening to show something to the Sewards got me thinking about the possibility. As in, wasn't it odd that her phone was suddenly available when she needed it and I wasn't around? But I was pretty sure Burke Cunningham would make the point just fine.

"So," I said. "Can the museum survive without Eleanor Seward?"

"An interesting question," Lillian said. "Before this, I would have had my doubts. But the board's rallying around us. A couple trustees have already texted, despite the hour. I supposed that was my biggest miscalculation all along."

"What do you mean?" As I waited for her to respond, I tried the chardonnay. She was right. It was nice, for wine.

"In the end, no one person is bigger than an institution. Don't you agree?"

"Makes sense to me." The world was about to find out, though I didn't tell her that. After hanging up on Fawcett, I texted basics of the incident to Suzanne Gregory, as promised, and told her I'd be available in the morning to go on camera, no matter how bad my hair looked.

"May I ask you something, Andy?"

"As long as it's not a request to participate in more skulduggery."

"Lord no. But I am curious about something. Do you find Patience Hampton attractive?"

I glanced at her, unsuccessfully hiding my surprise.

"No offense, but that's a very odd question."

"I'm aware of that." Even as she spoke, her eyes told me she was looking for an honest answer.

"Well, since you're asking, yes."

"That's what I assumed. Why is that?"

Odder and odder. "I suppose because she's convention-ally pretty and has a nice sense of style, setting aside the whole criminal conspiracy thing for now. Which reminds me." I related the story Patience told me, about Lillian tweaking her about her weight.

"Good God." She sat up, outrage in her eyes. "I would never say such a thing. Especially to an employee. How absurd."

"I figured as much. It was all part of the con, in hind-sight. Setting you up as the bad guy."

"Disgraceful."

"Without question. But if I may, as long as we're on the topic, why in the world did you ask me that question?"

She relaxed, looking a little sheepish. "To be frank, my husband left me for a woman who looked quite similar. He denied that my looks had anything to do with his decision, but I'm sure he was lying. You've confirmed my suspicions, so I appreciate your forthrightness."

"Your looks?"

"'An elegantly dressed crane.' That's how a girlfriend in graduate school once referred to me. Quite drunk, of course. But she was right."

"I'm sorry that happened."

"Don't be. It's who I am."

"You know, besides the fact that 'Elegantly Dressed Cranes' would make an excellent band name, they have their own attractions."

"You're just teasing now. Or drunk yourself."

"On a sip of chardonnay? I don't think so."

"Then what?"

"Unconventional beauty and style. A vastly underappreciated subject of study."

"I'm not sure whether to be flattered or insulted."

"It was meant as a compliment."

"You have a funny way of expressing esteem, or whatever it is you're getting at."

"Guilty as charged. Would this help back up my argument?" I leaned over to kiss her.

"You can't be serious," she said, pulling her head away.

"Why not?"

"You're just having pity on me. Which is something I absolutely cannot abide."

"For the record, I only have pity on animals, old ladies crossing streets on windy days, and Michigan fans. Since you're obviously none of those, I reject the accusation." I drew close and kissed her on her cheek. This time, she didn't pull away.

"This is quite unexpected, Andy. And undeserved. I fired you, for heaven's sake."

"On Eleanor Seward's orders. Either way, that saves us the awkwardness of a workplace romance."

"Is that what this is?"

"It's whatever you want it to be. Or not. We can also finish our wine and call it a night. It's been a long day. If I've overstepped my bounds, I apologize."

She hesitated and then took my hand. "No apologies necessary. But I am an elegantly dressed crane. Don't deny it."

"Whatever you say."

"But I think . . ."

I waited.

"I think, just this once, I'm willing to accept a compliment about my appearance."

"Just this once?"

"The thing is, you never know how people will react to a new exhibit. What if it doesn't appeal?"

"Only one way to find out." I set down my glass of wine.

"I suppose that's true," she said, pulling my face to hers.

40

I PAUSED as I stepped off the elevator to catch my breath, then walked the rest of the way down the hall.

"That's the last of it." I set the cardboard box down in the middle of the living room. "You do know there's such a thing as a library?"

"Since it's one block from here, yes, as a matter of fact, I do," Alex said. "I reread a lot, especially books Mom gave me."

"I'm on board with that." I walked into the kitchen to retrieve glasses of water. Mike and Joe looked up briefly from their phones, both wearing T-shirts nearly soaked through from the morning's exertions.

"You're sure you don't mind living this close to head-quarters?" I said, handing Alex a glass as I settled myself onto a chair. "Seems like you'd want some breathing room."

"It's fine. It's not like I'm going to be based there. And I like it downtown. It's cool. A lot cooler than the burbs."

I nodded. I couldn't fault her for the new apartment, one of hundreds constructed in recent years as the Columbus building boom continued unabated, even during the pandemic. Alex had already declared her intention, weather permitting, to ride her bike up the Olentangy Trail to her police academy classes whenever possible, a commute made possible by the new apartment—and by the administrative decision that her actions that day on the trail saved my life, a ruling bolstered by multiple cell phone videos shot by rubbernecking drivers. Whether the taint of the shooting would hamper her career down the road remained to be seen. But that was all in the future.

Meanwhile, to Alex's dismay, I'd found a used Honda Odyssey two years newer than my last model whose cost my insurance would mostly cover. Maybe I am a soccer mom at heart.

"Hey, Dad?"

"Yeah," I said to Joe as he walked into the room.

"Are we still going for pizza?"

Before I could reply, Alex said, "What about ribs? There's this place at the Continent I've been dying to try."

"The where?"

Alex and I shared a glance. A thousand unspoken words flashed between us. Then she grinned.

"Just kidding. I think pizza's still the plan. Right?"

"Yes," I said. "We're going for pizza. But I may order anchovies."

"Ew," Joe said.

I checked the time; just past noon. Plenty of time for pizza—anchovies or not—followed by the Tuesday night Blue Jackets game I was miraculously taking all three of my children to. Wednesday promised to be a little quieter. I had a Zoom meeting scheduled with a woman from Milwaukee whose husband would be in town this weekend for a convention, and whose extracurricular activities she had some questions about. With my art museum gig over for good, I had hung my investigator's shingle out once more. Joe's agreement to attend a school this coming spring closer to German Village had taken pressure off my need for a semi-normal schedule.

"Whenever we're ready," I said, right before my phone rang.

"Andy Hayes?"

"You've got him."

"Andrea Chamblin. I'm with the Department of Public Safety. The PISGS office." She pronounced it piss-gizz.

"The what?"

"Private Investigator Security Guard Services. We hold your license?"

"Right. How can I help?"

"This is a courtesy call to let you know we're launching an investigation into your status, based on a formal complaint."

"Wait now. What?"

"You'll be receiving official notice by mail within ten business days. You have thirty days after that to respond, including setting up a formal interview."

"What's the complaint?"

"Improper conduct."

"Based on what?"

"Based on your discharge from the Columbus Museum of Art."

"What are you talking about?"

"Your employment was under the aegis of your state-issued license. Termination from employment related to your license triggers an automatic investigation."

"You've got to be kidding."

"That's nothing I would kid about."

"I saved a valuable painting."

"That would be something to tell the investigator assigned the case. I'm just informing you of the situation."

"This is bullshit."

"I would advise you to refrain from verbal abuse as the probe proceeds."

"Oh for God's sake—"

"Also, you need to update your contact info. It took me a few calls to find this number," she said, and disconnected.

"What's up?"

I looked over at Alex, who had posed the question. But all three kids were staring at me.

"It appears the shit has hit the fan." I gave them the short version of the conversation.

"That sucks," Mike said.

"To use my least favorite expression, it is what it is. Let's go. I'm hungry, and there's nothing I can do about it right now."

Joe and Mike preceded us out the door and raced to the elevator.

"Are you going to be okay?" Alex said as she locked up.

"I'm sure it'll all come out in the wash. Maybe just a little wrinkled."

But what if it didn't, I thought. What if my career as a private eye were over—the only thing I'd ever been good at besides hurling pigskins down fields. What then?

"I feel responsible," Alex said.

"Don't. If anyone's to blame, it's Eleanor Seward, and she's got her own problems now. Trust me, no matter what happens, I have no regrets about that day. About saving that painting. About us saving it."

"Sure about that?"

"I'm sure."

"Okay. Thanks, Dad," Alex said, as we joined her brothers at the end of the hall.

Acknowledgments

I started this book in August 2019 well before I learned of something called the novel coronavirus. Although early drafts included wrongdoing in a hospital, the themes and plot evolved as the upheaval of the pandemic—both socially and medically—became clear. Many health professionals helped me redirect *Sick to Death* into a world with COVID by reading the evolving manuscript and answering multiple questions, including Jen Axe, Emilee Barrett, Sarah Cazares, Michele Elkins, Barbara Mogren, Melissa Royero, and Scott Mackey, with extra thanks to Kelly Dodd. I'm deeply grateful for their assistance. I'm also indebted to several people who answered police procedural questions or offered comments related to art museums, traffic investigations, college football, and weapons, including Eric Delbert, Glenn Jambor, Gary Lewis, Adam Nemann, Mitch Stacy, and Jane Ann Turzillo, with a special shoutout to Bill Parker for his assistance with this and many other books. I so appreciate their help. As always, any errors are mine.

I'm grateful to the amazing team at Ohio University Press for their continued support of the Andy Hayes series—which celebrates its tenth anniversary this year!—including director Beth Pratt; publicity manager Laura André; managing editor Tyler Balli; editor in chief Rick Huard; sales and events manager Jeff Kallet; and acquisitions and rights administrator Sally Welch. Big thanks to my agent, Victoria Skurnik, for her help and encouragement. Finally, as always, I reserve my greatest thanks to my wife, Pam, whose support of Andy Hayes, and of this Andrew, has never flagged.